A Glass Darkly

Jean Goulden

Transcendent Publishing

TRANSCENDENT

For Ann and Heather

1

Glen – 2014

"**C**ome on, Mom! I'm right, aren't I?" I urge.

She takes a rattling breath, reaches a trembling, scaly hand for her cigarette, inhales slowly, and smiles an enigmatic, annoying Mona Lisa smile ... And did she give a shallow nod? I'm not sure.

Mom's propped up on Brandi's recliner. She always was slight. Now, she's not much more than a skeleton clad in leathery skin and cocooned in an old, crocheted blanket she made by unravelling wool from the worn sweaters Aunt Mon knitted for us the year Dad died and our lives turned upside down.

I stay with her awhile, perched on the folding chair Brandi got out for visitors. The room's claustrophobic. The recliner and the sickening commode are crammed into an already modest room that was Brandi's den before Mom got so sick. Mom can't stand the cold, so the heat's cranked, the window's shut, and trails of cigarette smoke spiral languidly to the popcorn ceiling.

I don't say much. Mom's watching the TV that's been moved to Brandi's desk. An inane game show—even so, the expressions that flit rapidly across her pinched face tell me she's following it.

I watch her reflection on the screen, her eyes dart about, her lips quiver, she frowns, she pulls a face, perhaps of disgust. She's frail, yet she's still herself, she's got all her marbles. So why can't she find a way to answer my question, damn it? A contestant shrieks hysterically after pulling the ridiculous correct answer out of thin air, remembering in the waning seconds she needs to hit the flatulent buzzer three times for a correct answer.

Frustrated, I decide it's time to leave, and I bend to kiss Mom, my lips barely brushing her parched skin. Agonizingly slowly, she tips her cigarette into the ashtray at her side. Her faded green eyes search mine, she reaches out her bird-claw hand, and very deliberately gives mine an almost imperceptible squeeze. She does it again. And a third time.

And I know.

Trying not to crush the delicate quail bones of her hand in my excitement, I squeeze it back. Three times. Immediately, I feel her relax. She's understood that I know and I'll keep her secret. Soon, her head begins to nod, and her rackety breathing evens out a bit. She's taking a nap. I pause to make sure, then I tiptoe out of the room.

Adrenaline is coursing through my veins, I can't talk to Brandi for a moment without betraying what I feel, so I go to the little bathroom and splash my face with cold water. *Christ! It's true! Oh, Christ, it's true!* I think, gazing at the cracked primrose tiles above the sink without really seeing them. It explains everything!

I sigh all the tension out, as I'd learned back in my swim team days, and then I take several slow, deep breaths to calm myself. Once my heart rate begins to steady, I go and find Brandi.

She's in her functional, near-sterile kitchen. My subconscious registers that there's music playing, the old Talking Heads hit, "Once in a Lifetime." Somehow, I note the irony of the lyric, "Am I right or am I wrong?" Just a few minutes ago I didn't know.

The upper windows are open, and it feels chilly after Mom's stuffy, smoky retreat. In spite of the hospital cleanliness and the minimalist furnishings, there are odors here too, incompletely masked by the bleach and disinfectant. Brandi's leaning over a large cat carrier, fussing with a Burmese cat. It's gorgeous, the color of dark chocolate with huge honey eyes.

There are two other Burmese in the kitchen—one, similarly draped in dark-brown velvet fur, is curled in a pool of light from the windows; the other, wearing a perfect coat of pale cream satin, is under the table where Brandi keeps their food bowls. A hint of the pungent food hangs in the air, mingling with traces of ammonia from the litter tray.

Brandi notices me, but her attention's with the cat in the cage. She's rhythmically rubbing its abdomen, and the cat, who would have scarred me for life for much less, seems to be enjoying it. Her purr's a sustained, rumbling alto like an opera singer drawing out a low vibrato.

"She'll give birth in a couple of days. I'm hoping for at least one platinum kitten. Donna Alvarez says she'll pay double for a platinum," she tells me.

This no longer sounds strange to me. I've learned that Burmese, like decorator fabric, come in a range of luscious finishes. Brandi breeds prize winners, and they're all fabulous—and a fabulous price! My wife Lisa thinks Brandi loves breeding them because she was never a mom herself. I sneeze violently despite the slightly-too-fresh air. *Hell!* I forgot my allergy pills when I rushed out to come over here.

"Forgot your Benadryl?" Brandi asks with a note of amusement and a hint of criticism in her tone. I guess my allergies remind her of Julian, and they're not all such good memories. "I thought you seemed in a hurry when you dashed into Mom's room—what's so important?"

I struggle for a convincing lie and mutter an unconvincing one. I tell her going through Mom's things hit a raw nerve. I had a sudden need to reassure myself she's still alive. Brandi lets it go with a half shrug that lets me know she doesn't believe me. She's my sister, and oftentimes we read each other well. I don't miss a world of weariness in her sigh.

"Can we sit on the porch a bit? Mom's okay, she's taking a nap," I suggest, hoping it'll help my allergies and revive her spirits.

Brandi pulls a shapeless hoodie from a plastic hook at the back of the door, and we head outside. There's a miscellany of weather-beaten chairs on the porch—all Brandi's—I recognize them from way back. The guy who owns the other half of the duplex doesn't have access to this porch; he has an upper deck at the back overlooking the tracks. It's in such poor shape, Brandi swears he'll fall through it someday.

I take a mildewed Adirondack that Dad bought after he'd had a good quarter, part of a set with a bench swing and picnic table. Brandi takes a frayed, old wicker chair that was once her pride and joy when she struck out on her own with Julian. She sits back, her right ankle crossed over her left knee, like a man. Her big toe (no polish) peeks out of a hole in her espadrille—she isn't wearing socks.

Dragging the hoodie on has messed up her hair. She runs her fingers through it and shakes her head like a dog. I idly wonder if she picked up this gesture over the years she'd worked at the vets, and I'm surprised I notice these things with my mind still racing over the news I learned from Mom. Brandi's hair is shorter now than when we grew up, and it's lost some of its fire. Even so, every now and then, it sparks alight when she's riled up or does the dog shake.

"How do you think Mom is?" she asks.

"Well, it's a helluva lot worse than laryngitis," I say.

When Mom first got sick, she'd pretended she'd got laryngitis—didn't want to upset us with the "C" word, I guess—who was she kidding? It was unlike her. Mom's used to facing facts. Maybe she was trying to protect us. Maybe herself.

"God, yes! D'ya think her mind's going? She recognize you okay? Glen, how long do you think she's got left?"

I hear her fear—it echoes my own—and her exhaustion. Her pretty face is drawn, her freckles bleached away with worry and sleeplessness. She spends her nights on the couch next to Mom's room, scared to sleep in her own bed upstairs in case Mom needs her. I'll bet she never gets more than a catnap.

It's useless to remind her we can pay for caregivers, or Sherri or I, maybe even Carling, can give her a break. She won't hear of it. It's in her nature to look after others, stray animals, weary folk—she says it's a big sister thing. Sure wish she'd let us take care of her once in a while.

As we've all been doing these last few months, I mostly sidestep Brandi's question. "Dunno, hard to tell."

Irritation at my pathetic evasion skids across her face, but it doesn't land. I've seen this with Lisa when she doubts me and then decides to let it pass. We're shit-scared about Mom's passing, and at the same time, we can't bear not knowing when it will happen.

Brandi changes tack, turning practical. Although it sounds callous, I'm relieved. Focusing on the details takes away some of the fear. Something we can control.

"I've talked with Sherri. We should think about the wake and her funeral mass," she says.

"Ahem," I reply, knowing if my sisters have already discussed this, they probably have it all worked out down to the hymns and the sandwiches at the reception. The burial plot's no issue, we've had it ever since Dad died, behind the church near the old, big maple and the ragged forsythia, fluorescent yellow in the spring. I start a little—it's the first time I've thought of visiting her grave.

Apparently, I'm to give the eulogy. I'm secretly pleased. At last, there's something I can do for Mom, though I protest feebly. "Hey! I'm the youngest. Whatever happened to feminism? You know I'll choke!"

"Glen, you always were the sentimental one. You cried over a dead chipmunk I brought home when you were little. Get over it! You'll be fine— just speak up!"

She says this in that half-amused, half-admonishing tone I caught earlier. Part big sister, part exhaustion, part resentment that crept in years ago. She's not entirely fair either—squeamish, yes—God! You'd never in this world catch me assisting the vets amputate dogs' legs, or putting tubes down their stomachs, or breathing dog breath, septic pus, vomit, and feces like Brandi did all those years.

I'd say I'm sensitive, not sentimental—more manly—at least it is these days when a guy's gotta be strong and in touch with his emotions. God knows what Dad would've made of that! Goes down well with Lisa anyway. Brandi can be a bit sharp; she's had it tough. Christ! Look hard, there's marshmallow inside—like her precious cats, at one moment she's taut to pounce, the next sleepily purring by the fire.

She chats away, and I shiver, not having grabbed a jacket when I dashed over here. Like I guessed, Sherri and Brandi have covered a lot of ground, chosen the funeral director, put a deposit on a coffin. Oak.

"That okay?" Brandi says.

I nod, dumbfounded.

"We're hoping the heating in the parish hall will be fixed in time—if not, the Lions Club's available—unless someone reserves it. May Linn will play the harp—the organist's away for six weeks, so it will have to be a substitute. Shame, Mom loves how Sean O'Connor plays, and he adores her. Can't be helped ..."

She goes on to ask what I think of ham sandwiches, finger food, and if we should offer vegetarian. After a while, I'm not paying much attention, my mind swerving back to the secret Mom shared. It's hard to take it in all at once. With an effort, I drag my thoughts back to the arrangements, and it occurs to me to offer to pay for all this.

"No way!" she jumps in. "Mom's been saving. It's what she wants. Call it her last gift."

She grabs my hand at this, then we cling to one another, both tearing up, sentimental Glen and marshmallow Brandi. Feeling the grief that already has us in its grip. Going through the motions of living even as she's dying, as if our ordinariness could push back the extraordinariness of her death. How can any of us bear to live without Mom? Watching us you might not catch it, yet we all love Mom.

Even, and perhaps especially, Dr. Carling.

As I start the engine to drive away, I realize I am humming the song from the radio in Brandi's kitchen.

"Where does this highway go ...?

"How did I get this life?"

2

Brad – 1963

I exaggerate my swagger as I walk into the lunchroom. It's five o'clock on Saturday, and I just closed a sale. A big grin spreads across my face, and I hook my thumbs through my belt loops as if I'd just taken out the O.K. Corral.

"You cocky bastard!" Gord says.

I laugh and reach out for the cigarette he's offering. Ken takes one too and slaps me on the back. They're sick with jealousy, especially Ken 'cause he's had a bad week, but they're relieved too. Passing that Falcon on to the woman who strutted in "just looking" (they're never "just looking") is more than a fistful of greenbacks for me. It's the end of the quarter, it means the whole team's made quota, and we've all got a nice bonus coming.

It's not long before Chad, the manager, comes in. He's been finishing off some paperwork. I think he's a mean bastard, and he doesn't much like me either, though he won't get rid of me. I'm the best salesman on the team. I bet I'm the only reason the dealership keeps him on as manager.

His belly arrives in the room before the rest of him. Wiry belly hairs poking through the gaping triangle of his crumpled, straining shirt, where the blubber's sprung the last button, and it sprawls over his belt. There are sweaty tidemarks under his wobbly armpits. His pen's wedged above a fleshy ear. We'd pass out from his rancid body odor if it wasn't smothered by the cigarette smoke and the burned wood stink of stale coffee in here. There's a rusted can of vanilla air freshener in the corner—if you spray it, it only makes you want to puke.

"Nice one, Brad!" he says, clapping me on the back with his pudgy hand. "Holy cow! This calls for a beer."

Now, this is definitely against procedures—we're a car dealership, for God's sake; we can't show up for a test drive reeking of Coors. Who gives? It's become a Saturday night ritual anyways, drowning our sorrows or celebrating our (mostly my) little victories. Chad goes and locks up the showroom and comes back with the six-pack he keeps in a cooler in the broom closet.

"How'd you swing it?" Gord asks. "You offer her a movie and a roll in the hay?"

If you take one look at Gord's missus, you can guess his nights in the sack have come to an end. He gets his kicks wishing he was me (the fantasy version of me).

Well, what d'you know? It's not such a bad question. It almost never happens like this, actually never before in my experience; a woman walking into the showroom alone, and one with enough dosh to pay for a car. She wasn't that bad-looking either, generous hips, nice ankles, pasty skin—a bit stuck up.

I straighten my tie, slick back my hair, sidle up, flashing my charm-school smile, and hold out my hand to shake hers. She looks me straight in the eye, no avoiding my gaze or trying to sidle away.

"Pleased to meet you, I'm Mrs. Bernstein," she says, squashing any thoughts my brain might be cooking up of asking her for a date.

After the usual pleasantries and the "just looking" line, she zones in on the Falcon straight away. I take an almighty gamble and introduce her to the technical features right off, engine capacity, acceleration, braking system, transmission. Stuff I might not kick off with even with most men. She doesn't give me a blank, uncertain stare or try to edge away, but nods as if she might even understand what the hell I'm talking about. Seems she's done her homework.

I grab the keys, and we take a test drive. Not many women drive, few with any degree of confidence, but she's right at home behind the wheel. Not fazed one little bit that I'm watching her or that the car's unfamiliar. We head out of town to the highway. She isn't afraid of the gas pedal, but she's no lead-foot either.

We take the first exit, and we're back at the dealership in no time. It's looking promising, and I haven't met a dame yet who isn't interested in the springiness of the seats, the color of the exterior, the trim, how the car will look on her driveway. When I tell her the blue matches her eyes, I think I've blown it. She stops talking and nodding, wrinkles her brow, pauses, and then she laughs out loud. Her laugh's annoying with a weird goose honk at the end. Thank God, she isn't offended, and I know I'm home and dry.

I name a good price (we're desperate for the sale after all). She's probably guessed that, she's that smart. So, without blinking a bright blue eye, she low-balls me. I make a big show of going off to see Chad, who's hogging the phone trying to get someone out to fix his leaking toilet, and I draw up the paperwork myself.

Back at my impressively tidy desk, I tell her she has the deal of the century (she does). With a hint of laughter in those eyes and only a slight smile, unlike the euphoric glee of most buyers, she signs and writes out a check for the deposit. I notice it's a joint account—Mr. Michael and Mrs. Esther Bernstein—and wonder at the husband who trusts her enough to get a better deal when she's alone. We shake hands again, I look into those eyes and think, hubby must be something else. She's out of my league, that's for sure.

Well, you can bet I don't tell the guys all that.

"You gotta know how to turn on the Brad charm," I say. "Anyways, she's off limits—hubby's at home."

"So who's the lucky lady tonight?" Gord asks in a lascivious tone.

"Don't you worry," I tell him, "it's the Lions' dance tonight. They'll fall at my feet."

We carry on the banter for a while. Chad produces more beer—the cooler must be bottomless. He really must not want to go home tonight, but I don't drink any more—no sense in arriving at the dance loaded. I'm planning on flirting with a pretty girl, not barfing all over her.

With a little lubrication, it's Ken who asks, "When're you gonna get tired of the chase, Brad? Hey, isn't it time to settle down?"

I know he's genuinely curious, but I'm not going to tell him that part of me's terrified of settling down, losing my freedom, having to measure up in someone else's eyes ... And there's the other part of me that wants that so bad it's like a physical pain.

"You won't catch me with a ball and chain," I reply a tad too loudly since I'm anxious to hide the truth. I almost follow up with a dig about bossy mothers-in-law, then I suddenly get a mental picture of the old battle-axe who came with Ken's wife and who's always telling him he's not good enough for her sweet darlin'.

Instead, I shrug and say, "Suits me, playing the field. Get a little action and no reaction."

I leave with Gord not long after this, who's giving me a ride home—it's too cold to ride my motorbike, and the only car I can afford, even with dealer discount and bought on a desperate day, is so beat up that it's in the shop. Driving with Gord's like being in a motorized trash can. Pop bottles roll around the floor, orange crackers are ground into the upholstery (which is coated in dog hair), the lining's Scotch-taped to the roof, and the ashtray's overflowing. Ugh! The sole of my shoe's stuck to the greasy mat with gum.

I don't say anything. I'm glad for the ride, and I'll need him to do me the favor for another couple of weeks until the bonus comes in and I can pay off my car repairs. It's just like Chad's desk at the dealership, piled with crap. And the guys all wonder why I make the sales.

I twist my head to figure out what's leaking out of the door pocket, and I catch a glimpse in the wing mirror. *Who is that?* The mirror's cracked, and there's glare from the headlights, so it takes a second to register. *God, it's me.* I look older than I feel, like someone who deceives himself. Gord pulls up outside the newsagent. It's still open.

"Get me a pack of Winstons, you bastard!" he says with a laugh. It's our agreement, I'll keep him in fags, and he'll give me a ride. I live in the apartment above the newsagents anyway, so it's no hassle.

I turn on the gas fire when I get in. I always like the little explosions, the pop and fizz as it spurts into life. The place heats up fast, it's real small, a couple of rooms with a bathroom out on the landing. I rent it furnished, and I've only added a few personal touches.

In the bedroom, I tacked up a poster of a babe straddling a white horse, her long hair barely covering her big bare breasts. You can't see her privates, but you know her sweet butt's slapping up and down on the saddle, naked as the day she was born. There's another poster of the red Corvette I'd like one day; the car leaps out of a floodlit darkness like a red flash in the night.

I've a row of paperbacks in the other room—all sci-fi, and some photos I brought from home. Me at high school in my football gear just after I made the team, Pat as a little girl with a gap where her front teeth used to be, and one of Mom and Pop on their honeymoon looking crazy young and eager, too eager.

Most of the time I like hanging out here, I can do things my own way, and I can always head over to Mom's if I'm bored or hungry for decent food, or I don't want to go to the launderette. Mom's always pleased to see me. She's pissed I moved out. "You'd save a lot of money, you know, if you lived at home—or even got a roommate."

She doesn't get it. I want my own space, and there's not even a broom closet for a roommate here. I need my hang out space. I'm not the great sex athlete I make myself out to be at work, but now and then I'll bring a cute girl here, and I don't want my Mom or my baby sister butting in.

I stretch out on my bed and pull out a porn magazine from underneath the mattress. Another benefit of leaving home—though I did find hidey-holes for them when I was at Mom's (and not under the bed—far too obvious). I flick through the pages, and for once, they don't turn me on, they're too raunchy. After Esther Bernstein, I'm looking for a class act. A woman who knows her own mind.

Now, I need to eat. I'm not thinking a real meal like Mom'd cook … I heat up some chicken noodle soup, eat a couple of soft Hawaiian rolls, a few Little Debbies, and a bowl of ice cream. I wash up, dry the dishes with the towel with Christmas elves on it that I lifted from Mom's, and put the dishes away. I don't want a mess if there's a chance I'll get lucky tonight. Not too shabby for a bachelor.

I take my time showering and shaving and splash a generous amount of Old Spice around my neck and slap it on my cheeks. There's a pleasant sting that stokes my excitement. Then, wrapped in a towel, I make the mad dash back to my apartment. I don't know why I run like this, there's never anyone around; all the same, I feel exposed.

I've worn a suit coat all day and I'd like to dress down, but this is the Lions Club dance. I joined the Lions 'cause I thought it'd be good for business—another move the other guys didn't think of because it can be a tad boring, but I've broken into the old boys' network, and it's beginning to pay off.

I reach for my other suit, a clean shirt and tie, and put them on. I make sure I've pocketed my wallet, the dance ticket, a few business cards, and a couple of rubbers just in case. My good shoes need a polish, but I hear Sandip on the stairs, so I rub them on the back of my pant legs and grab my heavy coat. We're gonna walk there and get a taxi back—if all goes well, with a couple of cute chicks in tow.

Sandip's been my buddy since he was the new kid in high school. It wasn't a slam dunk we'd get along. He was the only Indian I'd ever met, and I was wary at first. He was too slight to be any good at football and too quiet (or so I thought) and too different to be popular, so I figured I'd leave him alone. A lot of the guys gave him a hard time, calling him names, messing with his locker, body-slamming him in the gym corridor.

Well, what d'ya know, Mr. Cousins made him my lab partner in chemistry. Perhaps old Cousins had a hunch we'd be good for each other. So, it wasn't long before I found out Sandip has a wild sense of mischief to match my own.

We were always up to something, fooling around mostly, but the best and the scariest was when Sandip suddenly turned up the Bunsen burner when Cousins was leaning over it and his beard began to char. It smelled wicked bad. Sandip looked real innocent, and he threw a beaker of water at Cousins to staunch the singeing. Cousins was dripping from the eyebrows to the belt buckle, and I got the blame—a visit to the principal's office and a phone call to my parents.

Sandip said his folks would've died of shame if it'd been him. They wouldn't have punished him—they'd have punished themselves, maybe fasting for a few days, 'cause they'd failed in their duty to raise an obedient son. He couldn't live with that. Worse than a thrashing. My folks started off mad, then they couldn't help seeing the funny side after a bit as old man Cousins didn't get hurt.

"How much water was in the beaker, Brad? Did Mr. Cousins keep on teaching soaked to the skin?" Pop couldn't help asking.

Sandip did my homework for me for a couple of months after that. No surprise, he got an A at the end of the year and I got a C; I flunked the exam. I made sure nobody messed with him anymore, and we've stayed friends ever since—even though he went to college and got a decent job, and I stayed in town and joined the dealership.

"Hi, Brad. What's up?" he says with a grin.

"Same old," I say. I don't try to impress him with my last-minute sale. He's known me too long. "What's with you, mate?"

"Same old!" he parries, and we head off at a brisk pace, the three miles to the Lions Club across town.

Turns out it's far from "same old," in Sandip's life. His folks have been fixing to find him an Indian wife, and he's had a blazing row with them 'cause he turned down their latest pick. Evidently, they'd already talked with her folks ... Some shit about honor and stuff. They needn't worry. For all his talk of meeting his future wife (a knockout American girl with big boobs) at the dance tonight, we both know he'll follow their customs soon enough.

And what about my prospects tonight? I wonder, as Sandip, with a fair imitation of the Everly Brothers and a shit-eating grin, whispers in my ear, "All you have to do is dream."

3

Rita – 1963

T he face squinting back at me in the mirror looks dog-tired. I've been rushed off my feet today, teasing beehives, curling flips, a fancy up-do, and I squeezed in a couple of grandpa guys who walked in wanting crew cuts. The older dude wanted a shave as well, but I told him where he could stuff that. Jesus, Mary, and Joseph, I'm kinda glad Mrs. P's running late as ever, lets me catch my breath, take the weight off.

Margaret, who owns the salon, asked me to close up tonight. She put most of the takings in the safe deposit box, leaving enough for my wages and to make change. I'll put the rest in the cash drawer and lock it up. It's been a good day for tips, apart from the tight-fisted men. And Mrs. P's always late, but she's always generous even though it's only a boring old shampoo and set.

One day I'll rent a chair, then the takings'll all be mine, and after that I'll get an up-to-the-minute salon and sell all the latest products. It won't be dowdy cream and brown like this place, it'll be sunshine yellow with a bright green door to lift everyone's spirits, especially through the long winters. There'll be a big sign outside. What'll I call it? Something eye-catching ... like "Snips." In my dreams!

Margaret's gone off to pamper herself for the dance tonight. She put her hair up in a bun, and I checked the back for her. She looks way too formal for my taste. She needs to hang loose. She's got tickets to the dinner and dance, and she had a spare "Dance-Only" ticket, so I'm going too. I'll wear my hair down ... hmm, *Holy Mother of God, do I have time to dye it after Mrs. P's done?*

I lock up the salon nearly three hours later. It's taken a bit longer than I planned, but the results are fab, and I didn't forget to tint my eyebrows a little to match. I swish my newly dyed, fabulous red hair around my shoulders as I hurry up the street. Holy Mother of God, I'm gonna need to change fast or keep Maria waiting while I get dolled up.

"You ready yet?" Maria, my friend, calls up the stairs, making me jog the mascara brush at the sound of her voice. Maria hates waiting with my Dad and Aunt Monday, they can't chill around each other.

I fix the mascara, blot my lipstick on a Kleenex, and do a quick twirl in front of my dresser mirror. I don't get a full-length view ... no problem. My eyes flash back at me, hair streams aflame like maples in the fall. I'm so taken with the perky young woman in the green dress and stunning red hair that I begin to blush. I forget all my tiredness from earlier on and, dress swishing, heels clattering, I hurry downstairs.

"Christ!" Maria screams when she sees my hair.

"Shush!" I say, even though I know Dad's overheard. Maybe Aunt Monday too, although she's in the back kitchen. They can't stand it if anyone says "Christ!" or "My God!" if they're not praying. It's partly why they're uptight when Maria's around. Never mind her family's even more Catholic than ours.

Maria's jangling her car keys ready to be gone. She's smoking hot too in a red dress I helped her make and heels so high I wonder if she can walk (let alone dance) in them. Hope to God she's got some flats for driving. I sniff her perfume. I can't place it, a hint of jasmine, I think ... And I remember I forgot to dab any on. Too late now, and so what? It'd be lost in the sickly mix of old-lady scents, cigarette smoke, a sea of English Leather aftershave, and spilled beer.

Dad comes into the hallway. "Let me take a look at you lovely ladies." Then, he notices my hair.

"You didn't say you were planning on coloring your hair, Rita. My! That's a fine color on you. Suits your eyes." Then he can't resist adding, "Take care, and don't be late back!" as he's done since we were eleven, off to a birthday party or the roller rink. I roll my eyes, but I don't mind really. I'm well past being embarrassed because he cares.

Maria lives in a row home with about a hundred of her family, so there's no spare money there. I've known her since we were at school, doing our nails under the desks and giggling when Mrs. Jenkins came to class with lipstick on her teeth. Gross! Maria dated a car mechanic for a couple of years. They even got engaged. He taught her how to drive and fixed her up with a car.

Mother of God! The paintwork on it's really weird, different shades of gray that feel as if they've been buffed with a wire brush. But the motor works fine. When she broke off that engagement, after she found him in the back alley with Angie Todd, she threw back the ring, but she kept the car keys. She's given me a few lessons, but I haven't taken my test yet—backing up's a nightmare.

As we're driving to the dance, I'm getting excited. Like I said, all my weariness has worn off—even though I didn't get to eat properly tonight, just the PB sandwich I took to work with me. It's been a while since I went out with a guy. I'm just too picky. Perhaps tonight's my lucky night.

The Lions Club's on two levels, the dining room above and the dance floor downstairs. Maria drives down the ramp to the parking lot on the lower level. It's almost full, we're late because of my hair, so Maria creates a spot in the cinders round the back. We totter to the side door—no sense in using the main entrance as we're "Dance Only." We check our coats, they're buried amongst the furs and the black overcoats (how do men tell them apart?), then we step into the Ladies' to check our hair and lips again.

There's one helluva crush, and it takes a while to work our way to the mirror through the sweaty bodies. The mirror's pretty fogged, so I wipe it with a Kleenex. Christ Almighty! We look amazing. The dash from the car put color in our cheeks. We're two hot chicks, and we're ready to party.

It's like a wall of noise and the heat hits us full force when we go into the dance hall. They've already opened some of the windows even though it's cold outside, and the drapes are flaring out like ghostly dance partners. Even so, there's still a swirl of smoke and a musty smell. Mary, Mother of God, there's a whole heap of people here—a crowd around the bar and more on the dance floor.

I spot Margaret and some of the women who come to the salon, one of the beehives, and a bottle blonde, together with their guys, who look as if they've loosened up quite a bit already. I wave, but I don't go over, I don't want to get trapped with the oldies, I want to join the young crowd.

In no time at all, Maria's whisked up to dance with car mechanic's friend Boxer, who's always been sweet on her. Good luck there, I think ... Maria's never been that keen on him. She loves to dance, so I guess she'll put up with him for a while. I make my way to where my old high school friends are hanging out. My hair's a sensation, although they've seen me color and frost it so many different tints, no one can remember what it's naturally like. Even me! (A paler shade of mouse, I think.)

"Swell hair."

"God, Rita, you're on fire."

"Feel the heat, Reet!"

I lap up the attention. It gives me confidence and makes me feel I've stepped out of my humdrum life and I'm about to blaze.

The band's great, and no surprise they're playing, "Let's Dance," the music throbs, and I dance until I'm dizzy and much too hot. It's been no sweat getting partners—on the other hand, no one's swept me off my feet. I'm about to drag Maria, who's escaped Boxer by now, to the bar when I see car mechanic's there with Angie. He's wiped and she's flashing a rock, so I sidle up to the bar on my own. I'm not too crazy about this. The bar staff are rushed off their feet, and they try to ignore a girl on her own, but eventually I get my vodka martini and a glass of water.

I'm being careful with my first drink of the night, given my empty stomach and the fact I'm not much of a drinker. I'm taking my first gulp, when something, or rather someone, catches my eye. Out on the dance floor, just to the left of the band, is one of my regulars—Mrs. Bernstein's dancing with a drop-dead gorgeous guy. I know he's not her husband. She's told me he's quite a bit older than her, and I think he's in a wheelchair. This guy's closer to my age, maybe four or five years older.

He's stripped off his suit coat and loosened his skinny tie, his shirt's sticking to him with sweat, and you can tell he's in fine shape, the clinging cotton defining a flat stomach, broad shoulders, and strong arms. His hair's dark auburn and, although he's flushed, he's fab looking—open features, inviting moist lips.

Did I really think "inviting"? Must be the vodka. There's something about the way he snakes his hips when he dances that's well, seductive. *Seductive?!* There's the vodka talking again, I never use words like that—Dad would have a fit.

Mrs. Bernstein's having nothing of it, she's keeping her distance. I make a sudden decision, and finish the martini right off. The number's ending, and they're walking to the edge of the floor. I toss my head up and walk over to them, plastering what I guess is a bright, confident smile on my face, that I hope covers up all my jitters. Really and truly, I don't actually know Mrs. Bernstein all that well. She's not a tattletale in the salon, keeps her private business private.

"Well, hello, Mrs. Bernstein, I didn't know you were coming. Are you having a nice time?" I say in a voice that comes out with a squeak. Then, I can't quite believe I'm saying, "I'd like to meet your partner! Will you introduce us please?"

And yes! I've said it, bold as brass—*Mother of God! Do I look like a fool?*

"Oh, Rita, I almost didn't recognize you," she replies a little breathlessly. "Your hair looks very pretty. This is Mr. Brad Lenox, he offered me a sweet deal on a car this afternoon."

He smiles at this, a smile that hints there could be more to the story than she's letting on. "It was my pleasure," he says smoothly. "And your friend is?"

"Meet Miss Rita Doyle," Mrs. Bernstein replies. She doesn't correct him and say that we're not really friends, and she adds, "Thanks for the dance, Mr. Lenox. Let me know when the car's ready. I need to get back to my party now." She heads off to the other side of the room, giving me an arch look as she goes by.

For some reason, we both burst out laughing. We're not quite sure what to say when the band strikes up again, and Brad asks, "Wanna dance?" He leads me onto the floor before I've had a chance to accept. If only he knew how much I want to dance with him.

They're playing the twist, and we have a wild time, losing our inhibitions as the music rises and falls. He's the best twister I've ever been with, and we gyrate back and forth, up and down, my hair and my skirt flying, and I hear him laughing and singing, "Let's twist again," above the band. When the pulsating music finally stops, I have a second's fear that he's going to abandon me. I needn't have worried, we dance a couple more, and then he says, "It's sweltering in here. Wanna go outside?"

He threads his way through the crowds, holding my hand so we don't get separated. I've only just met him, not even said a dozen coherent words directly to him, and he's holding my hand! Mary, Mother of God, this can't be happening to me. We make our way round the back of the dance hall, past a few couples making out, some old dudes having a smoke, and a girl I don't know who looks as if she's about to hurl.

Brad pulls out his cigarette packet and offers me one. We smoke and we chat, and it's as easy as anything. Before I know it, he's telling me about his family and some funny story about his grandpa, and I tell him about my Dad and Aunt Monday. And my dreams of a salon one day—and a driving license. After a bit, he notices I'm shivering. He wraps his arm around me and draws me close. Through the sweat and the cigarettes and the beer, I can smell his aftershave. I think it's Old Spice. I approve, beats English Leather.

His arms are around me and I feel his rib cage and those strong chest muscles rise and fall as he breathes. I shift in a little closer, and he tips my chin, so he can kiss me. It's a tender, sweet kiss, his soft, "inviting" lips brushing mine. I want more, and I think he does too, but it's too soon, I don't want to give him the wrong impression, so I hold back. We exchange a few more delicious little kisses. He gently strokes my hair away from his face so it doesn't tickle him. Such a little gesture, yet a thrill tingles through my body, as he does this.

"Rita, my bud and I have a taxi booked. Come back with me, and we can take you home, or hang out some more, pop a couple of beers?"

I think this is a step too fast, and I'm glad I came with Maria. He's not put off when I decline, and he tells me he wants to see me again. I feel as if the whole of me, body, mind, and soul's cheering as we make a date.

Before I go off to find Maria, I look up at the sky.

I swear on the Holy Bible, there are shooting stars!

4

Brad – 1963

Oh my stars! She's there already, waiting for me! I'd had a few beers last night, and it was so far out, I thought maybe I'd dreamed it.

She came walking across the dance floor right up to me … And I realize I'm holding my breath at the memory. Her perfect little body, her flashing hair, her smile, her poise. I can hardly breathe now thinking about it. Just like last night. And she walks up to Old Ma Bernstein, chock full of confidence. She wants to meet me! I don't know if I can hold back my cock's response to her—should I put my hands over my crotch? No, that's sure to put off a dame.

She's on fire. I can always find something to say—I put that on my resume—but I'm almost speechless, stunned, and brimming with desire. Well, what d'ya know? The music comes on, and we're spinning like dervishes—whoever they are. Get this, the dancing's out of this world. Her hair's whipping around wildly, and we're twisting away into the night.

When the music stops, I feel like pinching myself. Can this really be true? She's a firecracker. Stardust! After we dance some more, I take her hand and we head outdoors—and she doesn't call for a spotty, overweight friend to come too. She follows along as if we've known each other for ages. Then, oh, how I want to kiss her, to stroke her cheek, to nestle into her. And then I do take her in my arms and it's warm and sweet, and I long for more. I think I can taste her like a sweet strawberry hanging in the air.

I don't want her to run. I don't want to scare her. So I hold back. I brush her hair from her face and nuzzle on her neck. Hell! There's the moment when I think I've blown it—asking her to share the cab, come back with me.

It's better the way it turned out, that she went back with her (clear-skinned, slender) friend, and we have this first "date" alone together any minute now. Oh Christ! She's really there—in a heavy coat that hides her gorgeous bod, but not her light-up-the-world smile.

Caught up in the moment, last night, I couldn't think where to suggest, so we're here at the bandstand in the middle of Warner Park. If I thought at all, I guessed we'd just stroll around. It's pissing it down! She didn't stand me up or play hard to get. She's here waiting for me. God! It's not a dream, I might have to pinch myself again. I'll be black and blue at this rate.

We sit on the bandstand steps—the roof overhangs just far enough to keep the worst of the rain off us. She tells me she can't stay too long; they have a special dinner on Sundays, and she needs to help her aunt out. She's brought a little notepad and a pencil so we can exchange phone numbers. After she writes down hers, she sucks the end of the pencil, and it drives me wild. She gives me both her home and work numbers. I do the same, though I think what a ragging I'll get if she actually does call me at work.

The chatter comes naturally, I've got the gift of the gab back, and she's fond of a good story. We squeeze hands, she snuggles into me. She's shivering again, even in the thick coat, the rain making it feel raw. I put my arms around her and hug her close. She puts her face up to be kissed, and I gently trace her lips with my tongue.

This sends tingles all over me and I'm aching for more, but this is so delicious, I can hold back until the time's right. She runs her fingers through my hair, along my jaw, and then she breaks the spell by feeding her hand into my jacket and tickling me under the armpit, and we both giggle like teenagers.

Even though I get soaked to the skin, I walk her home. It's a couple of miles and in the opposite direction from my apartment. We barely see a soul as we're walking—except, as luck would have it, Gord's out walking his dog. He gives me a knowing look and taps a finger alongside his nose with a smirk.

We pause a few doors down from her house, and I gently sweep the hair from her face and kiss her, one of our chaste, exquisite little kisses.

"See you next week," she calls as she hurries home.

Next week! My stars! How am I gonna wait that long?

When Gord picks me up the next morning in his cesspit of a car, his eyes are popping out of his face in excitement like blueberries in a muffin. "Dish the dirt, Brad," he says. "Who's the chick?"

I take a deep breath, knowing this will be all around the dealership the moment we arrive, and then I tell him what I told Sandip on our ride back from the dance on Saturday night. "I think I just met the girl I'm going to marry."

Gord whistles, his breath draining from him like a sagging balloon. He turns to me, gives me the raised eyebrows look (I wish he'd keep his eyes on the road), and he mutters, "Oh, Christ! Brad, what the 'ef' did you get yourself into?"

There's a lot of barracking in the showroom when Gord spills the beans—Chad has to waddle out of his office to calm us down. It's always slow on a Monday morning, so they bait me for a couple more hours until the prospects (or pisspots, as we've been known to call them) start to straggle in.

The week drags by, and our numbers aren't that good. Chad gives us a talking to when we close on Saturday. "And you, Mr. Lenox,"—his name for me when he's not well pleased—"you need to get your mind back on your work and away from the skirt, or you're missing our drinking session for tonight." The guys make some choice lewd remarks as I leave.

"Be good, Romeo, and if you can't be good, be careful!"

"Give her one from me!"

It's warmer tonight, so I walk and leave Gord to his filthy car. If the weather stays this way, I'll soon be able to ride the Honda Trail again. I get to the Odeon before she does, and I've just begun to pace, wondering if I look like a wanker, when she shows up.

"Hi, Brad. Hope I didn't keep you waiting too long. I had to do a permanent at the end of the afternoon, and you know how long those take." (I didn't—I guess I do now.) "Did you have a good week?" she asks.

"Fab," I lie, and I take her hand and we're swallowed up in the theater. I lead her to the back and take it as a good sign that she doesn't complain. We find our seats along with two or three courting couples, all younger than us. She squeezes my hand, and I balance the popcorn between us.

The movie, *Through a Glass Darkly*, is not bad, but you could say I'm not giving it my full attention. Not even half my attention. It's locked on Rita. I'm deciding how soon I can creep my arm over her shoulder (very soon), how soon I can feed her popcorn from my hand (very soon), from my mouth (quite soon). How soon I can kiss her (quite soon)—and I take the opportunity to roll my tongue inside her mouth pretending to hunt for popcorn. How soon can I ease my hand down to feel the juicy breast beneath the blouse.

This takes a while, but she helps me by taking her jacket off and leaning in towards me over the awkward ridge in the seat, and my stars! It's worth the wait. She's firm and soft and warm all at the same time. Jeez, she feels so good, I start to throb.

I'm tempted, but I don't reach my hand over the stupid ridge towards her inner thigh. I don't want to break the spell even though all her lights have been on green. She's run her fingers through my hair, traced my jaw with her finger, and fed me popcorn kisses too. I don't give a damn about the movie anymore, the action around here's grabbing all my attention. As the credits roll up, our lips are locked, and I'm running my tongue over her delicious teeth. She gives a little sigh.

Then there's a cough, a clearing of the throat—the movie's over, and one of the other courting couples pushes past. "Disgusting ... at their age!" sniggers the girl, who looks about twelve.

We keep going out. I'd guess you'd say we're going steady from the get-go. It's always magic with Rita whether we're out for dinner, at the bowling alley, the rink, or just walking in the park. Whenever she takes my hand, it's like a jolt of electricity ripples through my body, jerking me alive.

In a couple of weeks, I invite her round to my apartment. I've spent a lot of time after work spiffing it up. I'm tidy, even at home, but I'm not into cleaning. I figure I haven't cleaned the bathroom in months, and the kitchen area's smeared with a light film of grease and dust. I open the windows to air the place out now the weather's better. I vacuum, not too crazily—I don't go rooting in the sofa for popcorn and crackers and God knows what's in there. I do pull out my stash of "Vixen" magazines and hide them in the loft space above the bathroom (just where I used to hide them at Mom's). I try to look at my girl on the horse poster through Rita's eyes. Will she think it's a "guy thing"? I can't tell. All I know is I can't part with it right now.

It's a bit like playing house when she comes round. We cook Spaghetti Bolognese—well, she laughs as I cook. I pour the whole box of spaghetti into the boiling water, fry the ground beef, and pour a jar of tomato sauce over it. There's enough spaghetti to feed a small starving nation—one that doesn't mind it's all sticking together. The pan hisses at the meat and hisses and spits a lot more when I tip in the sauce, so I have little splatters all over my light blue shirt, and one smear Rita licks off my nose. Yum.

I can't pretend the meal's delicious, but we wash it down with a couple of beers (well, I drink a couple, she has a half glass). Then we wash the dishes together, and I flip suds on her nose, so I can pretend to lick them off and get my own back. She tugs at the neck of my shirt and plops some down there, getting a glimpse of my manly chest hair at the same time.

Then we curl up on the sofa, like an old married couple, to watch TV. She snuggles under my arm, and my fingers go a-wandering. After a bit of fumbling, I slip my hand inside her bra and toy with the weight of her breast, squeezing it and weighing it as sparks explode in my head. She wriggles her hands behind her back and unfastens her bra clasp. More sparks. I find the nipple and roll it between my thumb and forefinger. Hard and taut to my touch. She gives a little gasp and I think I've hurt her, but there's anticipation and joy in that gasp that makes me tremble.

I bury my head in her cleavage and move her nipple into my mouth. Is it Rita who's moaning or is it me? Maybe it's both of us. After the sparks and meteors fade a bit, I lead her to the bedroom. She's already seen it—she didn't say a word about the "girl astride horse" pic. Wordlessly, she starts to pull off my shirt. I ease her blouse above her head, and the loose bra falls from her shoulders. I've been tempted to rip off my shirt myself 'cause I don't like stained clothes. I'd held back so I could feel her hands running up my torso.

Christ! She's a knockout. A small frame but with fuller breasts than you'd expect. We fall on the bed, and she rubs those breasts up and down my chest as if that glimpse of my hair turned her on. The friction's wonderful. I feel her chest rising and falling, the darling breasts quivering. We're moving quickly now, and she lets out little gasps and sighs. And the warm heart that beats so fast—mine or hers? We make that moaning sound again in unison. I need her. God, I need her.

The thinking part of my mind has shut down. I'm all touch, all feel, all desire. I undo my belt and struggle out of my pants. *Why is this so clumsy when there's a girl around?* And I toss my Y-fronts on the floor. I help Rita shimmy out of her jeans, and I'm a bit surprised when she keeps her undies on. They're white cotton and, in this moment, sexier than black lace or red satin. I slip my hand inside and feel the steamy hair, the full mound, and the moist cleft.

She sighs, and I press my hips into hers so she can feel my erection. Then she stiffens and says, "I'm sorry, Brad. I'm so sorry, I can't go any further."

I'm not sure I heard her. We've opened all the doors, it's time to go inside. Then it flashes across my brain, "Is it that time of the month?" I ask—thanking my lucky stars I have a sister so I can sound sensitive and knowledgeable, even though there was no indication, no pad, no tampon.

"Nothing like that, and I really want to—but, well, I'm Catholic," she tells me.

"What's that got to do with anything?" I ask.

"We don't ... well, nice Catholic girls don't—it's a sin unless you're married."

I want to shout, protest, remind her it's the sixties. We've come this far, I'm aching to climax. I don't tell her this. Instead, I excuse myself and run to the bathroom on the landing, where I quickly finish myself off in the shower, clean up, and make a big show of washing my hands, before I wrap a towel around me and dart back to Rita.

Turns out she's stubborn about this. "You're twenty-three, Reet, you mean to say you've never done it? You're a natural for fuck's sake."

She laughs at this, and I love her and want her even more. I have to swallow my frustration and respect her boundary. God! I'm frustrated, I've hit a barred gate.

All the same, over the summer I teach her a few tricks to make sure she and I get our kicks. I long to be inside her, move with her, feel her pleasure, yet the delay, the tension makes what we are doing a pretty good substitute. For a while, I make the sprint to the bathroom, then I realize she's not repulsed—she's only repressed, by the church, a church that wants her to believe there's something wrong in loving like this. And, oh, my stars, no one has ever made me feel this good, this sensuous, this right.

5

Rita – Summer 1963

The summer's a blur. I'm with Brad every spare moment, and my friends all whine that I don't hang out with them anymore. Brad buys me a flashy motorbike helmet—I feel like an astronaut when I wear it—and we go places on his Honda. Holy Moly! The rush's awesome, the scenery hurtling by like a speeded-up movie, and me holding on to his strong body for dear life. I don't tell Brad, I clutch my rosary so hard it dents my palm, I swear that's what keeps us safe. It's heady, intoxicating, exhilarating—like we're launching into space. And lots of fun to get out of Dodge.

I get Mondays off—the salon's closed—and since he works Saturdays, Brad can often swing a Monday too, so we ride to the ocean and spend the day on the beach. Sometimes we pack a lunch, sometimes he treats me to a lobster roll at the clam shack just up the road. I can't believe I'm saying this, I guess it's love! I'm in love!

There's never been a summer like this, day after day of bright sunshine, salt sea air, warm breezes, and no jellyfish! We barely hear the kids' shrieks as they charge in and out of the water. We do hear the gulls' and the sandpipers'' catcalls when we're sunbathing or making out in the dunes, like they're broadcasting a play-by-play of us.

Other times, we go to the lake; the water's warm enough to swim in at this time of year. Brad likes swimming well enough, but really and truly, I'm in my element, slipping and, now and again, slicing through the pristine water, dipping under in a duck dive, and surfacing to shake off the drops like a puppy. Brad loves to see me in a swimsuit. (He'd rather see me in less—I guess that's a guy thing.) My skin thrills when I leap into the water, splashing Brad as I go, and there are more thrills when I come out and he rubs me down, slipping a hand inside my clingy suit. Jesus, Joseph, and Mary!

One time this endless summer—we spend Sunday on the beach with friends—it's time to stop their whining, and I want mine to get to know Brad. I intend on keeping him around a while. I invite Maria and Amy from school days, Brad asks Sandip (also from school), his sister Pat, her boyfriend, and a coupla guys he played football with back in the day.

Brad and I always travel light—there's a limit to what you can fit on the back of a motorbike, so it's wild to see the others hauling beach chairs, coolers, and heaven knows what to the beach. Sandip's even lugging a volleyball net, and we annoy a whole load of other beach-goers marking out our court and yelling and leaping around. It's a whole load of fun, though most of us take it seriously. Hmm! We've got the competitive instinct—and raging hormones?

Brad's in shape, he jogs a few times a week. The football guys have run to flab, and they're cursing themselves when they're out of breath, or can't dive to the ball. A summer of swimming and a job where I'm on my feet all day, and I can keep up—Maria's falling down and panting like a dog. She joins the guys shouting, "Jeez!" "Christ!" and "Shit!" Thank the Lord, Dad and Monday aren't here.

I can't avoid noticing Maria and Pat are almost falling out of their miniscule bikinis, and Pat makes a huge show of asking her boyfriend to massage her with sun oil. He's all for it, and slips his hand under her bra whenever he thinks no one's looking. Don't give Brad ideas; he hardly keeps his hands to himself as it is. When Pat's all wet after a screaming dip in the icy ocean, she can't find her clothes. Amy and Maria add to the drama, shrieking, "Oh my God! There's a sex pervert, stealing women's clothes!"

Sandip and Brad look way too innocent and soon can't smother their giggles. They keep glancing at the lifeguard's chair, and I wonder, for a moment, if the guard, a hot guy with slick black hair's in on it, too. Then I get it, they're trying to distract anyone from looking at the little platform by the boardwalk. I scurry over there, my feet stinging on the hot sand, as the guys yell at me, "What the fuck, Reet?! Come back!" And there, screwed up under the bench are Pat's underwear (barely worth bothering with), her floppy hat, an apology for a sundress, and heeled sandals (yes, heels).

Later, when we're all hot and bothered, covered in sand and salt, we go into the little town in search of ice cream. First, we have to haul all the paraphernalia to the cars. Mary, Mother of God! It just makes us all sweatier and bad-tempered. Pat's play fights with her guy are on the brink of turning nasty,

"Well, I didn't ask to have sand down my cleavage and up my butt!" she complains, even though we all saw her making a big show of stuffing sand up his boxers. Amy's feigning exhaustion so she can drape herself round one of the footballers, and Sandip's trying to annoy everyone. Good God! If we didn't need it earlier, we really need that ice cream now.

It's a picture-perfect New England fishing village with a ripe-smelling port, marina, and quaint Main Street. The stores all look as if they were built with the ark—overlapping shingles, crazy angles and bottle-glass porthole windows. Wherever you look there are bobbing flowers, squawking seagulls, and loads and loads of people!

There's a huge line outside the ice cream hut that looks so unsteady it'll tipple over with just a little push. You bet the football players hurry over and lean into it, but it's sturdier than it looks. I guess it's held up against nor'easters and has a good few years left.

As we're hanging out, I see Mrs. Bernstein and her husband slowly making their way up the street. He's on elbow crutches today, and having a hard time negotiating the cobbles. They find a bench with, miraculously, two empty seats. I nudge Brad, "Hey, that's Mrs. Bernstein, you know, the woman who introduced us?"

With a quick glance, he registers Esther and her husband. "Oh! I didn't realize," he says, noticing Michael, and it's as if I can see the cogs of his brain click into gear, that car purchase suddenly making sense.

He's almost at the head of the line now, and buys two mint chocolate chip ice creams.

"Get us some too!" he tells me, heading over to the Bernsteins to surprise them with the ice creams. When I join them, ice cream dripping through my fingers, he's chatting about the Falcon. Mrs. Bernstein's laughing her rich, gurgling laugh. That's my Brad. Always working a deal.

❖

Brad comes to dinner with Dad and Aunt Monday almost every week. She's not really named Monday. When I was little, before Mom was real sick, she'd come over on Mondays to help Mom do the laundry (it was a heavy job then, before the new machines). I got to calling her Aunt Monday, and the name stuck.

Although Brad turns on his salesman charm, I can tell they're none too keen. Dad's worried about me on the back of the motorbike. He tries to give Brad holy water to sprinkle over it to protect us. (Brad doesn't even know about my rosary yet.) He politely declines.

"Mr. Doyle, I appreciate your concern, I really do. You can trust me to take care of Rita, there's no call for divine intervention."

All the same, it's pretty obvious he's taken aback, and trying to stifle scorn. Dad's always been a worrier, or maybe that started when Mom got sick, I don't remember and, as I'm an only child (yes, we are Catholic, but Mom was sick a long time), he's over-protective. Aunt Monday doesn't say as much, but I guess she thinks Brad's too brash, too old (he's twenty-eight), too careless with his words—a few "My Gods," "Christs," and a "Jesus H. Christ!" have slipped out even though I warned him.

They're both embarrassed when he touches me, holds my hand, strokes my hair, or gives me a peck on the cheek, which is all we do when they're around. A weird or maybe a mean thought crosses my mind. Aunt Monday might be just a teeny bit jealous. She's Dad's big sister. She moved in after Mom died to help take care of us. She never married, and I didn't think of it until now, but I haven't ever seen anyone make a fuss of her, pay her attention, flirt a little with her.

She'll give me a quick hug now and again though—Mary and Joseph, I see now—we're not a touchy, huggy sort of family. Even so, no one can doubt that she loves me and Dad to bits. What d'ya know? There's all kinds of ways to love in this world.

It's a different story at Brad's house. His mom ("Call me Phyllis, dear"—it doesn't seem right, but I manage it after repeating, "Phyllis," to myself in the mirror about a thousand times) and sister Pat treat me as if I've always been part of the family. There's one thing. Bless my soul, Phyllis and Pat, they're always wanting me to give them new hairdos—it gets old since that's what I do all the livelong day. They're so pleased with their new do's, I don't mind too much.

After dinner, we all go into the TV room and watch game shows. They're all shouting across each other when they know the answers so I can hardly hear the show. It's not like that at home, where everyone's got to take their turn.

Phyllis and Pat take me shopping when we're all off work. Phyllis can't resist buying Pat and me little treats; a pair of flip flops for the beach, a little necklace that looks as if it's made out of candy, a juicy strawberry dipped in chocolate. They tell me things about Brad, like how he led his high school football team to the state championship, or about the pranks he played on his teachers. One time he "accidentally" set the Bunsen burner on high and it set the chemistry teacher's beard on fire. (Pray heavens no one tells Dad and Aunt Monday about that. They'd lay an egg.)

You can tell Phyllis and Pat are really fond of him and, at the same time, they want to baby him. His dad, Jack, travels for business, so I don't see much of him. When I do, I get the feeling he's a bit relieved Brad's got a steady girlfriend. Like the rest of them, he's super friendly, and I should be grateful. They're all a bit too friendly for a girl like me, if you know what I mean. Takes a bit of getting used to, and I do wish Jack'd keep his hands off me. Mary, Mother of God, I swear he's always patting me on the bottom stroking my hand, or touching my hair.

I can't say anything, that's rude, and they all mean well enough. Now I know why Brad likes to touch me up so much, it's what Lenox men do. And don't get me wrong, I adore when Brad does it. It's just when his dad tries it on, it gives me the creeps. I glance at Phyllis when Jack's too familiar—she can't like it. I catch her eye for a fraction of a second, then she looks away. Does she accept it as something all men do and all women have to deal with? She needs to meet my dad!

When she does, Phyllis gushes over him, "Oh! Mr. Doyle, may I call you Wilf? I'm sure I never met such a sweet man. Make yourself at home, you're part of the family. Rita's just darling. We all just adore her. You must be very proud. Please, let me get you a glass of iced tea—or would you prefer something stronger?"

And she tells Aunt Monday what a wonderful job they've done raising me. Dad and Aunt Monday are a pushover for Phyllis—and they don't meet Jack until the picnic.

To celebrate Labor Day, Brad's family invite us (and a huge crowd of their close friends and neighbors) over for a cookout. It's one of those glorious, late summer days. Cotton puff clouds drift across a clear blue sky, a little breeze whistles in cool hints to remind us that fall and winter are waiting in the wings. Here and there, a few leaves are beginning to turn. The Canada geese sound their horns and practice formation flying. The Lenox backyard is surprisingly big for the size of the house, and it's buzzing with guests, who all come armed with picnic chairs, food, drinks, and raucous voices.

Phyllis and Jack (he of the wandering hands) make an effort to include Dad and Aunt Monday, who actually look like they're having a good time. Aunt Monday made her signature sour cream and chocolate chip cake, and Dad, a bit to my surprise, brought a six-pack of beer and another of hard cider.

The guys make a big show of cooking, flipping burgers, and burning the hot dogs. Jack manages to singe his chef's apron (he's not wearing his favorite featuring the woman in a bikini, thank God) and a neighbor kid drops a whole plate of chicken, but he bends down and picks it up and slaps it on the grill before his mother notices. After we've eaten (we all claim it's great although it's charred and gritty—especially the chicken)—and it is great because, really and truly, it's all about hanging out together.

We all kick back and somebody puts on some music—the Everly Brothers' "Devoted to You." I mouth the words, "I'll never leave you, I'll never lie, I'll never be untrue," and I feel like dancing, when Pat corners me and wants to talk about the latest styles. Out of the corner of my eye, I watch Brad sneaking off to one side to talk with my dad. I'm pleased about this, he's making an effort, though they look a bit serious. Pat whispers to me she's just met another special squeeze, and she blushes a deep red. *How far did they go?* I wonder.

I glance away from her for a moment to let her calm down, and notice Brad shaking Dad's hand, they're all smiles now. That's odd. He slips through the crowd, and I think he's headed my way, but he nods at his mom and dad, who have amazingly drifted together. Jack usually claps his arm around all the other women's shoulders before he gets round to Phyllis. Odder still, Jack bangs on his glass with his knife, Pat smothers a giggle, and when he's got everyone's attention, announces, "Quiet, quiet, everyone. Brad has a question to ask."

There's a bit of a buzz, then everyone does quiet down, and Brad comes over to me. Then he does it.

"Rita Marie Doyle, I love you forever. Will you marry me?"

Holy Mother of God! He's down on one knee, fumbling in his pocket for something. I pull him to his feet, my heart pounding through my chest fit to break a rib, and tears already pricking in the corners of my eyes. Jesus, Mary, and Joseph! I drag him upright and give him a big, smoochy kiss. Right there in front of everyone!

When we pull ourselves apart, he says, "I take it that's a yes?"

"Yes, Brad Lenox, let's get married!" I manage to stutter in a wobbly voice as the tears have really begun to flow. The ring's a tiny diamond solitaire, sparkling like a star—and it fits! Phyllis and Pat must have had a hand in this—maybe the other day when they gave me a manicure.

Everyone's cheering, dogs are barking, car horns blaring, even the geese are honking! I find Dad, who looks as proud as punch and holds my hand super tight—it's the left one with the ring, and, oh my! That hurts. Aunt Monday hugs me so hard and for so long, I wonder what's come over her until I realize she's trying to hide her tears.

When I finally drift off to sleep that night, I dream that I'm clinging on to Brad on the bike and we are soaring across the night sky, flying through shooting stars.

We marry just after Thanksgiving. Brad couldn't afford to miss Black Friday at work. It's such a whirl in the weeks before the wedding, I can hardly remember it. Just flashes. I'm at my sewing machine buried in mounds of fabric, making the bridesmaids' dresses, or I'm addressing piles of invitations, or I'm off with Brad checking out apartments.

Aunt Monday makes my dress while I'm at work. It's all froth and foam like you get on top of steamed coffee, and I adore it. I can't wait to see Brad's face. Aunt Monday and Phyllis and some other Lenox relatives cook up a storm for the reception.

There's a moment when I think Brad's going to burst a blood vessel and call it off! I tell him I'm thinking of going blond for the wedding.

"Holy smokes, Rita, don't do that. I love your hair. I'll be at the front of the church dying to turn around and see you coming down the aisle with a wisp of your insanely gorgeous, red, red hair curling out from under your veil. That's my Rita," he tells me.

The ceremony's in his family's Unitarian church. Then we make our way across the street where an icy wind tugs at my veil and turns the bridesmaids blue. Dad and Aunt Monday wanted a Catholic wedding mass, but Brad told them we couldn't wait while he took instruction. I know they were hurt. Brad makes it a bit better by promising our children will be little Catholics. Father Patrick comes to the reception and offers a nice blessing. That's the second time I see Aunt Monday cry.

I think Dad is more nervous than me walking down the aisle, but we don't trip or have a nosebleed or anything, so it all goes well. When I get to the front, I lightly brush back a little of the veil so

Brad gets a glimpse of my hair. He stops shaking, grins, and brushes it ever so gently.

A whirlwind of chatter, hugs, kisses, laughter, and tears. I throw my bouquet and everyone (except Pat) cheers when it's Aunt Monday who catches it.

We're off.

A couple of nights in an inn looking over a gray, windswept ocean. No worries, we have an open fire, and we have each other. And that first night in our marital bed together? Mmmh!

6

Brad – 1966

I tuck her damp hair behind her ear, I kiss her brow, and I brush my lips across her sweet mouth. I'm wiped with all the pacing up and down, so she must be exhausted. I see it in those forget-me-not eyes, she manages to smile and draws some energy into her voice, "Did you see her already?"

"You bet I did! She's a stunner, like her mom and her big sister," I say.

Tears well in her eyes at this and, all at once, I'm choked up with love for her. They've taken the baby to the nursery to give Rita some rest. She was in labor a long time, nearly as long as with Brandi—I didn't think it'd be this bad with a second baby. I paced a couple of marathons in the waiting room. Now, I stroke her hand until her eyes begin to droop, and she settles deeper into her pillows. Time to let her sleep.

I make a few phone calls from the lobby although it's late. "Yes, it's a girl. Both doing well." Excited voices on the other end, joy bubbling up, relief all went well. My mom sobs, Aunt Monday's thanking God, the Virgin Mary, and all the blessed saints, and Pat wants to know all the gory details. Her own baby's due in three weeks. I don't have much to tell her, they don't let the dads watch. Hell! We'd all pass out, throw up, and get in the way.

I drive to our new house. Seems like the removal van only just pulled away. My God! We cut it fine! We were unloading our shit only two days ago. We got the beds set up, and Rita's dad stocked the fridge for us. All that activity must've brought the baby on. She's ten days early. We thought it'd be a race between Rita and Pat.

I'm hardly out of the car when Mom rushes down the front steps in her old chenille robe. Thank God the outside light works even if it's dim. Brandi's asleep on her shoulder. Mom can't stop hugging me—Jeez! Hope Brandi doesn't slip off. I wriggle an arm free and put it 'round both of them. Mom's sobbing an entire ocean of tears—my shirt's soaked and I'm shivering. *Mom—don't wake Brandi up, or squeeze the two of us to death.* I'm knackered, but I know why Mom's reacting like this. It's the first good news since Pop passed, nearly six months ago.

He fell asleep driving home from one of his business trips, drove slap-bang into an eighteen-wheeler. He couldn't have known a thing about it. Mom's not been herself since the policewoman knocked on her door. The officer didn't need to say a word, Mom knew. Pat completely lost it, fell apart, convulsing like she was having a fit. We thought she'd miscarry—she'd only just told us she was pregnant. I'm not sure Pop even knew that, he'd been gone awhile. Must have. Mom would've called him.

Hell! It took me off guard. Poof! Pop's gone. I'm the man now, Christ Almighty! And Mom's taking it so hard, growing old and helpless overnight! What with Pop being away all the time *and* a ladies' man, I'd not realized their love ran so deep. Guess you never notice when it's your folks.

Next day, I wake up around nine o'clock, feeling groggy from the Jim Beam I slammed to help me get to sleep—and celebrate the baby. Jeez! Hope Brandi's alright! When I stagger into the kitchen, I needn't've worried. She's with Mom, playing with a set of zoo animals on the floor. Her shirt's on the wrong way round, but it's not bothering her.

Mom found the coffee pot. Smells great. Thank God, the baby came on a Saturday night, and I don't have to go into work! It's a missed opportunity—customers, especially couples, love to buy from a brand-new dad, and they don't try to beat you up on price. I'll work that angle for all it's worth next week.

Aunt Monday and Wilf are going to the hospital this morning (you bet they went to five o'clock mass yesterday to be on the safe side). Mom, Brandi, and Pat are going this afternoon, and I'll visit in the evening. Poor Reet, she'll never get to rest. Never ever again now, with two little ones to look after—and a sexually demanding husband!—how long before she reaches for me again—or I can reach for her? I call the hospital, and they tell me she's a little uncomfortable, (like hell she is,) but she's doing well. The baby's fine, took the breast—no problem—wish I could too.

I take a second mug of coffee to the ugly, new bathroom. Who chose the revolting puke green tile, the mismatched avocado sink? (What is avocado anyway?) I take a shower. We're still getting used to everything here—the water's fucking hot and I get third-degree burns until I figure out how to adjust it. It pounds on my scalp and my shoulders, scouring the sleep, the sweat, and the booze from me. It's much more intense than our old dribbling shower, and I feel a deep clean. Like a baptism. My God! That's another thing we'll have to arrange. Catholics don't hang around about that—not with a precious, immortal soul to save. Who'll we get to be godparents? Better choose someone with some readies.

I rub my hands over my chin; I'd like to skip the shave, but Brandi'll scream if I don't and I try to kiss her. The mirror's on an extension arm that reminds me of my grandad's music stand. Miss him and Nan. Miss Pop. Miss him a shitload. He should be here. A huge version of me leaps from the mirror; I look like an alien, greenish and gross! Shit! I nick myself alert and wonder, *Brad Lenox, husband, family man, head of the household, mortgaged up the wazoo! What happened to me?*

The guys at work rag me about this all the time.

"Yikes! You're an old married man, Brad. Lost your roving eye and your roving dick, eh?" This from Gord.

"Swapped your bike for a fucking family sedan? No time to have a few beers with the guys! She's got you right where she wants you," crows Ken.

They can't lay it on too thick. I'm the manager now. Chad got caught with his stubby fingers in the till. Surprised they could reach that far over his big belly. I'm building a new team, working longer hours. Oh, my stars! *Oh, my stars!—why am I still saying this dumb phrase?* It's all Sandip's fault. He and I were forever mimicking Ma Grady, the school secretary. *Oh, my stars* sounded a whole lot funnier when Sandip said it. Anyways, I'm glad for the work. We need the money.

I go and check on Mom and Brandi—Mom shoos me away. "Brandi's going to need a lot of your attention when her little sister comes home. Give yourself a break for a couple of hours. We're fine."

Mom's tone is lighter and sharper than it's been in a long time, she's not looking quite so drawn. Wow! Thank God! Guess there's healing magic in a new grandchild—that, together with the need to be needed, it's working wonders. Brandi looks up at me with her wide green eyes. Her mouth's covered in pudding or yogurt and it's disgusting!

And when she flashes me a great big grin, she's the most beautiful little girl I ever saw. She's feeding the stuff to a walrus, and suddenly pokes the spoon at me, missing my mouth and jabbing into my cheek. I open walrus wide, and she shovels it in. Yuck! Revolting! I gulp it down, lick my lips and tell her, "Yummy yummy in my tummy."

Although there are a thousand jobs to be done, I can't settle. I walk to the creaky old bench on the back porch, sit there, take out a cigarette, and my mind drifts ...

I think about how cute Brandi is and how much she's changed since we brought her home from the hospital. My stars, she's not the only one who's changed. Look at me! I had to grow up, stop running home to Mom. Hell, it seemed like I had to grow up overnight. One moment I'm speeding down the lanes with a knockout chick straddling the bike behind me. Blink, and we're married—a bigger apartment, bigger bills to pay.

I make a small salary and commission now—not long ago it was all commission. My God, it's hard to pay regular bills without regular income. Rita didn't make enough to cover it if I went through a lean spell. I pulled it out. Rita doesn't know how close we came. Damned hard work and a stroke of genius.

Late one evening at the end of the quarter, I rang Sandip and a football bud I haven't seen in years—not since that beach day. I sweet-talked them both into dropping a deposit on a car. We all knew they'd cancel after the weekend. Hey! We made quota, and the landlord didn't throw us out on the street.

That's likely the night Rita got pregnant with Brandi. I was throbbing, ready to explode—I couldn't hold back until she got the diaphragm in. We were young, naked, and on fire with desire and relief. I wanna have sex with Rita all the time. It's like pop rocks exploding in my mind and my body all at once. Babies don't come cheap, but if Brandi's anything to go by, they're worth it.

We started looking for a house as soon as we knew our daughter Carling was on the way. Needs to be in a good school district, so you bet your bottom dollar, the sticker price goes up. I talked big to Rita telling her we'd find a place. Inside, I wasn't sure we'd make it.

Pop left most of his money to Mom but, thank God, there was some for Pat and me. Pop was savvy with his money. He paid off their mortgage before the smash, and Mom gets his life insurance and some savings so she doesn't have to worry. She's real lonely in the house, and she can't keep up with the big yard. I'll bet she moves within a year. Too soon now.

I light up another cigarette and walk around our house. *Our house!* Unbelievable! We haven't lived here anywhere near long enough to make it feel like home. Jeez! I've stiffened up. No time to go for a run these days, and horseplay with Brandi doesn't cut it. I'm 'round the front now, taking in the street. It's a nice neighborhood—ours is the end house, the smallest, and the least maintained. That's why we could afford it—and we were damn lucky. The others are pretty big, all neat with nice yards. There's a lot of basketball hoops and swing sets—kids for our girls to play with.

I check out the cars. I'll work some deals with the neighbors. I don't know them yet. Rita met them briefly when we came round to measure up, and then on moving day when they brought a pie over. Middle-aged, foreign—Hungarian, or maybe Polish. I'm not sure. There's some large trees between our lot and theirs—maples, I'd guess. Rita will know. A bit of privacy, shade in the summer, color in the fall—God, I hope they don't blow down in the winter. Gee! I hope they're on the neighbors' property.

I'm gazing at the trees when a florist's van pulls up with pink and white flowers for Rita. Wow. The news spread quick. I'm just taking them from the driver when the foreign couple appears.

"Your wife had the baby I'm thinking?" the woman asks.

"Congratulations!" says the guy, and he looks down at the flowers. "Ah, another girl, I see. "

Their English is perfect, but they have quite the accent. I guess we all do, come to think of it. I'd say they're about fifteen years older than us, both a bit pale, especially the woman. She's taller than her husband (poor sod!)—yellow blonde to his dirty blond. (Rita's trained me on this.) We talk for a while. They have a daughter, too—all grown, not around a whole lot. She's off in college.

"Too bad!" I tell them. No way are my girls going to college and leaving us. I'd miss them to bits—I feel this in my gut. I haven't even got to know Carling yet, and I already have this strong urge to protect her.

"Can't complain," the man says with a little smile lighting up his long face and deepening his dimple. "She's a good girl. Never in any trouble."

Hell, I was no angel myself, but I can't imagine what he means by "trouble." When it comes to the kids, the worst Brandi does is slap Jell-O on my face and throw a fit if I move her animals around. The neighbors offer to bring more food. I thank them and say no, I can't deprive Mom and Monday of overfeeding us!

Mr. Sarva (Jarek, as we find out later) nips back next door while his wife (Zofia) chatters on about the baby, weight, length, hair—that kind of thing. Jarek comes back carrying a bag with a few bottles of stout—stimulates milk flow, he tells me, and I realize these are for Rita, who will pull a face. There's also a half-bottle of something with an oily-looking foreign label.

"This will put dad to sleep when the baby's been crying half the night," he says with a wink and that wicked smile. I can't help liking him, although I'd been disappointed at first because they don't have little kids.

There's a flurry of activity when Pat arrives and the womenfolk head off to the hospital. The phone never stops ringing, Rita's friends and clients mostly. When it's finally peaceful, I realize I could be watching the game. A local derby. Working six days a week and running errands with Brandi on Sundays, I don't get any time to myself anymore. (No, I don't go to mass much, though I feel bad about that since I promised Rita's dad we'd bring the children up Catholic.) I settle in with one of Rita's stouts. The game's a nail-biter. Even so, I don't see that much of it. Brandi leaps on my stomach to wake me up when they get home. She has no mercy.

"How's the baby?" I ask her.

"Mama! Baby! Wah! Wah! Wah!"

Then she beats me up, not with the nice new doll we bought her in case she was jealous, but with the old eyeless giraffe she carts around. Luckily, it's not one of her wooden zoo animals, but I'll get whiplash if I don't put up a pretend fight.

"I'm gonna get that giraffe. Love you, sweetheart."

7

Aunt Monday – 1968

I stuff my mittens into my pockets, hang my coat up inside the door, and change into the moccasins I keep here. As I bend down, I can't help but notice how grubby the floor is. Any reputable builder would've included a mudroom or a front porch. Shoddy workmanship. That's what I call it. The girls' shoes are strewn across the floor, I'll trip over them one day and, although they have pegs they can reach, their jackets have fallen too. Graying pink and baby yellow. I pick everything up and make a mental note to wash the jackets when I have time.

Carling almost bowls me over in the hallway. "Mon Mon, Mon Mon," she chants over and over again, and I can't help feeling how nice it is to be wanted, even if it's by a toddler with a sticky face, sticky hands, and sticky hair. I carry her into the kitchen, some of the stickiness spreading to me. The kitchen's modern with lots of countertop space, yet there still isn't room to put anything down. I know this gets to Brad, he used to be a neat freak. Now he's too tired to tidy it up himself, just like Rita.

Ah! That's why Brandi didn't charge down the hallway to meet me too. Rita's cutting her bangs. She's sitting on the kitchen table with Rita leaning over her. Brandi hates the feel of the scissors across her forehead, so Rita's given her a candy pop, and she's hard at work sucking and licking it with a tongue stained—what color is it stained? Blue? Purple? Brown? The pop's fairly well covered in little red trimmings from the haircut, but Brandi doesn't care, and this way Rita can get the job done.

"Hi, Aunt Monday!" Rita says, a little preoccupied with what she's doing. Brandi squirms as she opens her mouth wide to show me her tongue. It's repulsive!

"Don't move, Brandi, I'm almost done," Rita says, and I can tell she's trying to mask the irritation in her voice. She's pregnant again—baby due next spring.

I hope it's a boy this time, then maybe Brad will lay off her. Can't say I've a lot of experience in that department. The few times I've tried it, I didn't think it was up to all that much—a lot of sweating and moaning and a different sticky mess. Rita works two afternoons a week when Grandma Phyllis babysits, and I come in on Mondays—just like I did when Rita was a little girl—and sometimes Friday afternoons, to give her a hand.

"Doing for others" hasn't quite been my entire life's work though it seems that way sometimes. I was the secretary at Cameron Mill and then at St. Joseph's, what seems like a lifetime ago, bless my soul. They gave me Mondays off from the church, so when Faith needed help, I used to go there. That's when Rita started calling me Aunt Monday, and now her little ones do too. Can't say I mind—Betty, my own name, is a bit plain.

"I thought I'd do some baking with the girls this afternoon, so you can put your feet up for a bit. Then when Carling goes down for her nap and Brandi has quiet time, I'll put the laundry on and make a start at cleaning the kitchen," I say.

"You're a saint, Aunt Monday," she says as she finishes Brandi's bangs. Very neat—Brandi looks a bit goofy but awfully cute.

Brandi wriggles down, a ball of excitement. "Make muffins, Monday!" she shrieks, hopping up and down.

I can't help smiling, even though I tell her, "Make muffins, please, Aunt Monday."

"Pweese, Mon Mon!" Carling joins in, and Brandi remembers her manners too.

I march them to the bathroom to wash their hands. Pretty pink fingers emerge from the layer of grunge. Whatever happened to hygiene, I can't imagine.

"I'll turn the oven on then to heat it up. You girls be careful. It's going to get hot-hot," I warn them, wagging my finger like a school ma'am.

We clean and roughly tidy the kitchen counters, moving away pacifiers, (I'd like to ditch the germ-ridden things, Carling's too old for them surely), stuffed animals (blind giraffe and his sidekick, Stu the rabbit), raisin boxes, and crackers. Then we set about finding the ingredients, when there's a terrible, acrid smell and chemical blue smoke starts pouring out of the oven vents.

"Fire, fire!" Brandi screams, dropping an egg, splat onto the floor, and she and Carling start to cry. Like a blessed fool, I open the oven door, and more smoke billows out. Mother of God! There's a pink, plastic potty in there, and it's started to melt.

I turn off the oven, but it's too late, Rita's already called the fire department. Our eyes are streaming with the smoke, the girls are spluttering and yelling, sliding on the smashed egg. I grab their jackets and my coat—make sure that Rita's okay, scoop up the girls, and we dash outside.

We're all gasping for breath and Brandi's still screaming, "Fire! Fire!" It's cold out here, and I try to get their jackets on but end up draping them over their shoulders. Rita picks up Carling, and I heave up Brandi onto my hip. Even though I'm strong and wiry for my age (like an ox), she's really too heavy for me now and I can only hold her for a few minutes. It's enough to calm her down a bit until we hear the sirens wailing in the distance. Renewed sobbing, crying, shrieking, and shivering.

The neighborhood's athrob with blue lights flashing and fire trucks thundering down the street. The men jump off the truck and run up the path. Oh no, a couple of them are unrolling the hoses.

"It's all right," I cry, but Brandi shouts, "Fire, fire!" again.

Two of them burst into the house, trailing mud inside.

Rita goes over to the men unrolling the hoses and explains it's a false alarm. One of the firefighters comes out of the house. He's got great big, thick gloves on, and he's carrying an oven rack dripping with molten plastic. Most of it's charred black, but sickly pink oozes out in places.

"Poddy, poddy!" Carling wails pathetically as if her heart is broken.

The firefighters are evidently amused. "Well, we've seen everything now!" one of them says in a surprisingly jolly tone.

Rita's infuriated. "Brandi, did you put the potty in the oven?" she yells.

Brandi's still scared, and her lip puckers, her little chin trembles as she sobs, "You cut hair, Momma. Carwie put poddy in." She's usually more articulate than this, but it's all she can splutter among the gasps and gulps.

Rita gives Carling a dark look and she's about to yell, when I put my arm on her shoulder. "Rita, we're alright."

"She could have killed us, burned the house down!" she snaps back, and she's crying too now.

"No real harm done, Mrs. Lenox," the firefighter says quietly. "Let me have a word with the little ones, and we'll make sure this doesn't happen again." His voice is steady, calm, reassuring, thank heavens.

Rita sniffs and nods, she's still hyperventilating, so I say, "That's very kind of you, officer." I don't know if you should address a firefighter as "officer," it just slipped out.

He crouches down to the girls' level and very calmly explains that they mustn't put anything at all in the oven until they've been to the big school and taken cooking classes, and they mustn't go anywhere near the stove when it's on.

They both nod very seriously, gulping and hiccupping at the same time. Then he calls out to the others, "Jose, Frank—got any coloring books for these two young ladies?"

Brandi and Carling each get two Freddy the Fire Truck coloring books and two red crayons, and the lead firefighter slips them a Werther's Original candy as well. He turns to Rita and me.

"No need to worry, ladies. Everything's going to turn out fine. You'll need to scrape out the rest of the plastic from the oven with a knife, and use a wire pad with some bleach on it. We've opened the windows to get rid of the smell. Do you have anywhere to go for an hour or so until the smoke and the fumes go away?"

I'm about to say we should go to my house when the Polish neighbor, Mr. Sarva, I think it is, comes up.

"I couldn't help hearing the commotion. Please come next door."

"That's so kind of you," Rita tells him. She's pulled herself together now. "We can't impose, the girls will be a nuisance. I'm sure you'd rather try and get some peace and quiet."

"Miss Brandi and Miss Carling. They'll be fine. They can see my fish, and I can turn on the TV. I'm sure I can find something they'll like."

We go next door to Mr. and Mrs. Sarva's immaculate house. I'm glad at least the girls' hands are washed and, pray the Blessed Virgin, they didn't use them to wipe the snot from their faces. I burrow in my pockets and find the handkerchief I keep there just in case. In the somewhat austere family room, they have a large tank of tropical fish, and both girls are mesmerized by them. Brandi's thrilled.

"This one's like a ze-*bra*!" she squeals. (Is Brad responsible for that pronunciation?) And Carling likes the little shoal of lightning-blue fish. I think perhaps they'll be okay without the TV, but Mr. Sarva fiddles with the channels. He can't find any children's programs, but there's an undersea nature show, and Brandi and Carling settle down fascinated.

I'm concerned they'll sully the good furniture, so I help them kick off their shoes and give their hands a quick wipe. Mr. Sarva smiles a cheeky little smile that shows his dimples when he notices me doing this. He turns the volume down low.

"We'll keep the sound down. My wife's not feeling well. She's trying to rest," he explains. Rita's mortified we caused the uproar, and I feel bad we didn't head to my house.

"Not to worry. My wife will be sorry to have missed you. We're really very lucky to have such delightful neighbors. Now, please no more worries. Can't complain!" he says.

Keeping the TV to just above a murmur is exactly what the girls need. They're both asleep within a quarter of an hour. Mr. Sarva offers us coffee; we both decline and take a glass of water instead. He tells us he's a professor at one of the local colleges—civil engineering, maybe. Rita seems to know this and a few bits and pieces about their background. He's quite a bit older than she is—then so are most of the neighbors. It's too pricey around here for most young couples. Never could figure out how Brad affords it.

After a while, I tell them I'll go back to the house. I say it's for security purposes with all the windows open—but really, I want to clean the oven and the floor (there's congealed pink plastic drips along with the grime and the eggy mess) before Rita brings the girls back or Brad gets home.

◆

Brad sniffs the air suspiciously when he walks down the hall. "What the hell happened here?"

I wish he wouldn't swear, especially in front of the girls—but I don't say anything. I can hold my tongue. Some of the smell's worn off, and we've got used to it by now, but it's definitely lingering.

"Dada! Dada! Poddy, poddy!" Carling tells him in explanation as she launches at him.

Brandi runs up too, fights for a place on his lap, and gives her version. "Carwing put her potty in the oven and the fire truck came and the man said we'll have cooking classes and we got coloring books and Uncle Sarva talks funny and ze-*bra* fish and he didn't have juice and he didn't have no cookies and we got crackers."

Brad's eyebrows shoot up, questioning, but he's smiling too, and I watch Rita's expression change from apprehension to relief. He's not going to make a scene. I can't help wondering when we grew wary of Brad's moods? Holy Mother! They're both worn out. A fancy house, hard work and too much going on upstairs if you ask me!

Once we've gone over the afternoon's excitement again and again for Brad's benefit, I realize that I haven't thought about dinner. Usually, I have fish sticks or mac and cheese ready for the girls, and Rita and I are working on something a bit better for them by the time Brad's home.

"Let's go out for pizza!" he suggests enthusiastically.

He's trying to be nice, but Rita's not up for it. "There's been enough excitement for one day. Let's order takeout."

A momentary look of frustration crosses Brad's brow before he gives in. "Okay, I'll call it in a few when Miss Brandi here stops climbing all over me. Hey! I've got a coupon in the car. It'll have the phone number on it—I bet your life it's still valid."

"Carling needs changing," Rita says. "Aunt Monday, would you mind going to the car?"

Brad tosses his keys to me. I'm quite pleased to catch them with one hand. There's life in the old girl yet.

"It's in the car door pocket—driver's side," he tells me.

I hurry down the path—it's even colder, and I didn't pause to get my jacket, or slip my shoes on. I slide my hand into the door pocket. It's not filthy like most men's cars. Like I say, Brad's neat, picks up after the girls have been in the car. My hand lands on something. It's a small packet with an odd, squishy feel. I take it out and squint at it. Then, embarrassed, I put it back. I'm not used to seeing these things. Bless my soul! There's a rubber in the little foil packet.

"Why in heaven's name would he need that now Rita's expecting?" I wonder. The answer's staring me in the face, but like the old fool I am, I couldn't see it. "Must have been there a long time," I tell myself.

I return it to its place, and slide my hand around until I find the coupon. Brad's right, it's not out of date. My word! I'm flustered, and suddenly I realize how tired I am. It's been quite the afternoon, and I'm not getting any younger. I take the coupon inside, return Brad's keys, (he misses the catch,) and hug Brandi, though she's not much bothered with me now her daddy's home. I find Rita, she's just finished with Carling. The animal smell mingles with the toasted plastic aroma. Disgusting. I need to be somewhere fresh and clean. I kiss them both on the forehead and tell them it's time for me to head home.

Rita's not keen on me leaving, she wants me to have some pizza with them because she feels bad about losing it earlier, and for all the extra cleaning I did. I tell her it's all part of the "Monday Service," but my heavens, I've had enough and all I want is a quiet supper with Wilf and a peaceful evening doing the crossword.

"I don't know what I'd do without you," Rita says as she waves me off. I guess she knows that sometimes it's all a bit much for me—and I wouldn't miss it for the world. What was it the Polish man said? Can't complain.

8

Wilf – 1972

C all me old-fashioned (and many folks do), but I like order, everything in its place, so I do a nice job parallel-parking part-way down Rita's street, even if I do say so myself. There'll be more room at her end for all the other cars, and with any luck, we won't block in the neighbors.

I do a walk-round check of the car like I always do, I'm driving a Galaxy these days—can be tricky to park. Brad sold it to me last year when the gray Fairlane gave up the ghost. Brad's always trying to fast-talk me into a new car. Well, I'm not like his mom—ready to trade up every eighteen months. I'm comfortable with what I know; Faith was the adventurous one.

I get the box of decorations out of the trunk and the little gift I have for Cheryl—Sherri, as they've all slipped into calling her. I hope these girls don't turn into alcoholics, the names they've got. Even Carling's named for a brewery! Can't imagine what they were thinking. I wanted "Faith" for each of them, like Rita's mom, but even Rita wouldn't go for that, and Brad said it'd set them up for failure in life if they didn't have any faith. That Brad talks a lot of rubbish if you ask me (nobody ever does).

No matter, Sherri had the good sense to put in her appearance around St. Patrick's Day. So, in honor of the Doyle family's Irish roots, I've brought the shamrocks and the leprechauns. Brandi calls me Grandpa Wolf—she overheard her dad "mispronounce" my name one time, and now the little ones call me Grandpa "Wuff!" I must say I've taken a liking to that. Mon Mon (*how did I slip into that? It's the girls*), I mean Betty, is here already—been here most of the morning, helping with the food and trying to keep the girls calm.

The whole world's invited—or so it seems to me. And Sherri's only three! It's the way Brad's family is. They all love a good party, a lot of fuss. His sister Pat, her husband, and the two kids—Tessa and Kevin, I think they're called—(I'm not so good with names as I used to be)—are coming, bringing their neighbors' kids too. And I expect Phyllis will have her beau, he's always very well turned out, and he has the good sense to stay mostly in the background.

I have to admit I'm shocked at the speed they got together. I couldn't think of another woman after Faith, and when Jack died, Phyllis was torn apart. I thought it was the same for her (but what do I know?) Rita told me Pat had a hard time seeing another man in her father's place, at first. Brad just rolled with it, glad his mom wasn't lonely anymore.

I pause by the mailbox to blow up the balloons—pink and green. *Was it always this hard to get them started?* I've no problem knotting them and tying on the ribbon. No arthritis. My hands are strong and agile from working all these years at the butcher's counter at Market Basket. No sense in hacking, like the younger guys do. Most of what they work with's already frozen. You've got to respect the meat, go with the grain.

Once inside, I notice how Betty and Phyllis have spruced it up for the party. Picked up, wiped down, and tidied everything away. Everything in its place, neat and tidy, just the way I like it. I give Rita a peck on the cheek. She gained a few pounds with the babies—no, never mind, she's still a head-turner. My girl! We're all used to her with red hair, forgotten what she looked like before—Brad won't let her change it, and with three carrot-top daughters, it seems only natural.

Brad's auburn's beginning to show some gray. He's put on the pounds too over the years—likely all the responsibility he's taken on. Right now, he's at work, hoping to get back in time to catch the tail end of the party. Like I said, Phyllis's been here for hours.

She never misses a minute—I can see she's getting on Rita's nerves, forever rearranging the food.

I glance in the den, Mon Mon's reading quietly to Sherri and Carling. Brandi's nowhere to be seen, my guess is she's playing horses up in her room with her best friend. Carling's looking flushed—probably had a hectic morning—and little Sherri's eyes are drooping. She'll do better at the party if she can take a nap. I nod and smile at Mon Mon—I mean Betty. She puts her finger to her lips, so I don't greet the girls, I tiptoe past, and something I can only call joy fills my chest and rises up my throat 'til there's a lump developing. What a sentimental old fool I am.

I spent all those years nursing Faith, and when she died, I thought I couldn't carry on. Except for Rita's sake. Betty moved in, she's such a trooper—and now I have the three best granddaughters in all the world. I know there's some who think I'm a weak man, they're not wrong there. I had to hold tight to my pain growing up, couldn't breathe a word. It scarred me—never been much good at speaking up since then. All the same, I count myself a lucky man.

I swallow the lump down—silly to come over sentimental. Anyhow, there's work to be done, so I start putting my decorations up ... a twist of green crepe paper across the mantelpiece, shamrocks in the windows, leprechauns either side of the fireplace, nice and symmetrical. I have a couple of rainbows to put in the light fixtures. I'd like to have a pot of gold under them, but it'll get in the way. Instead, I brought the party favors, chocolate coins wrapped in gold foil nestled in a net bag tied with green and pink ribbons.

Next, I head into the screened porch to set up the puppet theater. Brandi and a couple of her friends are planning on putting on a show for the "littles." It might not happen—we'll see. The theater's a hefty thing, and I'm not sure I'll manage on my own when Phyllis' friend joins me.

"Need a hand?" he asks, and I'm grateful for the help. Mr. Insurance Man (I've forgotten his name if I ever knew it), tosses off his navy jacket and helps me heave the heavy panels into place. We're both panting when we've hooked them together.

"Thanks ... er?" I say, breathing heavily.

"Anton, call me Tone—it's Wilf, isn't it?" he says.

The women finally decided on setting the food on the dining room table, buffet style—no good for my digestion, but there's no room to sit down. Rita and Betty are going to spread a quilt over the floor in the den for the little ones to sit down on and have their treats, and the adults will mill around and mingle. Well not me, mingling's not my style. The centerpiece is the pink cake Betty made. She found some plastic ballerinas to put on the top. Sherri's in love with it.

She's mad about dancing, always twirling around and around. Now she's three, she can start taking dance classes if Rita can find time to take her and Brad gets enough commissions to pay for them. My gift's a little music box. When you open the lid, a dancer pops up in a tutu. I know it's far too old for Sherri, but like the old fool I am, I couldn't resist it.

The party's in full swing. Among the first to arrive are the neighbors from next door, Mr. and Mrs. Sarva. I know Rita really appreciates them even though they're older with their own daughter back in college in Poland. Must be hard. They don't get to see that much of Krystyna.

Jarek (yes, that's his name) will come over and fix things when Brad's at work, or I can't get over, and Zofia used to watch the girls for a little while when Rita went to pick up milk or something she'd forgotten. They both look strained, and Zofia's clearly unwell. Jarek makes sure she has a chair, but they don't stay long.

I catch a glimpse of them walking back to their house; they're painfully slow, Jarek's almost propping Zofia up. They must love Rita and the girls to make the effort. And they brought a little gift for each of the girls to keep them from being jealous, sparkly bracelets for Brandi and Carling, and a tiara for Sherri. Bless them! I say a little prayer that Zofia gets better soon.

Phyllis has taken charge of the little ones. They've all agreed that they can't have the kids running wild—especially as it's too chilly to go outside—so there's a craft table and a few singing games, "Ring Around the Rosie," "The Farmer in the Dell," and the like.

Then Pat arrives with her crew. It seems like a whirlwind's burst in. Not much hope of keeping the kids calm now. Pat must've brought half her neighborhood with her.

"Hi, Tone," she calls to Anton, who's been helping the adults to soda and juice. From her easy tone, it's a jolt to realize that Anton's evidently accepted as part of the family now. People move on, I suppose. Not me. I'd feel like I was betraying Faith.

Betty takes over the kids' games since Phyllis is distracted with Pat and her other grandkids. Betty's good at this. I wonder for the first time, I'm ashamed to realize, if she regrets not having children of her own, not having a husband, that special bond.

In no time, the magic moment arrives. Rita pulls out a coffee table, the right height for Sherri, she puts the pretty pink cake in the center and lights four candles, three for every year of Sherri's short life and one for luck. I've lived long enough to know that she'll need some luck in life, we all do.

She takes a big breath then, all of a sudden, she stops and screams, "Daddy, Daddy!" Her eyes flash, the candle flames reflected in the deep puddles of her pupils. Brad grins. He's looking hot and disheveled, but he's here, and Sherri's ecstatic. Would you believe it, as if it's been prearranged, some of the other little ones sneak up and blow out the candles. Pandemonium breaks out!

Eventually, we get it all sorted out, and Sherri gets to blow out her candles for real as we serenade her with an off-key, drawn-out, "Happy Birthday to You!"

"Were you born in a zoo?" Brandi mutters under her breath, her two friends giggle, and the rest of us ignore her.

"Make a wish, Sherri," Aunt Pat shouts.

"More birfday amorrow!" Sherri cries without missing a beat.

Brad scoops her up and swirls her around, narrowly missing the sea of birthday gifts and wrapping paper that are strewn in his way. He wobbles a bit. Must be dizzy with the heat that's built up in here. Tone notices too and opens a window.

Finally, the crowd dwindles and Betty notices Carling curled up on the sofa. Even though it's cooler now, she's looking hot. Betty feels her forehead and whispers to Rita so the remaining guests don't hear, "Think she's running a fever."

Tone and Phyllis and Pat's mob take their time leaving. Thank God, they took a bag of cupcakes with them, there's so many left ... It's a sin and a shame if you ask me. I tell Rita and Betty to sit down and rest. I want Brad to help with the clean-up, but he grunts, "Helluva mess, damned kids, Carling's sick, now we're all gonna get sick," and he goes to the kitchen and cracks open a beer.

I'm glad Rita and Betty didn't hear that little outburst. I bet they won't rest. They'll be searching for Baby Tylenol and apple juice for Carling. Poor little thing, there are tears dripping off her nose.

I spring into action, I've always liked restoring order. They call me OCD at work, like it's dumb to be neat and clean. I throw most of the trash into black plastic bags, a cascade of pink and purple wrapping paper, napkins, and matching ballerina plates and cups. I take down my St. Patrick's decorations. I'll bring them home— if I store them properly, maybe I'll use them again another year. I clear the rubbery, vile-smelling Play-Doh from the craft table, scrub it down, and fold it up. When I've put it in the garage, I'm ready for the puppet theater.

Brad's pretty reluctant to help—he's watching cartoons now with Sherri on his lap. Tiara aslant, she laughs infectiously every time Jerry mouse gets beaten up and even more when he extracts revenge. I watch with them until the cartoon's over—well, really I'm watching Sherri, not the TV.

It's plain even to Brad I can't manage the theater on my own. When he wanders onto the porch, I notice there's something off about him. As we bend down to unhook the panels, I smell his breath. There's more than a couple of beers on it, something a whole lot stronger. And a sickly whiff of lavender too.

When he stands up from crouching down, he staggers, and I guess his head's swimming. We finish the puppet theater without saying a word. But when we're done, I gulp hard. Although I chop up carcasses all day long, like I said, I'm a coward at heart, a weak man. Too many incidents in the vestry with Father O'Brien when I was his altar boy made sure of that.

All the same, this is my precious family, so I screw up my courage to say, "You've had one too many, Brad, you need to watch that in front of the girls. And that's not Rita's scent either. She's not partial to lavender." My heart's beating wildly, I'm holding my breath, and I wonder if I've gone too far.

He gives me a slightly bleary-eyed laugh, and then he scoffs, "Can't a guy have a beer in his own home after a hard day's work now, Wilf? And hell, the lavender? I let Sherri shampoo my hair this morning with her baby-doll stuff for a birthday treat. Felt a real wanker at work."

Feeling a fool, I tell him I'm sorry, but he probably knows I'm not. All those good feelings I had earlier on have flown away. I don't believe him, and I begin to dread what's going to happen to my family.

9

Brad – Summer 1972

I've just shown a client out—a scruffy black kid, off to college. He says he's looking for his first car. Treading carefully, I suggest he might have more luck across the street. I don't buy his story for one second; he's a time-waster, on a dare, or casing out the joint, but I treat him with respect. You never know. Can't afford to lose a sale over not taking a client seriously or risk Laidlaw's reputation.

It's only moments later when, what d'ya know, I'm extra glad I acted professional when I see Cameron Laidlaw coming into the showroom. Old man Laidlaw owns the dealership, and he's a stickler for good manners.

"Got a moment, Brad?" he asks, and I make sure a couple of the team are watching the showroom for walk-ins before I take him to my office. I keep it tidy, no coffee mug rings on the desk, empty ashtrays, no sleazy calendars on the walls, a squirt of vanilla air-freshener every morning. I keep a stack of folders in a neat pile on my desk, so it doesn't look as if I'm wasting my time.

Laidlaw takes it in, then he notices my dark gray suit and black tie. Pretty much all the sales guys wear sports coats and slacks these days.

"My condolences, Brad, who passed? Was it someone close?"

"Our neighbor, Mrs. Sarva. I'm going to her funeral this afternoon," I tell him.

"Taking time off for a neighbor, Brad?" Laidlaw says. "Doesn't that set a bad example to the team? They'll all be off to funerals if you don't keep them in line."

"The Sarvas—they've been really good to us—the girls think of them like their aunt and uncle," I reply to him. "They're Polish, and they don't have much family. Mr. Sarva asked me to be a pallbearer. I couldn't refuse."

"I see. Quite right."

His tone's changed, so I know we're on friendly terms. I've made a good impression on Laidlaw over the years, and he isn't the easiest man to please. Served in 'Nam. Forgets he's not in the Army anymore and barks at you when he's having a bad day. We opened a used car lot across the street, with a service department. He appointed an assistant manager over there, but I'm general manager of both operations.

We put in a nice room for people waiting for service. We call it the "customer lounge." It's got a TV, and there's always a stack of new magazines there, not the ancient, dog-eared ones you get everywhere else. I brought in a crate of the girls' old toys, so there's something for kids, too. The receptionist rinses them in bleach once or twice a week (the toys, I mean, not the kids, but my God some of them deserve it!). I smile at my own little joke, then quickly wipe the smile off my face, Laidlaw wouldn't get it and he'll think I'm being insubordinate.

Laidlaw tells me he's made an offer on a body shop across town. For a moment, I think he's going to ask me to manage that as well, and I see the dollar signs, but hell, I don't know anything about that side of the business. No fear, that's not what he has in mind. He's going to launch Laidlaw's Body Shop with an advertising campaign on local TV and in the Odeon and the Rex movie theaters downtown. It'll include the new and used car dealerships as well. Should bring in a lot of traffic.

This is a big deal for us. We've only done the local rags before, and we talk about it for some time. I suggest he consider the theaters in the neighboring towns, too. He seems to like this idea and agrees to look into it. Perhaps we should do billboards as well—and again he seems keen. We're going to set up a tracking system of new customers to find out where they heard about us. I feel more enthusiastic about my job than I have in months until he bursts my bubble.

"I've one more thing to discuss, Brad," and he's turned gruff. "I've had a complaint concerning you."

Oh, God! What the hell has he found out?

"Dr. Arosa mentioned he smelled alcohol on your breath when he came to pick up his new Torino last Friday—I've put a lot of trust in you, Brad. Seemed out of character. It crossed my mind, Dr. Arosa might just be mistaken. What do you have to say for yourself?" he asked.

I struggle to keep my composure as I tell him that the guys and I go to Al's bar after work on Friday nights to unwind a bit. No one overdoes it since, depending on the rota, they'll be working on Saturday. I let him know I don't tolerate alcohol on the premises. I assure him Dr. Arosa must be mistaken. And I suddenly remember eating a Sloppy Joe sub with a heap of pickle and mustard just before the doctor arrived. That must be what he caught on my breath. I try not to say all this too defensively, and he watches me closely. I think he just about buys it.

"Alright, Brad, but if I hear another word, you'll be out on your ear. Is that clear?" he says.

"Of course, Mr. Laidlaw." I almost call him "sir," but hold it back. It'd be a sure sign of nerves. We part with a genial handshake—my palm's not too sweaty, but thank God, he can't see my heart's racing.

Oh, my stars! I wait 'til I'm sure he's driven off before I let out a big sigh of relief. Jeez! That was too close. I doubt I'm the only one to have a hip flask in the desk drawer. Need to transfer that to the file cabinet or somewhere safer. We don't have beer on the premises like we did in the old days—unless the others have a hiding place I haven't found. And you bet your life, I've looked.

On the other hand, Friday nights can get pretty heavy. Al saves a table for us in the back room; it's dark and dingy even in summer. I stand them all the first round—and no, it's not from the takings—then we drink and joke around a lot, gets loud and off-color.

One Friday, a few months ago, I was the last to leave. I'd been to the john, and I didn't much want to head home—Rita'd expect me to bathe the kids and get them ready for bed, and hell, I was wiped.

We'd had a shit week, then somehow, I'd got the team fired up and we were fucking pulling deals out of thin air to make quota. If we hadn't pulled it off, I wasn't sure where the mortgage was coming from. Rita doesn't appreciate how hard I work for her and the girls, and what a talented bastard I am. Drains a guy dry.

Anyways, I went back to the bar to have one for the road. I swear I wasn't on the make, until I glance down and I'm staring at an enormous cleavage. She slips a hand up my thigh and, heck, just like that, I have a hard-on. I don't edge her hand away and she squeezes tight. Fucking hell! She takes me to her truck, and she wriggles off my pants right there in the back lot.

I didn't even think of Rita. And I wasn't consumed with guilt afterwards either. Rita's always pooped after a day with the kids, she doesn't reach for me that much anymore. A guy needs to feel appreciated, like he's a man. And that's how it all began. Thank God, Laidlaw doesn't know all my secrets. Wimpy Wolf's caught on and, my God, he watches me like, well, like a wolf.

The morning ticks by. I make an easy sale, the black tie bought me a lot of sympathy, and the folks are so naïve, they pay full price. Then I head across the street to the used car lot. Sales are about average. I consult with Trev, the assistant manager, and we lower our offer for a trade-in. The client looks annoyed, jaw clenched, color rising, and I think we low-balled him too far. So after some fast talking, I sweeten the deal, lowering the price on the car he's looking at as long as he signs right away. Trev and I leave him in the rep's hands looking like he's won the lottery.

◆

A colleague of Jarek's and two funeral directors shoulder the coffin along with me. It ought to be easy as there wasn't much left of Zofia when she died, but Christ, we're all different heights. The professor's about six inches taller than me, and one of the funeral guys isn't much above five feet four. He warns us not to touch the tinny handles, they'll break off! The organ wails as we process solemnly down the aisle, our footsteps echoing against the stone floor as if we were all wearing army boots, and we manage to deposit the coffin ceremoniously on the bier.

The service is about as awful as it gets. Jarek and his daughter are in the front pew. Like her mom, she's blond, skinny, and on the tall side. She'd normally be a good-looker. Now, she's strained, struggling for control, and her face is set as if it's hewn out of granite.

It's steaming hot outside, the church finally heated up like a furnace. So, the janitor added supersize fans. They whir noisily like you imagine a plague of locusts, and you want to swat at them. The women sitting nearest them shiver in their cotton dresses, but I'm sweltering!

After my duties, I join Rita. She's wearing her Sunday-best black dress—wish she'd show some leg. I guess it's a sin to think that at a funeral. That's the trouble with this church. Too many goddamn sins.

My mom's looking after the younger girls, and Brandi's going to Grandpa Wolf's straight from school. Monday's spending a few days with her cousin who's just out of the hospital. A "woman's complaint," they tell me. Sounds gross. Mom's got a dentist appointment later on, so Rita isn't staying for the reception. I don't want to stay either, but Rita says we owe it to Jarek, and maybe I can help take down the trestle tables when it's all over.

Tears are rolling down Rita's face, she had the good sense not to wear mascara. I pass her a handkerchief—at least this one doesn't smell of lavender. From the front row, Jarek's shoulders are heaving, and the daughter's losing the battle to hold back her sobs.

Father Francis gives the eulogy. A lot about setting suns and boats going out on the tide to a new horizon and a safe harbor with the Lord. Then, he switches back to the liturgy, and people line up for the elements. I never did convert, so I stay in the pew and everyone shuffles past me.

We pallbearers form up again, not so steadily this time, but we shoulder the box as the organ drones a horrible wailing tune. I make a mental note not to volunteer for this role ever again. We head to the graveyard, fortunately behind the church and not too far to shoulder the coffin on this stifling day. Rita takes her leave, holding Jarek's hands in hers and, more formally, shaking hands with Krystyna, his daughter. Another waterfall of tears.

The burial's even worse than the funeral mass. Father Francis tries to inject a note of triumph in it, but we're all fixated on the "dust to dust, ashes to ashes" part, especially when Father Francis hands Jarek, and then Krystyna, a shovel to cast the first batch of earth over the coffin. It's hotter than hell, and after all the exertion, deep pockets of sweat bloom under my armpits. Can't help thinking it's like the fires of hell! No way—this one can't be heading there. Hell's reserved for even worse bastards than me.

We all traipse into the Parish Hall, and the mood lightens with the air conditioning and the spread. Our family had a hand in that, and Jarek and Krystyna come over to tell me how grateful they are. They're looking a tad better now, perhaps relieved that the worst of the horror show's over.

There's a reasonable turnout after all. Some other folks from our street, a few colleagues, and a student of Jarek's, some women from Zofia's quilting group, and some gawpers from the congregation. I'm surprised to see Dr. Arosa in the crowd. On a regular day, I'd head over and ask him how he likes his new motor, but I decide to leave him be, thankful that this time I'm stone-cold sober.

Jarek seeks me out again before he leaves. He takes my arm and tells me, "We were so lucky when you moved next door. Such good neighbors. You never know what comes around the corner. You take care of your beautiful girls and your wonderful wife. Such a wonderful family. Take good care." More tears well in his eyes, and I'm choked up too, as I pat him on the back and nod.

Eventually, most people leave except me, a couple of quilters, and the tall colleague. The women deal with the leftovers, packing it into foil containers, and we fold the tables and store them in the spooky closet near the furnace. I find a broom and am sweeping up when the janitor arrives. This is good news. I'm the only one left who knows the church, and I was sweating it over resetting the A/C and locking up.

It's hot as blazes outside, and I'm craving a cold Dr Pepper and a smoke. I cross the street to the five-and-dime. I'm all shaken up from what happened today and what Jarek said to me about taking care of Rita, so I don't notice him right away.

"Brad, hey, Brad!" It's Sandip. Haven't seen him in forever. "How you doing, my man?"

We start to chat. There's half a lifetime to catch up on—he invites me to his place. When I get there, I call Rita and tell her I won't be long—which is true as I've got to pick up Brandi. She doesn't make a fuss, since it's Sandip. She sounds a bit distracted, must be thinking about Zofia's funeral.

My stars! Sandip's condo's super cool. Modern appliances and contemporary furniture. It's clean as the hospital and neat as a pin, with books and records in alphabetical order. He offers me a beer, but Laidlaw's scared me today and Jarek pricked my conscience about Rita. I'm gonna show up sober as a damn judge to pick up Brandi. (Who says they're sober? Should see them at the Lions Club!) Snoopy Wolf will be on the prowl. We smoke and drink Dr Pepper.

Sandip's married too now; his wife's visiting family in India. They don't have kids, and he's kinda jealous when I tell him about the girls. I'm jealous of him too when I hear about his business trips and where they go on vacation, not counting visits to India. He's my bud—and he and Astra live in a different universe.

I'm thinking about this as I drive over to Wolf's. Is this the life I wanted? What kind of a man am I? I've secretly enjoyed the deceptions, made me feel I was getting one over. Now, I think I'm full of crap. Feel cheap.

Brandi and Wolf are in the neighbor's yard when I pull up. There's a woodpecker with a broken wing. It's really scared, making a pathetic noise, and shitting all over the place.

"Dad, we can't let it die! Can I take it home? Please, Dad, please!"

Her big green eyes open wide, and she's begging 'til it tears my heart. I cannot imagine life without her and the other two, but I surely can imagine what Rita will say if I bring home a mealworm-infested, dying bird. Wolf helps me out.

"This bird needs a vet, Brandi. I'll take it tonight. If the vet can save him, we'll let him fly free."

Fly free! I think to myself. *Do I ever fly free, or do I build my own cage?*

Rita seems dazed when we get home. She kisses both of us absentmindedly on the top of the head. I'll bet she's still thinking about Zofia—maybe her mom too—women are like that. There are cushions all over the floor, scribble on the tablecloth. After Sandip's stylish condo, my house is a dump, the furniture's dated, nothing matches.

I'm strung out, there's a battle raging inside my head, *Who the hell am I? What do I want?* In spite of everything, it's good to be home.

10

Rita – The same day—and late summer 1972

My neighbor gives me a ride home after the funeral. She didn't know Jarek and Zofia as well as I did, but Jesus, Joseph, and Mary ... She carries on as if they're joined at the hip. I'm glad to get out of her car even though a wall of heat hits me. I need to be alone with my grief. Phyllis is so anxious to head out to the dentists, she doesn't stop to hug the girls goodbye. She's nervous of the dentist at the best of times, and she needs a big filling today.

I feel a deep well of sadness inside me, and I'm relieved Carling and Sherri decided to make a "boat." It's one of their special games. They throw all the cushions off the sofa, drag an old tablecloth over and make a kind of shelter—or is it a sail?—I never figure it out. Two of their favorite teddy bears, Grouchy and Ouchy, sail the boat together with their stuffed toy cat, Miss Meow, who's lost her tail, whiskers, and most of her fur.

She's a hand-me-down from Brandi and unhygienic for sure. I don't dare wash her, she'll fall apart like blind giraffe did. Unaccountably, there's also a large, shiny, plastic apple that rings a bell when it wobbles, and a nurse's bag with a broken stethoscope and a yellow plastic syringe the size of a soccer pump.

Usually, they invade Pirate Girl Island, and they chatter away mainly to the toys rather than to each other. One time, they gave themselves pirate tattoos in felt-tip pen. Imagine that! We had to ban it. All the same, Brad'll complain they've made a mess, but I'm thankful they're not screaming for my attention right now. Jesus ... I'm all in.

I kick off my sling-backs, and I'm about to change out of my sweaty funeral dress when I hear a car door slam. There's someone storming up our driveway. I go outside barefoot to intercept the intruder—I don't want a scene in front of the girls. A scene in front of the neighborhood's bad enough.

"Can I help you?" I ask.

"Looking for Brad Lenox. I need to get my hands on him." This from a squat, red-faced man with a neck the size of a bull.

"I'm Mrs. Lenox, are you sure I can't help you?" I ask, alarmed.

"I've been to his work, and this slimeball told me he's home. Didn't say nothing about a Mrs. Lenox. Shit's gonna start hitting the fan," the stranger yells..

"My husband's at a funeral," I say flatly.

"Fucking hell—I can't take a swing at him there!" the man shouts in exasperation, a big vein pulsing in his neck.

"Er—could you keep your voice down? There are young children inside. How about you tell me what this is all about," I suggest, sounding a deal more confident than I feel.

"Your husband's been messing with my wife! That's what this is about. I'm fixing to give him a knuckle sandwich and chew off his bleedin' balls!" he growls.

"Oh!" is all I can manage, swallowing hard to fight back hot tears that are brimming, and regain some composure.

"Jeez! I'm sorry, I didn't mean to hurt you. Your husband's a son of a bitch. You shouldn't ought've heard it like this," he says.

He stomps back to his car (an import, not a Ford, so he's not one of Brad's customers), and he slams the door hard. Foolishly, I look around to check if any of the neighbors overheard. Fortunately, it all seems quiet. Too hot to hang outside. Instinctively, I cross myself and thank the Blessed Virgin for small mercies.

I walk back in, heart thumping, mind racing, and I blink back the tears so Carling and Sherri don't see me cry. Thank heaven they're so absorbed in their game, shipwrecked now, like me, and they're oblivious to what just happened. Oblivious maybe that I even came home, that I went outside. Thank you, Jesus.

I go to the screened porch—it's hot but bearable when I turn the fan on full. I slump in one of the mismatched chairs. Emotions are ripping through me so fast I don't know which one to feel. I'm furious, sad, humiliated, hurt, afraid, ashamed, defeated, and even a tiny bit amused, all at the same time. Inevitably, at one level, I already kind of knew Brad was cheating.

There've been signs for over a year now. Brad smelled funny, a mixture of sweat and sickly perfume he'd try to pass off as a new deodorant. Some days, he'd dart for the shower as soon as he got in ... "A/C's on the blink at work again," or "Been out on the forecourt all afternoon," he'd mutter. There were a couple of times he had to go into "work" at the last minute when I was sure he wasn't on the schedule. For Christ's sake, he's the one who sets it. And we all pretended not to notice he's drinking more.

Maybe I cried all my tears at the funeral. I feel flat and deflated now, like I don't have the energy to fight back. The phone rings. It's Brad—stopping over at Sandip's. Is this another excuse? He hasn't seen Sandip in years. I'm not sure how I'd react to this visit in normal times. Will there ever be normal times again? It's hard to picture. I say something noncommittal, and realize I'm glad to have some more time to pull myself together, figure out what to do.

The mention of Sandip brings me back to when Brad and I met—love at first sight, an amazing, romantic future ahead. I can't go down that memory lane right now, too painful, and Jesus, I'll probably cry. I've got to be practical. My thoughts spin, but I force myself to think logically.

There are three precious girls at stake here. I can't just tear their lives apart. I can't support them on my own, and they'd hate me for leaving Daddy. I decide I'm going to try not to confront Brad with it tonight. I'll try and pass off my mood as sadness for Zofia and Jarek. I'll decide what to do another day.

And even as I process this, I can't just switch off from thinking about Brad betraying me, humiliating me. It whirs round and round in my head 'til I've looked at it from above, below, and every which way. Whatever happens, Brad's sown a seed of resentment in me. I hate myself for understanding this so fast. I don't want to be the bitter, resentful, angry woman I'm becoming. *Holy Mother of God, where did I go wrong?* It's way too much!

I've just told myself to let it drop for the umpteenth time when the girls start throwing a fit. "Apple" apparently destroyed the boat, and Miss Meow is nowhere to be found. Cat overboard? I smile wanly as I think of that, surprised I can muster a smile.

I decide the game's over and bribe the girls with Goldfish and Skittles until I can get their dinner ready. The Goldfish are ground into the sofa cushions, and there are Skittle smears on the tablecloth. Brad'll complain about this mess. Other days, I'd clear this kind of thing up or half-hide it before he gets home. Today, I think, *What the hell?*

◆

"SuperSmiles Circus" always comes to town around Labor Day. Brad's taken the girls to the matinee performance. They love it, even though it's the same every year. Unfunny clowns, a woman in faded sequins and fishnet tights riding a mangy horse bareback, pretending to drink a bottle of bourbon and shoot a target all at the same time, wobbly tightrope artists, and a trapeze act where all the performers miss their tricks and fall into the net.

I decide to stay home and take some time to myself. I didn't exactly confront Brad after the man came to beat the living daylights out of him, but I know he knows I know—and he's acted contrite these last few weeks. Hope it lasts.

I take an iced tea and a couple of hairdressing magazines onto the screened porch and turn the fan on high. It judders, sprays off a collection of dead bugs, a couple of flakes of rust, and then rips into life. I'm in shorts and a strappy little T-shirt. The fan's tornado flaps the magazine pages like a manic bird and makes my nipples rise. I slipped off my bra when they all left to be more comfortable.

I turn the fan down a notch, to ocean breeze, and focus on controlling my magazine, leafing through the new styles, and figuring out how they've been layered. I like to keep up to date. I still only work two afternoons a week, but when the day finally arrives that Sherri goes to school, I'll add more hours. I don't want to be behind the times.

After a while, I put the magazine down. Mother of God, it's too hot to concentrate, even with the fan. I'm not as relaxed as I figured I'd be. Restlessly, I get up and stroll around, leaving the porch and wandering across the yard, heading vaguely in the direction of the oasis of shade cast by the old maples.

An odd sound catches my subconscious. I think I hear a low moan, perhaps an animal in pain. Then, through the branches I see Jarek's out on his deck, sitting with his head in his hands. I think he's sobbing as quietly as he can. Without thinking, I go through the gate that links our properties.

"Jarek, is there anything I can do?" I ask, tentatively patting his shoulders. "Some iced tea?"

"You are too kind. I'm sorry to make a fool of myself like this. I had no idea anyone was outside," he tells me.

"Don't apologize, you've every right to be upset, what with Zofia and everything."

I've no idea what "everything" might cover—but he tells me he failed to make tenure at the college where he lectures, and he's planning to go back to Poland. It's all muddled in his head, good to go back home and be near family and, on the other hand, terrible to leave this house where they were happy for a good few years and where Zofia spent her dying days. He says he's a failure. He couldn't save Zofia, and now he can't save himself.

"I shouldn't complain, Rita, life's been good to me. I can't give up, but just now, I can't carry on."

I shepherd him inside—he needs a bit more privacy—he's losing the battle with his sobs, and it really is too hot out there. I get him ice water and, after he's cooler and calmer, he surprises me and gets out a bottle of slivovitz.

"Don't think I make a habit of this, Rita. I feel I need a drop of Polish courage right now. The weeks have dragged by since she died, but it doesn't make it any easier. I miss her all the time. Sometimes it's as if I died with her, sometimes I feel I have a life sentence. I'm lonely without her."

I'm crying with him now. With him, for him—for me? I realize I am lonely, too. There's constant activity in my life, dropping the kids off here and there, figuring out babysitters, schedules, grocery shopping, my work, holidays, and all the rest of it. But I'm lonely in my marriage. Brad and I were so close in the early years that I swear our hearts beat in unison. Now, they're way off-beat, and we live emotionally distant lives like we're on parallel railway tracks under the same roof.

I don't tell Jarek any of this. I feel a huge lump of self-pity rise in my throat, and tears trickle down my face. I don't want him to see, so I give him a big hug and I rest my head on his shoulder. My T-shirt strap slips, and his hand grazes my breast to replace it. But somehow we don't replace it, somehow we are kissing, somehow my breasts press against his firm chest. Somehow we are on the sofa and he has slipped inside me. Somehow it's wonderful, tender, poignant, and comforting. Somehow he shudders and we both gasp, then I tremble.

I want to curl up in his embrace for a long time, feel safe in his arms, but he remembers himself quickly. "Oh, Rita. I am so sorry. I was overcome."

"Please don't spoil it. Mother of God! That was sweet. Believe me, I didn't plan this, but I'll never forget it. Brad, well, Brad's not ... well, you know ... and Zofia, I'm sure she wouldn't mind you taking a little comfort," I say.

He nods, weeping quietly, and then he pulls himself together again. "Thank you. Bless you. I promise I won't let this happen again. I'll be leaving for Poland by the end of the month."

I hurry back next door, shower, and change. My mind's exploding. *Did I just do that to get back at Brad? Am I just as bad as he is now?* The Catholic guilt swirls. *Oh, no! Will I have to go to confession? Mary, Mother of God, no! Am I damned?* All my years of Catholicism, you'd think I'd know what a mortal sin is. There's no way this felt like any kind of sin. Only two adults being tender and kind and caring with each other. I decide I should stop worrying about it, and I set to cleaning the bathrooms and the girls' bedroom. Trying to distract my circling thoughts with work.

Brad's surprised about the cleaning binge when he brings home three awestruck girls, all brimming with excitement and sugar! Brandi's bursting to tell me all about the horses, but she's drowned out by Carling and Sherri giggling and pulling their noses at the horse poop.

"I thought you wanted to relax," Brad says.

"So did I, but I got restless, and it's too hot to work on the porch or in the yard. I just thought I'd neaten things up a bit."

The girls are super hyper, so I decide to set up the paddling pool, and even though it's beneath Brandi's dignity, she joins in. Brad runs off to buy hot dogs and beer. We have an impromptu barbecue. By a miracle, we don't burn anything too bad, and we don't get mosquito bites or poison ivy. Instead, we sing "The Sun Has Got Its Hat On" and "Roll Out the Barrel," at the top of our lungs. We must look like the perfect family.

Well, all families have their secrets, don't they?

Much later as I'm drifting asleep, I think about my cycle. Jesus, Mary, and Joseph! It's just possible. Brad and I haven't slept together in a while and I'd lost track. Hell! Do I wait until I think I know? Or should I try and seduce Brad right away? My God! I was beginning to dream of more freedom. I should wait, it'll be okay, I tell myself.

I'm only a day late and not too worried when Brad takes it out of my hands. He bursts home mid-morning on Saturday. Cameron Laidlaw dropped by and told him to take the rest of the day off. Gord and a couple of new kids can cope. The new advertising campaign's made selling cars child's play right now. Laidlaw's given him a raise in pay and a bonus! The money's burning a hole in his pocket, even though it hasn't hit his bank account yet. He wants to celebrate. We pick Brandi up from her riding lesson—she looks so grown up in her velvet helmet and her leather boots.

We go to KidzPlay, the place that sells swings and slides and playground equipment. Brad buys the best he can afford that's in stock, no negotiating, no deal that I can see. Joseph and Mary, where's the famous deal-maker when he's on the other side? All the same, he bribes the manager to put it on the truck and deliver it right away.

He's sweet-talking the driver and finds out his brother, who also works for KidzPlay, can come over and help assemble it—for a kickback. Then, he calls Pat's husband, my dad, and Tone to come over and help set it up. Obviously, Pat's kids, Tessa and Kevin, hang out, and I dread having to watch them like a jailer. For once, they all play nicely together, and thank God, I don't have to referee any wars.

At some point, we order takeout pizza for everyone. Although it's late when it's set up, there's still enough light for the kids to try out the swing set. Wow! It's a blast! They're all in heaven, and no one breaks their neck! Brad's in heaven, too. I guess he's convinced himself he's a great guy again, a superstar at work, and the world's best dad.

The euphoria's still peaking when we go to bed that night. Brad's passionate like he was in the early days, throwing caution to the winds, never thinking to ask if I'm "safe."

The next day, I drag three sullen girls to mass. They want to play outside, no matter it's pouring with rain. I'm not concerned about the rain, I'm quietly thanking the Blessed Virgin for my night in the sack with Brad!

11

Glen – April 1983

Typical! My dumb English teacher, Tomboy Thomas, set us a real dumb assignment. "Write about your earliest memory." I can't do that—it's totally embarrassing. What I mean is—well, not that I can't write my earliest memory, I do know how to write. English isn't my favorite subject. Math is. I mean, the memory's super embarrassing.

I was about three years old. It was Halloween. The first year I knew what was going on. Look cute and you get a pile of candy. My mom had made me an "adorable," boring, stupid, pumpkin costume, but my big sisters had a different plan. They pulled out all their old "dress-up" clothes. They dragged a few different outfits over my head, scratching my face with torn net, frayed ribbon, and jagged buttons—see if they care—and we all giggled.

The outfits were all too big until they found a fairy costume Sherri wore in a dance recital when she was about four. It still had the wings and the wand. I liked the wand. I'm small for my age, so the costume was still a bit big, and I kept tripping over the skirt, and we all fell about laughing when I did. I was just bashing my sisters over the head with the wand (what did I care I might poke their eyes out?) when Dad walked in.

He went ballistic! He yelled and screamed and sent the girls to their rooms. He tore the costume off me, sequins pinging across the den. He crushed the wings and snapped the wand, and then he threw it in the trash. I was bawling my eyes out. I ran to Mom in my big-boy Spiderman underpants and grabbed onto her legs, sobbing and sobbing, hiding from Dad. There was no Halloween for any of us that night. No candy! (Except a dumb Kit Kat Mom sneaked us.) You see, there's no way I can tell my English teacher that!

In the end, I wrote about jumping off the high board at the swimming pool that Christmas, when the girls were off school. Dad was with us, which was lucky because the girls would've let me drown—no, they'd have drowned me. Anyway, they were climbing up to the high board and jumping off. I did it, too. There's this gigantic splash, and you shoot down to the bottom of the pool, and then you pop right back up. Totally cool. So what I couldn't swim? Grown-ups spoil all the fun.

Dad was there, he caught me and took me to the side. Then I did it again and again and again and again! Old Tomboy wrote on it: "An unlikely story. Stick to the facts and watch your spelling!" and he gave me a C+. He's so dumb. I was going to tell him that I'm a swim champion now, and a world-famous hero. Honest! No sweat. He couldn't care.

Cross my heart and hope to die. It's true. I'm on the Flying Fish swim team, age ten and under. I can do all the strokes. Coach usually puts me in 'fly. Some of the other kids are bigger than me, so they can catch me in freestyle. Not many kids swim butterfly, and being big sometimes slows you down unless you get the stroke just right, so I win a lot.

The meets are on Saturdays when my dad's usually at work, so sometimes my mom comes. She says it's dead boring, and she brings some crochet to pass the time—she never does it, she gabs with the other moms. I swear she's talking so much she doesn't even see me race.

When Mom can't come, Mon Mon and Grandpa Wuff bring me. The other kids crack up when they hear me calling Grandpa that. I've called him it for so long, it's stuck. No joke, they're so old I'm scared they're going to fall in the pool. Mon Mon can't see too well, and Grandpa's a bit deaf and a bit unsteady on his feet.

Funny thing is, they're wicked quiet at home, but they cheer like banshees (whatever they are) at the pool when I win. One time, Mon

Mon yelled at the stroke judge who was going to DQ me. The judge must have been blinder than Mon Mon. No one DQ's me!

We're in two divisions, the South Central Division and the Metros. Mom and Dad hate the championships because they take all day. And I mean literally all day. We kids hang out in the corridor and play cards for hours, and some of the older kids play music my mom and dad wouldn't approve of.

I feel weird in my Speedos with all the girls there, so I keep my running shorts on until I'm called for my heat. Can't help staring at the older guys. Am I gonna get a bulge like that? Gross! After you hang out literally forever, your name gets called and you line up for your race. You're shivering on the deck—it's not cold, it's nerves and excitement.

After you win, the team screams, and everybody hugs you like you cured cancer or saved the world from aliens. I was first in 'fly in the eights and under—hardly any kids do 'fly at that age—and I got second for the medley relay, that's where a kid from the different age groups does one of the strokes, then hands off to the others. So I *am* a champion, whatever old Tomboy thinks. I got a Flying Fish tracksuit. I can't wear it at school. It's against the law.

It's true about being a hero too. We were over at Jake's house playing ping-pong in his basement. His mom was in the kitchen getting dinner ready. Their basement's this ginormous space, and they've got this itchy old purple carpet and a ping-pong table at one end and sofas (literally for the dog) at the other, and a TV that doesn't work 'cause one of Jake's brothers spilled Cherry Coke all over it.

And there's a closet where Jake's dad keeps scotch and vodka stuffed under some old sleeping bags. The lock's broken—bet your life it was Jake's brothers again. Sometimes we take the tops off and smell the liquor—*gross*. We don't dare do it often, and we turn the boombox up so Jake's mom doesn't hear the stoppers squeak—she'd throw us out, call the cops, get us locked up. Swear to God! Some parents stress out all the time.

It was pretty boring playing ping-pong. Jake wins the whole entire time. His brothers and his dad are wicked good at ping-pong, so it's no fair. He can't beat them, but he destroys us. "Eye of the Tiger" is blasting out while he's smashing the ping-pong ball.

When he's creaming Will, I decide to see what I can find in the garage. There's this door from the basement into the garage, so I go in there and look around. Not much, just an inner tube, a few broken hockey sticks, a whiffle ball, a flat basketball, and bikes for Jake's whole family.

Turns out some of the other kids don't wanna be crushed at ping-pong anymore either, so we decide to take the inner tube to the river at the end of Jake's yard. Jake's not happy about this. He's having a blast showing off his "Rocky Balboa" ping-pong. He says he's scared his mom'll find out and she'll kill us. Literally kill us. We tell him not to be a wuss, it'll be cool. (Well, freezing actually.)

Luckily, there's a side door out of the garage, so we don't open the main doors and make a ton of noise. We drag the inner tube to the water. There's a broken-down chain-link fence at the bank, and we heave the tube over it—don't think we punctured the tube.

The water actually is freezing, worse than any pool in the whole universe, and there's a bit of an oil slick on the top. But the inner tube floats alright. Will hands me the hockey sticks—we're gonna use them as paddles. Jake looks as if he's gonna back out and tell on us. He's real nervous. I pull him to the tube and show him how to sit on it. It's dead spinny, but the others heave themselves on and it stays afloat.

We're all soaking wet, we don't even feel the cold, it's super cool—even Jake's laughing. The inner tube lurches and spins, and we bounce off of the banks a bit. Then we're floating down the river. Well, not exactly "floating," more of a soggy lurch. It's way more fun than ping-pong, until we hear a scream. My God! It's Jake's mom.

When she screams, everyone turns at the same time and we capsize. It's not far to the bank, and I swim over there. It's harder in your clothes than you think. The others scrabble a bit, then they make it too. Oh shit! Jake's not here. Oh my God! Can he even swim?

I see him clinging on to the inner tube. His hands keep slipping, and his head goes under. When I swim out to rescue him, he's freaked, and he's lashing out for me. I yell at him to stop. He doesn't. I kick at him hard. It might've landed on his nuts. Anyway, he stops fighting me.

"Jake, it's alright!" I scream, though I'm not sure if I've killed him. *Can you die of a blow to the balls?* I really gotta save his life now. I'm super, super cold. I drag him to the bank. It's way, way harder than I thought, and I panic a bit. His head goes under once. It flashes across my mind, I might not make it, and we'll both die. Then the others reach out like a human chain, and we get him on the bank.

Thank God, he's breathing. He coughs and splutters a lot. All of a sudden, there's a weird gurgling sound and he throws up—some of it splatters over me. There's a lot more screaming. It's his mom, and now half the neighborhood's here. A big guy, with a bald head and a beard, picks up Jake and kinda carries him home. He's gonna be okay, he's just shocked and shaky. The big guy tells Jake's mom to run a warm bath.

The rest of the gang's in the basement, dripping half the river on the yucky carpet, we're shivering like crazy, and our teeth can't stop chattering until Will finally creeps into the house and raids the linen closet for towels. Mine used to be white. Jake's mom is kinda mad at us, but she's totally relieved Jake didn't drown, so she doesn't seem to notice the towels.

She tells us to stay in the basement so we don't mess up the house, and she finds the old sleeping bags to wrap us in. "What the hell! Liquor in here!" she says like it's a big surprise.

I'm sharing a sleeping bag with Mikey, who's about a foot taller than me, so I mostly get zip and split binding. Hell, I'm so cold it hurts to warm up, and I've lost my sneakers. *Dad'll kill me, I know he will!* The big guy clumps downstairs with a tray of hot chocolate—we're all shaking so much we can't hold the mugs. When I get home, Mom's freaking and stressing out, and my teeth are still chattering so much I can't tell her I saved Jake's life.

"Your dad's going to hit the roof," she says. I know she's practicing what old Tomboy calls, "the art of understatement," and she's trying to be kind, but I wish I could die right here on the spot before Dad gets home.

Brandi's at work, and when she comes home, she and Carling tell me I'm the lowest form of idiot. Retard! I almost choke at this, and I'm super tired and shivery. Sherri gets home from dance later on—she gives me an embarrassing hug and says I'm her hero!

It's the next day when Grandma Phyllis and Grandpa Tone are over. I give them a tidied-up version of what happened—perhaps it wasn't all my idea after all, perhaps Jake was just a teencey-weencey bit excited about it. Grandma Phyllis hugs all the breath out of me so I literally think I'm dying all over again.

"Oh, you brave boy!" she squeals.

Grandpa Tone's got a camera in his car. He takes my picture. I'm in my Flying Fish tracksuit, and I look wicked cool. He gets it developed express, even though he hasn't finished the film. The next week, it's all over the Gazette: "Local Hero Saves Drowning Boy!" I don't think Jake's mom will ever invite me over again.

It's good being a champion and a world-famous hero when you live in a madhouse like mine. Everyone's real loud, especially Dad and my sisters (maybe not so much Sherri)—they're all older than me, so they either treat me like a baby, or they totally ignore me.

Dad's always wanting me to be just like him—a jerk. (I didn't say that.) I overheard him tell Mom, "Glen'll get a growth spurt right before high school. I was a shrimp at his age, and then, wha'd'ya know, I'm looking down on everyone. Glen'll make the football team. It's in his genes."

When I'm not at school or at swim practice, they pretty much leave me on my own. It's totally childish I know, but I still play with Legos. Not the build-the-biggest-tower-in-the-world-and-knock-it-down (ha ha) kind of dumb Legos. I make models. I was bored one day, and without thinking, I made a construction all out of red Legos. It looked quite a lot like the brick hardware store on the corner of Colonial Street. I left it out on the coffee table. Everyone thought it was lame, but Grandpa Tone kinda squinted at it and said, "I see what you mean."

He took me out in his car. Why is it old people never know they're too old to drive? Well, we didn't hit anything so I guess it was alright. He parked round the corner from the hardware store, and he made me go inside. My God! It was embarrassing. I could have died, *literally*.

Grandpa found Mr. Cousins, the owner—a scary, hairy guy, with these wild eyebrows and asked if it was okay to photograph his store. He told old man Cousins that I was making a model of it. I went bright red.

Oh my, was Mr. Cousins interested! (By the idea of a model of his store, not my face looking like someone poured beetroot all over it.) He told Grandpa to take as many photos as he liked and if he wanted to take measurements that would be fine with him. Then, he asked me did I know anything about scale, and he started to explain even though he had a line of customers waiting. When we got the pictures, it seemed as if a scale model was a bit beyond me, so I started with something easier—the public bathrooms in Warner Park.

I really needed yellowish bricks for them, but I had mostly red, so I used them, and I felt stupid going off to measure the bathrooms, so Grandpa Tone did that for me as near as he could. Even Dad helped a bit with the math. He's not bad with numbers. He's figured out car deals his whole entire life. I guess he thinks it's kinda sissy making Lego models, but he brings me huge bags of Lego when he's had a good week, and containers to keep it all organized. Mom and Sherri and all the wrinklies like the models now I've got the hang of it. Carling and Brandi shake their heads, roll their eyes, and mutter, "Pa-thet-ic!"

12

Rita and Brad – Summer 1985

"**B**rad! Brad, what in the name of the Blessed Virgin have you done now?" I snap.

It's been a difficult, long, hot summer, what with Pat's divorce—her second, or is it her third? I've lost count. Tessa and Kevin have been hanging out here, partly to give them somewhere stable to stay, partly to give Pat a break. She took this one hard, and she's in no fit state to supervise them and try and hold it together at work.

Tessa and Kevin are playing the latest break-up like it's no big deal, but they're lost souls inside. These "lost souls" are drinking and smoking marijuana on the sly when they think I live in la-la land. Pray God they don't get our kids into bad habits (heaven knows they've enough bad habits of their own). But unless I'm actually living in la-la land, drugs (well, they sneak my Winstons, but that doesn't count), *hard drugs,* aren't among their vices.

I thought life was getting easier. Sherri spent the entire summer at dance camp, home only two days ago. Glen had a couple of weeks' swim camp, then despised the summer swim team at the rec department ... They are pretty lame—the kids just want to hang by the pool and flirt and sneak off to smoke or make out when the lifeguard's distracted (and they're always distracted) since the lifeguards are more interested in flirting and sneaking off themselves.

Maybe I do live in la-la land. I think Glen's a shade young for that, his acne's bad, and his voice's cracking. He wants to compete, win something else, everything else—most likely for the hell of it—maybe to impress his dad.

Good luck there, son ... Brad has a hard time seeing swimming as a real man's sport. Glen already swims in his regular team at two years above his age group in backstroke and 'fly and, even though he hasn't hit that growth spurt Brad's expecting, he usually wins at freestyle in his own age bracket, and demolishes the opposition in IM.

Hope he'll be more chill next summer—though on second thought, I doubt it. He's intense. When he's not swimming, he's working on technical drawing or his models. My heavens, he's come a long way since the public bathrooms and the hardware store. He figured out Brad's dealership, Bradley's department store, and now he's working on City Hall.

Brad's not sure, doesn't know what to think. He was over the moon to have a son. Felt like we were starting over. Brad thought Glen'd be just like him—big, brash, extrovert, football player, a guy's guy, dreaming of speed, excitement, and living on the edge. Well, that's the way Brad wants to see himself, ignoring the spoiled, frightened little boy he tucks away inside. I was packing for our vacation when he came home with the shiny new Toyota. Jesus, Mary, and Joseph, what's he want with a Toyota? Laidlaw's a Ford dealership, for Christ's sake!

We're headed to the Beaumont Family Camp in Vermont, where Carling's been working all summer. She must think we'll never leave her alone. And she did need to get away. Hounding her's not exactly why we're going. Most likely, this'll be our last vacation all together. Brandi's bringing her boyfriend, Julian. I don't feel right about letting them share a cabin, so he's in with Glen, and Brandi and Sherri will have to put up with each other.

The girls probably won't want us next year. The camp's inexpensive, and there are a lot of us. We're taking my dad and Aunt Monday, bless their hearts, and Pat, Tessa, and Kevin. Pat's bringing a friend from work, Peggy, who moved here a couple of years ago to follow her guy—too bad he dumped her on Christmas Eve.

So we're a big group, and finances aren't great for any of us right now (you shoulda seen Brad's face when he got the bill for dance camp!) Pat never seems to hit gold in her divorces. Phyllis keeps having to bail her out. And we all know Brad's income's unpredictable ... Great times when the going's good and he can't wait to spend it—a pool, an addition to the house, a ritzy vacation. Or there's a slump, and we're tightening our belts.

"A Toyota! What the hell?" I ask him as I reach for my Winstons. This had better be a good story though I already know in my bones, it's not.

Brad

"Surprise!" I yell with a note of triumph that you bet, I actually do feel. "Come and look at this beauty."

Rita's incredulous. Can't say I blame her. I've worked for Laidlaw's forever. We've always had Fords, and now I've driven up in a brand-new Toyota.

"Hey, sweetheart, you know it's been one helluva drag selling Fords these days with all the imports flooding the market, so I told Laidlaw where to stuff it. I work for Toyota now," I say.

She's real mad that I didn't tell her I was thinking about this, didn't discuss it with her. How I never take her opinion into account. How we're supposed to be a team, only I never got the hang of that. She goes on and on, listing my faults ... She doesn't quite get how when I eat chips, bits fall out of my mouth, or how I never change the toilet roll, or how I leave my boxers on the floor—like she usually does when she's on a roll.

But she throws a good number of other darts that, hell, I hate to admit are right on target. When she's stopped spitting bullets, she asks how I know Toyotas sell any better than Fords, and thank the stars, I do have answers for that at least—you only need to skim the sales stats.

Then she worms it out of me that I'm only assistant manager at Toyota, when I'd been manager at Laidlaw's and in charge of the used cars too. Holy shit! I'm relieved to get this, to get anything, but I explain smugly that the Toyota dealership's a much bigger operation than Laidlaw's pathetic spread. The showroom's out of town, state of the art, on a huge lot with a service department, repair shop, and used-car lot all on the same site. There's plenty of room for inventory, so they can always meet customer whims. The cars have more features, and the price's right.

"I'll be back up to manager in no time," I lie. "And right away I'll be making more money than at Scrooge Laidlaw's," I lie again.

She's still mad at me. She blows a gasket when I tell her I can't go on vacation with the family now since I'm starting a new job. I try my charm-offensive, but Rita's wise to all my tricks. And holy hell, I can see why. I knew she'd be mad, feel betrayed. That's why I didn't tell her a week ago. I'd have got the cold shoulder treatment the whole damn week.

She doesn't talk to me for the rest of the night, and I take a slice of pizza and a six-pack to the screened porch. I'd have slept there too if Sherri wasn't home; she'd've guessed something's up. Glen's oblivious, playing with his Legos.

I'm okay with taking the rap. When we go to bed, Rita shuffles as far away from me as she can without actually tippling out, and she's wearing her passion-killer PJs in the summer. Ironic, really, she turns me on when she's mad, reminds me of her feisty side I fell in love with way back when. At least Rita'll never have to know how close to disaster we were this time.

I've been deadly bored at work for years now. I let my standards slip. I couldn't get motivated, let alone motivate my team. It didn't help that the new models were the shitty old models with a minor tweak here and there. Nothing to get excited about. Only the trucks compete with the imports, and there's not much fun in selling a truck.

What happened to the old me? In the early days, I'd find a way, a new incentive plan, provide the vehicles as courtesy cars for the seniors' golf tournament, make a deal with the local rental car company, sponsor a charity event for sick kids. I guess I lost my mojo. A few long lunch hours, and I missed a couple of early meetings when the hangovers were gross.

Then there's Barbie. She's not really named Barbie, she's a Danish doll called Helga, but the guys all nicknamed her Barbie when she came to work at Laidlaw's, for obvious reasons. Laidlaw (Cameron's sonofabitch son who runs the business now) had been pressing me to hire a woman for a long time. Said it was sex discrimination only hiring men.

I resisted him for the longest time. Didn't think I'd keep my hands off a woman if she was working with me (not just my hands either), and I didn't think a chick could pull in the numbers. Anyway, the day came when Barbie applied for a job.

Oh my stars! Drop-dead gorgeous, straight, split skirt, clinging blouse, smoking lips, and she had other assets—sold cars for years. She'd worked for Ford before, been sales"man" of the year three years ago. I couldn't say "no" in all ways, as it happened. My stars, I tried …

I lied and told her that my opening was at the used-car showroom across the street, thinking maybe then I wouldn't be so tempted. I moved Trev from over there to our showroom. She took the job all the same, and made a damn good fist of it. Couldn't sell to women (still not too many of them come buy cars), but the men eat out of her hand.

And you bet, so did I. We saw each other for months, and each time was better than the last. So, I got rash the other week, took her out for lunch—well, out of town where nobody knows us—that's what I figured. She's pursing her luscious lips at me and flicking the tip of her suggestive tongue as I feed her chocolate mousse, when guess who walks in—the "old man" himself, Laidlaw senior! I suppose it could've been worse, his boy might've found us on the sofa in the lunchroom after work. Anyway, he settles his guest, then comes over to our table and tells us he'll see us in my office in an hour and a half.

We're both out on our ear. Somehow, don't ask me how, I persuade him to let me keep the car for a week and, thank my stars, we paid off Rita's already.

In a mad panic, I head right over to the Toyota dealership. I should've been more professional about it, but I was shit scared—and, well, I got lucky. Lucky Lenox, lands on his feet. An assistant manager quit just that morning. References were dodgy, but they were happy to get one from Gord, who's been with me since the old days, retired six months ago before we hit the bad patch.

He told them I was a great team leader and all that. I said I didn't want Laidlaw to know I was thinking of moving on, so the other reference came from the president of the Lions Club—he owed me a favor. Thank God, he was in town.

They gave me a uniform—red polo shirt—told me to wear khaki slacks, and they'd get a car ready for me in a week. I let them know that with my sick leave, I'd only need to work out the one week at Laidlaw's. I've been pretending to go to work all week. I thought Rita'd catch me out. I've been leaving later and coming home earlier smelling of Burger King. Lucky Lenox—my luck held, she's been too busy keeping an eye on Tessa and Kevin, and getting ready for the trip.

Rita

Brad must think I was born yesterday to swallow that lie. Laidlaw's finally seen sense and fired him. Is this what's going to make him clean up his act? I doubt it. Why do I stay with this piece of shit? (Pardon my French.) What kind of a patsy does it make me? Too much to do before we leave tomorrow to worry about it now. Tomorrow—oh, Joseph, Mary, and Jesus! Now I'm in charge of all these kids and their rampaging hormones, and I need to keep an eye on Dad and Aunt Monday. When the hell do I get a break?

13

Rita and Brad – Summer 1985

I need to pinch myself. This is turning out to be an amazing vacation at Beaumont's. The cabins are pretty basic, but they're right on the lake. Aunt Monday and Dad only have a few steps to take to the Adirondack chairs where they read the paper and devour the view. It's spectacular, sunbeams sparkle on the ripples, deep, dark pines across the water, and all backed by mountains in the distance. If I'd ordered up the weather, I couldn't have done a better job, picture-postcard blue skies, a wisp of a breeze, all cooling off in the evenings so it's comfortable for sleeping.

We can take our meals in the main dining room or self-cater. The dining hall's rustic with beams and a huge stone fireplace. And the food's healthy—doesn't reek of pizza and fries like my kitchen, but we don't dine there often, we're on a budget. Pat and Peggy prepare most of the lunches, cold cuts, salads, hummus, and dip. Who'd've thought Glen would put away hummus? If I offer it to him at home, will he turn his nose up and beg for a cheeseburger and supersize fries? Brandi, Julian, and Glen like to grill in the evenings now and again with Sherri and once with Tessa and Kevin. Monday and I make pasta salad, coleslaw, whatever's easy. And someone always has a stash of Oreos.

Glen's found a buddy in Julian—the big brother he's always wanted, and Brandi's cool with having him tag along. She doesn't have much patience for him at home—maybe she's just too tired right now. She works in the vets' office, doing everything, I think, except major surgeries. And even though she loves it, she needs a break. Working weekends, always on call—it takes a toll. It's good to see her relax, soften her edges like she does with all the strays and stragglers.

Tessa and Kevin aren't my problem so much, now their mom's around. Tessa parades around in her minuscule bikini, and I notice she's attracted some male attention. Who wouldn't with your pubic hair showing! Sherri won't have anything to do with her, thinks she's a slut.

Sherri discovered there's a theater group and, although she can't stay for their performance, she's happy hanging out with them, choreographing their routines—even a fight scene. Not sure where Kevin heads off to—he's back for meals, and he's polite to Aunt Monday and my dad, so that's all I care about. He calls Dad "Mr. Wilf"—it's a bit incongruous. I've caught a twinkle in dad's eye when he hears it.

We don't see much of Carling, she works at the kids' club looking after the little ones, and she's always being asked to babysit at night. Sometimes we wave at her and a parade of rug rats holding hands heading off to some new activity, chanting, "We're the Munchkins, the mighty, mighty Munchkins. When they ask us, what do we tell them? We're the Munchkins, the mighty, mighty Munchkins."

Carling's likely embarrassed to see us wave, she never waves back. It's nice just to be near her and see how much the Beaumonts depend on her. When she's not babysitting, or kicking back with the other counselors, she comes over for a cookout. I almost don't recognize her! Even with her red hair and fair skin, she's deeply tanned after all these weeks outdoors, and she exudes confidence.

No one misses Brad. I overheard Brandi tell Julian he's "a fucking asshole." Since I feel the same way right now, I pretended not to hear, though I'm conflicted. Brandi used to adore her dad. Brad'd hate it here. Too rustic, not enough action—he'd be dragging the kids off to find motocross, an arcade, a waterpark, or a trip into Canada.

The farthest we all go is for an ice cream at Chillin'. I like seeing Monday and Dad demolish a banana split. They both end up with cream on their noses. We all laugh, and I realize we haven't laughed enough in these last—how long has it been?—weeks, months?

Peggy invited me to go on a hike with her. Sounded tame enough. I pulled on an old pair of shorts and a T and laced up my good sneakers. She's carrying a backpack. I find out there's all sorts of gear inside, lunch for both of us, first aid, spare clothes, water bottles, and God knows what else. She reminds me to put on sunscreen, a hat, and sunglasses. We both spray bug repellent until we cough.

I must look a sight in my old clothes, garish floppy hat, Walmart sunglasses, and embalmed in chemicals. Peggy looks pristine! Although her breasts are smushed into a well-fitting sports bra you can tell she's a full bust that makes her hiking shirt look as if it's been tailor-made.

She's only two or three inches taller than me, but those inches are all leg! Not quite legs up to the armpits, but strong and sleek like racehorse legs. Her hat's a pert little visor, so sharp it looks as if she just slipped it out of the package. It has little impact on her sleek bob. *Who did her hair?* I wonder. The cut's exquisite.

She's a bit younger than Pat—my age or a year or two less. I've got to admire her independence. I never lived alone like she does. Apparently, she can unblock a sink, lay a brick walk, and fix a carburetor. It's clear she's in great shape, too. She spends her weekends hiking whenever the weather's good enough, with a group who are planning on doing the Appalachian Trail next spring. I guess she has workout tapes at home and, from the look of her, she actually does them instead of using them as door-stops like the rest of us mere mortals.

Right from the trail head, she slows her pace to match mine, and when I'm not too winded, I ask her, "Don't you miss having a man around?"

Her reply shocks me. "I don't miss the man, I miss the sex!"

I can't help my nervous laughter—she takes it for genuine laughter, thank heavens. My life's been so confined, I've not met a woman as self-reliant as Peggy before. She's an accountant, works in the same office as Pat—I don't think Pat's her secretary, but I know she has one.

"I should never have trusted Pierre," she tells me as we pause to take in the view. It's unbelievable, and it's Peggy's way of giving me a breathing break.

I thought running after the kids kept me fit, and I've only gained a few pounds in the years since Glen was born, but I'm learning that climbing up mountains and cigarettes don't mix! My chest's heaving, my throat's dry, and my nose is running. Even so, I feel good, lighter, freer somehow, and how cool to see the camp below us with the people looking like ants and the buildings smaller than Glen's Legos. Other hikers pass us, breathing a lot easier than me—I hope Peggy's not humiliated. She doesn't seem to be impatient, drinking in the view.

We carry on, and she's on a roll talking about Pierre. I guess all of this was pent up inside her, and she hasn't had much of a chance to get it off her chest. She met him on vacation in the Canadian Rockies. He was totally infatuated with her, and she was more attracted than she'd ever been with any other man, (seems as if there'd been quite the list). He was smart, witty, darkly handsome, with the cutest French-Canadian accent.

She giggled when she told me about their adventures in bed. Athletic and yet playful. I'm glad we're outside, and I'm pink—no, red already—so Peggy can't tell I'm blushing. No one's ever told me about their sex life before.

Pierre was desperate to be with her and found a good job in downtown Boston. Soon Peggy moved out of her one-bed apartment to an upscale townhouse so they could hang out (make out?) in comfort, some awesome times slipped by, and life together was super fun. As Christmas approached, Peggy wondered about finally introducing him to her family (something she'd sworn off doing) and secretly hoped he'd choose the holiday to pop the question. Well, hell, she was leaning in to kiss him after an intimate dinner for two on Christmas Eve, when he told her he was heading to the airport to visit his wife and daughters back in Quebec!

I am so shocked, I blurt out, "Even Brad's not such a shithead!"

We're at the summit. We made it! Well, I made it—there was never any doubt about Peggy, who's not even broken a sweat, looks as if she's just been for a stroll in the park. It's wonderful—I can't believe it. I can see all across the western world, and I have a high that I don't get from smoking anymore and, at the same time, a sense of peace and tranquility that beats what the cigarettes do still bring. It's unbelievably fresh and clear up here. I'd not be tempted to light up even if I'd brought them with me.

I realize I haven't worried about the kids or Dad and Monday once. *Why haven't I done this before? How can I do this again?* I wonder as I eat the chicken sandwich Peggy made for me. Holy Mother of God, even this tastes out of this world! We're not alone at the top. A good number of other hikers are here—all very friendly—something else hiking does for you?

As we descend (not as easy as you'd think—kills your knees), Peggy quizzes me about what I said about Brad. I'm most likely feeling euphoric after all this fresh air and exercise, so I probably tell her more than I should.

"Why don't you leave him then?" she asks.

It's the question I've avoided asking myself all these years. Too scared? Have too little confidence in myself? Where did all that feistiness go? For the kids' sake? Brandi, at least, has figured her dad out. So Monday and Dad don't worry about us even more than they already do? Because I'm used to it? I don't know. As we're going down, I decide, at the very least, I'm going to be more independent when we get back home, and I'm going to get in shape!

I realize just how much I need to work on my fitness the next day when I'm as stiff as a board, and Peggy's off on a group hike on a much more challenging mountain. I linger at the lakeside, doing a little crochet, skimming a magazine, and then feel like getting a drink. I amble up the path toward our cabins. As I pass Pat's, there are unmistakable adult sounds wafting out, and I think for an instant, *Oh, Pat, you haven't found another man already.* But the voice that cries out is yelling, "Tess, oh, my God! Tess, I love you forever!"

Jesus, Joseph, and Mary. I'm shocked for the second day in a row!

We've only got a couple of days left! I've enjoyed every minute. I can't believe we've been gone for almost two weeks and we've scarcely had time to be bored. Strolling around, following the arc of a hawk, taking a dip, noticing insects murmuring, registering the clunk of a tennis ball in the background, watching little kids play. A trail of water becomes a river, sticks and leaves dams or boats—older kids learn to sail in a flotilla of lurching boats.

In the evenings, we gaze at the stars and Dad and Julian point out the constellations. Julian strums his guitar, and wondrously Brandi sings in a sweet voice I haven't heard in years, "Annie's Song," "Fernando," and "Song for Judith." It's kind of romantic, even though it's Tess and Carlos (yes, the guy from the passionate encounter,) who snuggle together.

This afternoon, Brandi and Julian are going kayaking, and Glen begs me to go out with him. I've never been in a kayak, and my body's still sore from hiking, even my arms. How did that happen? I wasn't even carrying a pack. Getting into the kayak's pretty precarious. It wobbles everywhere and Glen's laughing and rolling his eyes, as I slot myself in—a fit almost as tight as a condom! Heavens, did that really slip into my mind? Must be Peggy's influence.

We push out into the lake. Glen's doing most of the paddling, my paddle grazes the surface, or it digs a deep hole. Water swirls off the paddle and down my arm and seeps into my body. Cool and delicious at the same time.

After a while, I get the hang of it, paddling in a steady rhythm, matching Glen. In spite of my aching muscles, it's great to be in unison with my son. I can't remember this before. I promise myself it won't be the last time. All those years when I've been there for him, yet we've never done this before.

We're all four in the middle of the lake in our double kayaks, a good distance from the other boats. I'm taking a break from paddling, enjoying the view and the breeze against my cheek when, suddenly, water's cascading off my head down my chin, into my lap. Glen and Julian must have planned this. I'll get them!

It's an all-out water fight. Our kayaks are tipping all over the place. Brandi's joining in too, using her paddle deftly to kick waterfalls all over us. I'm pathetic, I only manage feeble little splashes, but Joseph, Jesus, and Mary, it's super fun. We're all laughing, caught up in the moment. Julian and Brandi are alongside us now.

They reach out and rock our kayak as violently as they can. We ship some water, but we're still afloat. Glen squirms out of his seat and stands up. He launches himself toward the other boat. Our kayak shoots sideways, rocks crazily, and he sends a tidal wave over Brandi and Julian. We're all in the lake, and the mom in me wonders if Julian can swim.

Our boat's upside down, and we drag it to the shore that way. It's a long haul, and Glen's doing most of the work—I'm in charge of the paddles. Brandi and Julian kind of nudge their boat from behind until finally, they join us on the shore. Okay, so it was an ambush, we're all fine, and it's a treat to feel young and silly again.

Carling's joining us tonight since she doesn't have our last night off. So we go to the store and buy hamburgers, hot dogs, and chicken patties for the grill. Aunt Monday makes an extra-special pasta salad—enough to feed the whole state of Vermont. Dad goes off with Sherri to buy ice cream, cream, and bananas, and Pat and Peggy make sure we have plenty of beer and soda.

It's an unforgettable evening, all the gang's here, including some friends we met along the way. Sherri's brought a couple of girls who have "alternative" hairstyles, zebra stripes and a kind of scruffy urchin look. Carling invited another counselor friend, Tessa has her beau (quiet and polite in our company), and Monday and Dad surprise us by inviting the watercolor teacher, a jolly man. We hadn't even noticed they'd moved from their spots all vacation, let alone learned to watercolor. Julian's in charge of the campfire, and s'mores appear although I don't remember anyone shopping for them.

I'm next to Dad when he says, "Wonderful vacation, Rita. I loved every minute. Just watching the kids—they're all growing up. They're so interesting. It's good to see them so happy. Brandi's young man's good for her, but I wish he'd keep his hands to himself. He keeps bothering Glen."

Startled, I glance in their direction. Sure enough, Julian has one arm around Brandi and the other loosely draped over Glen's shoulder in a protective, big-brotherly way. Glen's not having it, shrugs him off and leaps up to dive into the lake. The moon and stars glitter, reflected in the water like promises, and there's a hint of the trees on guard on the other side, keeping us safe. There's chill in the air, and even more chill when Glen emerges from the lake and shakes himself like a dog all over me!

Brad

They all troop home—they've grown closer to each other in the couple of weeks away. Fuck it! I'm more alone than when they were gone. Rita's trying to make nice, but the others don't even notice I exist. Hell! It breaks my heart. I missed them more than I'll ever admit, more than I ever guessed.

And it wasn't that time hung heavy. The new job's intense. I've had to go up a steep learning curve, learning all the unfamiliar models, all their finer features, the vagaries of the financing deals, leasing options, and fleet sales. Haven't worked this hard since I was wet behind the ears. I like the challenge—it's woken me up—thank God.

They credited me with a couple of "pity" sales the first two or three days, then I began to hit my stride, and it was good to get my touch back. I missed telling Rita and maybe Brandi all about it. Brandi's gone all cold on me since she's been hanging around Julian so much. We were best buds once upon a time.

The house seemed to boom like one of those New Hampshire loons without them. I didn't go to bars; I didn't hang out with women. I tidied everything up, did all the laundry, cleaned the bathrooms and the kitchen just the way I like. Then I found out it wasn't the way I like after all.

It was soulless.

Without them, I felt I'd lost my soul.

14

Brandi – 1985-1986

It's still freezing. God! It's a never-ending winter. I'm purple with cold, I press my numb fingers hard together to try and revive the circulation. Can you get frostbite in New England in March? God, yes! I just finished mucking out Manatee Bay. Steam rises from her flanks, but it doesn't do a thing to warm me up. We were only in the indoor ring—too cold outside. Glen calls her Mam-ma-ree Bay. Not even funny. He's a dork.

He doesn't even remember that cool vacation we had in Florida when he was little and Dad was flush. We stayed in an upscale resort, went on a speedboat, Dad let me steer, Glen threw up, and we swam with the rays, and there were real manatees in the bay. Weird and beautiful. I couldn't take my eyes off of them.

Surprising, Glen doesn't remember swimming. He's always bragging he swam before he could walk. A lie, but not a big fat one. That time with the rays, Dad realized it was shallow enough for us to walk, so he and I shuffled along trying not to step on a ray, but we didn't tell Glen and he was doggy-paddling for all he was worth.

The barn door creaks open, like a sound effect from a horror movie. It's Bev, the barn manager. She's wearing this enormous fake fur hat with ear flaps, Michelin-man layers of padding, and ancient boots. Her nose is red, raw, and dripping, and when she speaks it comes out as a croak. "Hi! Brandi, did your dad forget again?"

She doesn't have to say any more. I feel so bad she dragged herself out here with a bad cold to ask if Dad intends on paying the lease on Manatee Bay anytime soon. I like Bev a whole lot, and I give her a hug. We've known each other a super-long time. I used to volunteer with her riding for the disabled program, until the insurance wouldn't cover us anymore.

"Bev, I'm sorry. I guess Dad hasn't paid in a while?" I ask.

"Three months next week—I can't hold the owners off too much longer," she rasps.

"You go back inside, look after yourself, I'll bring the money over this evening," I tell her with more confidence than I have—and she must guess this. What'll I do if Dad can't pay? I hate to ask Grandpa Wolf, Mon Mon, or worse still, Grandpa Tone—I'd cross my frozen fingers if they'd move and hope it won't come to that.

Manatee Bay's my passion. God! I love her even more than Julian—I keep that to myself, of course. I can never resist animals, all kinds. We weren't allowed a pet, except when the old Polish dude who lived next door offered us his tropical fish when he moved back to Gdansk and, for once, Mom gave in. We had them for a long time until the power went out for three days one winter like this one, and they all died, smelled like rotten fish. We cried and cried as if one of our grandparents had croaked. It did no good, mom wouldn't buy any more.

I started working at the vet's when I was fifteen. I brought a lot of animals home then, bearded lizards, fancy rats, a pygmy pig. Mom and Glen used to scream, and Glen turned green when he saw their stitches. I only kept them until they got better. I had to take them back after that.

And no puppies or kittens, no fluffy rabbits or tear-jerker guinea pigs. Mom and Dad knew they wouldn't resist them. Sherri brought home a little dog once. It had a huge hole in its side from barbed wire. Glen actually vomited. I took it to Dr. Shirl and Dr. Dean, but they couldn't save him.

I'm off to the vet's office after I've finished with Manatee. It's my whole life—well, not counting Julian. I graduated from high school just to please Mom and Dad. Never thought of going to college, but Dr. Shirl and Dr. Dean signed me up for a veterinary technician's course at community college at their expense.

I try and take evening classes most of the time. It doesn't always work out, so I work extra on Saturdays to make up the time. I love my job—especially when one of the vets takes me with them on a field visit to castrate a llama or help with a difficult birth. I only wish it was better paid, I'd leave home then.

I've talked about it with Julian. He doesn't have any money either. He's at college. Started at community college and aced it, so he got a scholarship to Walden State. We met in the steamy cafeteria. How romantic! I say "met"—actually, he knocked into me with his tray, and I spilled a cup of hot coffee all over his privates. When he'd finished hopping up and down and swearing, holding his crotch, we were dating.

He's training to be a microbiologist, and I haven't the faintest clue where that leads him. He lives with his mom, who's a manicurist. He helps her out on weekends and on the vacations. He gets even bigger tips than she does, kinda odd for a guy. The clients think he's cute. They're not wrong!

Sometimes I feel he's more like a brother or best friend than a boyfriend. Guess that's a sign of a good relationship. I can be myself around him, don't have to pretend I'm someone I'm not—like all the other girls do to get a guy's attention. He's gentle and understanding, you can tell him anything, and I mean anything, even period cramps. He's really steady, not like Dad, who's either full steam or in a coma.

My dad used to be my world. I started realizing it was alcohol on his breath when he kissed me good night, and his promises were sad jokes, like vowing to pay for Manatee on time. Once you start seeing the other side of a person, you can't stop. I don't think he treats Mom right either, and I'm pretty sure he has a mistress. Julian's pretty cool in comparison. He gets on well with everyone, especially Glen.

I nearly died the first time I brought Julian home. Glen'd been folding the laundry. (Mom must've bribed him.) He put all his disgusting underpants and boxers on my bed and all our little bras and panties on his. He claimed he'd been concentrating on one of his models, and didn't notice. He was up to one of his pranks. Gets that from Dad, I bet.

Julian just laughed and was really interested in the models. They're kinda weird if you ask me, weird but harmless, I guess. This one's of the hardware store in town. I hadn't noticed that it's actually an interesting building, and it's uncanny how Glen's picked out the detail with Legos. Julian brought him a whole bag of his old Legos after that. Guys are dickheads.

That's another thing. Julian's not forcing me to go to bed with him, even though we've been dating forever. I don't mean that we don't make out, feel each other up. I stroke him until he comes, but he's not gagging for it like most men. I turned twenty-one last Christmas. I thought we'd do it as a birthday surprise.

Julian doesn't know it, but I'm not technically a virgin. I lost my virginity with Wiper Woods the day we graduated high school. A bunch of us told our parents we were staying at each other's houses. We made it super confusing so they couldn't check up on us.

They probably had our number anyway, now I look back on it. We all went to a campsite a few miles out of town. There was lots of cheap wine and vodka, a campfire, a starry sky, and one thing led to another. It hurt and kinda undignified, and I can't say I enjoyed it that much or remembered a whole lot about it later, thank God, but I'd like to have another go with someone I really, really care about very soon.

Oh! And on that subject—cousin Tess is getting married in a couple of months. She's only eighteen and, God yes, she's pregnant. The guy's the one she met last summer when we were all on vacation. He lives in Warborough, not that far away, and they "kept in touch." Evidently, his family goes to camp every year, didn't know Hispanic families did that.

He was bored out of his mind until he met Tess. The rest of his crew are all into birdwatching, fishing, and survival techniques. He's into video games, movies, and drinking. Left school last year. Works for his uncle as an apprentice plumber. He certainly plumbed Tess!

She'll graduate high school just before the wedding, and then it'll be Walmart for her until the baby comes. Carlos' uncle's renting them an apartment over his garage. They'll have less money even than us, and it'll be colder than the barn in winter. It'll never last. In the meantime, we all have to run around like headless chickens pretending this wedding's the most exciting event to hit humanity. She asked the three of us to be bridesmaids and her friend Trace. Dad's going to walk her down the aisle, (not sure where her real father is, Auntie Pat can't stand the sight of him) and, for some strange reason, Kevin's best man.

Mom's offered to make all the bridesmaids' dresses. She's in a panic. Tess wanted this apricot fabric, and it was back-ordered. Now it's arrived, it's tangerine. Mom says she hasn't time to make four dresses out of anything else, so we'll be tangerine dreams! Ugh!

Auntie Pat brought their dog to the vets the other day. Trusty was dragging his rear across the ground. "Blocked anal glands," I told her with one glance, but she insisted on seeing Dr. Shirl. I think she wanted a chat, they're old friends. She had to wait awhile as Shirl was doing emergency surgery on a cat that had been attacked by a stupid dog. It was quiet in the office, and Auntie Pat told me all about Tess's wedding dress.

"Well, y'know I was going to make it, but Tess had other ideas. She found it secondhand, beautiful, absolutely beautiful, and we'll soon sponge that drip of asparagus soup off the front. It's loose fitting round the waist so it'll fit her on the day. She'll look divine—I don't think anyone will guess. There's a lace veil, and a darling little tiara—not real diamonds, you know, but it sparkles and it'll catch the light. She decided on orchids for the bouquet. You girls better hurry up and sort out the bachelorette night, you know. And then, Brandi, you'll have lots of ideas for when Julian pops the question."

Auntie Pat never misses an opportunity to drop a hint about me and Julian, but I'm saved from a reply as Dr. Shirl pops her head around the door and calls Auntie Pat and Trusty in.

I shudder thinking about the wedding. Auntie Pat's making our headdresses out of silk flowers—a turquoise blue that would've looked okay with the apricot, but is vile with the tangerine. She's making silk posies too for us. Another shame, I like real flowers, though definitely not orchids. Aunt Mon Mon's making the cake.

She can't see well enough to decorate it, so Carlos' mom's going to finish it off. Everyone's cooking—even Grandpa Wolf. Turns out he can make a half-decent quiche.

Even with everyone helping out, the wedding's gonna cost a chunk of change. Dad said he'd help Pat out. Oh, my God! That's why he hasn't been paying for Manatee Bay! You'd better have a good explanation, Dad! We need to talk.

15

Glen – May 1986

Honestly, I'm super glad I'm a guy. Being a girl's gotta be exhausting! You only need to say the word "wedding," and the women start shrieking all over the place and whip themselves up like they're gonna explode. They fall apart, literally fall apart. End up a gibbering, blubbering mess. Take my mom, for example. She's normally completely sane (well, apart from needing me to be in bed by nine-thirty—which I am because I'm wiped from swimming). Anyway, Mom's always got everything under control, until these last few weeks when she's been out of her mind, stark raving mad—and it's not even her daughter who's getting married. It's my cousin Tess.

Mom's been a cross between an Egyptian mummy and a fetish doll wound up in fabric with needles in her mouth and pins in her top (when she's not smoking) and cussing under her breath at the vile material. (By the way, did you know they take the mummies' brains out through their noses? Ewww!)

Who thought tangerine was a good idea anyway? It makes you puke, and it's wicked bad next to my sisters' carroty hair. Mom insisted on piling it—their hair, I mean—up on their heads in a kind of woven bun, then she teased ringlets out to frame their faces. The turquoise headdresses look as if they're strangling the buns. (I just found out there's another meaning to "buns"—makes your eyes water.) What the heck—I'm only a guy, what do I know?

Tess's friend, Trace, is almost six feet tall. My mom had to stand on a chair to reach her hair. It's strawberry blond, so the gross dress doesn't do her any favors either. When the bridesmaids all stand in a line, they look dumb. The skirts are all at different levels since they're odd heights, and each of them dyed their shoes a different shade of turquoise to "match" the headdress and the fake flowers.

Sherri's in sandals with six-inch heels (They'll ruin her feet for dance. What was she thinking?), Carling's in wedges, Brandi's in pointy sling-backs, and Trace has these big, flat things. They look like something out of a freak show. Tess should've chosen full-length dresses—the effect would've been a lot less hideous. Then, Tess didn't have too much time to plan the wedding with a baby on the way.

Auntie Pat was bawling her eyes out over the phone when she told Dad and Mom, "How can a daughter of mine do a thing like that, y'know? And her timing's awful. Al, the guy I've been seeing, just dumped me. Didn't see either thing coming. Thought I had a future with Al."

It's a couple of days later when she's heard the "wedding" word and she's shrieking and fussing—and you know the rest—falling apart and going off her head.

So, Tess and Carlos did "it"! Wonder what "it" feels like. I think I've got an idea. There was that day when I was just a kid ... I'm standing in the lilac-colored shower in our house (yes, lilac, go figure), and I decide to let the water run super hard. The pounding from the shower beats and beats on my cock. It makes me throb and go all funny down there, and then it takes on a life of its own. There's this almighty thud that's something halfway between pain and the most fantastic feeling you've ever had. Made a bit of a mess. Good thing I was in the shower so Mom didn't find out.

Is that how "it" is for all guys? Is that what "it" felt like for Tess and Carlos? I bet they kept their clothes on and just undid their zips. Who'd want to look at "that?" Seems kinda gross to do "that" with a girl—and kinda cool, too.

The rain's slashing down outside the Lakeside Inn. Like God's having an almighty pee—oh! Hope Mon Mon and Wuff can't hear my thoughts. They'd need a lifetime of Hail Mary's. Auntie Pat's wearing a halter-neck dress splotched with sick flowers. She can't stop telling everyone Tess was hysterical this morning when she finally accepted the weather forecast was right for once.

Evidently, she screamed so hard she threw up—or is that something to do with the baby? It's a girl thing. Anyway, throwing up brought her to her senses. She has to get married today even if it can't be outside under the arbor, whatever that is, with the lake view in the background like she imagined.

She looks very pretty in her crinkly white dress. Holding her bouquet stiffly over her bulge doesn't fool anyone. I'd have noticed even if I didn't already know about the baby, and I'm just a dumb guy. The hotel set up the ballroom for the ceremony since we couldn't be outside. Dad thought it was a deal since he, Auntie Pat, and Grandma Phyllis had only sprung for the smaller function room.

Dad splashed out for a new suit for both of us in honor of the occasion. He's walking Tess down the aisle—she's not that pregnant she couldn't manage on her own, but Auntie Pat begged, "You've got to do it, Brad, y'know. Her waster of a dad's not coming, not likely—he's locked up."

Wish Dad hadn't bought the suits. I hate mine and can't wait until the reception's over to get rid of the jacket and loosen the tie. So, Dad walked Tess down the aisle between the spindly gold chairs the hotel set up. They look as if they'll collapse into splinters if you sit on them; hope none of the guests are fat. You couldn't hear the wedding march for the loud sobs from Auntie Pat and Carlos' entire family. Seems it's a girl thing or maybe a cultural thing.

Mom sat at the front with a space next to her for Dad. She's looking really good since she started taking aerobics classes after we went to Vermont. She cut her hair too, but she still dyes it red for Dad. Mom's wearing a pale green dress that makes her look young. I'm not sitting with them, I'm close to the back hanging out with Julian and a guy called Micah, Sherri invited.

The canned music fades (some sick-making thing) and the ceremony begins. Kevin's the best man—you'd think among all Carlos' relatives he could have found someone else, but it ends up being Kev. He makes a big show that he lost the ring. He's just messing with them, and everyone laughs even though it's not funny.

I nearly fall off my puny little chair when the leader guy says "Theresa Kaye, do you take Carlos Adam?" and all that. I think he's got the wrong woman, but Tess repeats after him, "I, Theresa Kaye ..." She's gone by Tess all her life—well, OK, the adults call her Tessa, but Theresa? Who'd've known?

It's not long before some boy genius is singing, "O for the Wings of a Dove," in a super-high voice that is awesome, and then they're signing the papers. Mr. and Mrs. Gonzalez-Who? are walking back down the aisle. And we're all on our feet clapping away—told you weddings make people go mad.

The child prodigy turns out to be the vets' grandson. He sang for free, which is most likely why he got the job. Brandi's vets are here, too. Dr. Dean's looking wicked old, almost as old as Mon Mon and Grandpa Wuff.

We shuffle into the function room. The buffet table's almost buckling under the weight of food piled on it. Seems the Gonzalez clan has been cooking up a storm too. Tess and Carlos look a bit stunned, and Auntie Pat's crying again. Her friend, Auntie Peggy (not a real auntie), fishes in her satin clutch and pulls out a handkerchief. It's a real cloth one with a lace edge. Who carries those around when there's Kleenex? Must be an antique.

So Auntie Pat dabs her eyes and wipes the snot from her nose, and then she tells everyone how happy she is and invites us all to load our plates. Most of the womenfolk, except Trace, pick at the food, but we guys pile it high.

Mon Mon and Grandpa Wuff are looking a bit helpless, so I take them into the "quiet room" and offer to get their meals for them. They're really pleased and tell me what a kind soul I am. Bless my heart. (So they couldn't read my thoughts—phew!) After we've all eaten and Kev's made a tasteless speech and Trace a shaky one (more tears—aren't weddings supposed to be happy?), the hotel staff come in and whisk the food away. There are quite a lot of crumbs on the floor. They don't sweep them up.

A few hairy guys heave in some disco equipment, and after a while (quite a long while), when the smokers slip off outside, we're ready to party! The time has come. I leave my jacket with Mon Mon and Grandpa Wuff—they're still in the quiet room shouting loudly with some dude who's forgotten his hearing aids. I loosen my collar and tie and roll my sleeves up. That's better.

There's quite a crowd of wrinklies gathered with Mon Mon and Wuff. Grandma Phyllis, Grandpa Tone, and the vets have joined them, some ancient Gonzalez relatives, and some doddery neighbors of Auntie Pat and Grandma Phyllis. The old women are all in super-bizarre outfits that look as if they've been made out of brocade curtains or lace tablecloths.

The men are in well-worn suits that have gone shiny at the elbows and across the backside, the stitches are straining too. I swear there must have been a sale on wingtips about thirty years ago. They're all in the exact same pair. The drinks are flowing. There's a free bar for a couple of hours, then everyone will have to pay for their own, so they're stocking up now.

The DJ's almost set up in the function room, and I drift back in there. It's kind of dated with faded, striped wallpaper that used to feel like velvet—most of it's rubbed off now, and what's left is matted and sweaty when you run your fingernails across it. The ceiling's pretty high with dirty leaf molding around the modern light fitting. They've hung a disco ball up there, looks lame in this light.

After the lousy squeaks and reverb, the disco's up and running, and Tess and Carlos shuffle around looking awkward until the DJ invites other people to join in. Brandi looks wide-eyed into Julian's face, Sherri's in a wrestling lock with Micah, and Carling's dancing with a Gonzalez relative. The ringlets have drooped, and the headdresses are beginning to lose their grip. Grandpa Wuff shakes a leg with Mom, and Dad whisks up Auntie Peggy. Funny, don't think I've ever seen Mom and Dad dance together. Maybe they're saving it for the slow dances at the end. Embarrassing. I won't look.

Finally, the soppy dance comes to an end, and the DJ plays some half-decent stuff. He makes a few off-color jokes. Grandpa Wuff's drifted back to the quiet room, so he doesn't hear—thank goodness.

Fairly predictably, the DJ chooses "The Power of Love" followed by "Crazy for You."

This girl comes up and asks me to dance. I have no idea what to do. She's quite good-looking. Then I'm walking across the dance floor with her, wondering what the heck. My whole entire life's been about swimming; I've never even been to a dance before. I'm more nervous than I am at the starting blocks, and I can't think of anything to say, which is not so bad as the music's so loud she wouldn't hear anyway.

I glance at the tangerine sisters, and they're all gyrating wildly. The old folks are all hopping from one foot to the other, waving their arms around in a deeply humiliating way. I choose to kind of sway from side to side. The music pounds so this doesn't seem quite right, but I'm so dumb I don't know what else to do.

The girl leans close, her brown hair swishing against my cheek so I go redder than a lobster. She's singing the words of the song in my ear, so I do the same. I've never seen her before, but that means nothing. Half the entire universe is here. The dance ends, and I can't get through the crowd to stand at the sidelines, so we dance again. I risk moving forwards and backwards as well as side to side. The girl yells into my ear, her name's Annamaria, and she's Kevin's girlfriend's sister. Something else I never knew—Kev has a girlfriend. Do they do "it" too? God! I'm going even redder at the thought.

After shuffling and swaying a bit, I edge to the side of the room, and when the dance ends I say, "Thanks," like a prize idiot, and we move apart. She tosses her hair and she looks a bit hurt. I feel dazed. The DJ's had a few by now, so his taste slips, choosing "If You Love Someone, Let Them Go" and "I Did It My Way." (Another "it"—it can't mean that.) No one else seems to notice the irony in these songs. (Irony's something we just did in English.) Pretty much everyone's lost all their inhibitions by now, and there's a lot of laughing and shouting going on.

When I hear pleas for "The Chicken Dance," I know it's time to make an exit, so I head for the quiet room and the Pac-Man machine. The old folk are huddled in the bay window. Rain's streaking down outside, and there's maybe a clap of thunder, but who knows? It's so loud in here that you can barely hear yourself think. The old dude without the hearing aid has nodded off. I'm good at focusing, so I'm gobbling up the cherries when the conga line snakes wildly through the room.

Annamaria's at the back, and she makes a grab for me, but I'm shaking her off just as there's a scream so loud, it pierces the din. Auntie Peggy's almost falling down the staircase sobbing hysterically and screaming, "Call an ambulance. It's Brad. He's collapsed!"

And that is how my dad died.

Taking a "rest" in one of the hotel bedrooms at the Lakeside Inn on the day of his niece's wedding. At least, that's how the family tells it. In all the confusion and shock, I am completely numb. It never crosses my mind to wonder why Auntie Peggy's zipper is down to her bra line, or why she's holding her balled-up pantyhose in her hand.

I don't think of it then; I'm too stunned to think anything. It's years before I realize, poor old Tess. Definitely not the wedding of her dreams, and, well, one nobody will ever forget.

16

Carling – August 1986

I'm serious, I'm never gonna have kids. Never ever. I swear parents' sole reason for existence is to embarrass their kids. I am never ever going to do that. It's shameful when they're alive. My dad was always showing me up, yelling, "Darling Carling," at the top of his lungs in front of my friends, flashing mirror sunglasses and a Hawaiian shirt—*in Massachusetts!!* Now he's managed to be embarrassing in death. Croaking at Tess's wedding with his pants down.

I was just back home for the summer after my first year at college. I'd got a job at the camp again, supervisor of the daycare this time—more responsibility and a tad more money. It was the absolute best time of my life, and now it's the worst. I love college—Franklin State. We couldn't afford a private school, but I didn't mind. All I wanted was to fly away, break free, find out who I am without my family around, telling me how to act.

My whole entire life, I've felt like the spread in a sandwich oozing out the sides. Peanut butter or cream cheese. Bland, uninteresting, predictable, boring. I'm the glue in our family club sandwich. The others are awesome fillings ... There's Brandi, who's amazing with animals; Sherri, who's amazing at dance; and little Glen, who's amazing at two things—swimming and making scale models. Even my mom's an amazing hairdresser, and Dad—he *said* he was an amazing car salesman.

And for the longest time, I believed him. Pathetic! I'm not amazing at anything, not better-looking than anyone, not cooler, not one of the "popular" kids. I wasn't Dad's favorite—it's weird to say it since he was such a dickhead, but I'd have liked that.

I was nobody. My life revolving round our stupid house and our stupid family. Sure, there was the cool trip to Florida that one time, and the summer we rented a house in Maine. (Dad was bored out of his mind until he figured out how to rent a sailboat, then he nearly drowned the lot of us—well, maybe not Glen and Mom.) But usually, we didn't go further than Cape Traffic-Jam Cod.

Dad wasn't smart about his money. Oh, boy! Have we found that out now. If he had it, he spent it. If he didn't, he just waited 'til he had it again. When he was flush, he was pretty generous, like helping to pay for Tess's wedding, Brandi's horse, me with college fees—but, honestly, he didn't have a clue.

Look at us now! We're moving into a dog kennel, honest to God. Our dumb dad didn't have life insurance—thought he'd live forever, ha! And hardly any savings. Never thought I'd care about this at my age—they were all screaming their heads off about how poor we are—I had to go to my room and turn the music up full blast.

Mom had to sell the old house. When the mortgage was paid off—something else I didn't think I needed to know about, I told you my whole entire life is ruined forever—this pitiful dog kennel was all she could afford, and even then Grandma Phyllis had to help us out. At this rate, Grandma Phyllis will have nothing to leave us when she dies,—and she's got Tess and Kevin and the new baby to think of.

Couldn't I have been born rich? Hey—there's a song about that from "Fiddler on the Roof," I saw at college. I didn't think I'd like it, a bunch of us went, and it was super cool. A junior who's an amazing actor played Tevya, and he sang, "If I Were a Rich Man." In my dreams! Even though Franklin State's not far away, it felt like a whole new life. I was an entirely different person. The only redhead in my dorm, for one thing.

My roommate, Madhur, lives in Northtminster, but her family came from India. She showed me how to wind a sari. The fabric's awesome, even if I felt weird with my coloring—a helluva lot less weird than the gross bridesmaid's dress. Madhur taught me how to cook all these great spicy dishes. We totally messed up the kitchenette and smelled out the corridor and all the guys came sniffing around. Oh, boy, those curries made me sweat. It was worth it—they were wicked cool.

I worked in the bookstore three nights a week to help with the tuition, and after a while, a whole gang used to show up there to keep me company. It meant three nights when I couldn't study. Not a problem. I'm an undeclared major, and apart from a few required classes, I could pick and choose whatever I wanted. Literature of the Caribbean was a fave. I'd picture a hammock and palm trees waving in the breeze. I'd have taken photography too, but I couldn't afford the camera, so I chose music appreciation, and it was a rap!

Now I'm signing up for community college, and I'll have to study something useful. Maybe finance, now I know about life insurance and mortgages, so I don't make the same mistakes as Dad.

◆

Mom's driving up with the keys to this place. She looks as if she just came out of a concentration camp, skinnier than she's ever been, dark circles under her eyes, lank hair. It breaks my heart in pieces, honestly, it does. She pulled herself together after the trip to Vermont. New hairstyle, aerobics, another day at the salon—so more cash for clothes.

She was in shock when Dad died, we all were ... Probably still are. She didn't yell or scream, throw insults at "Auntie" Peggy—or Dad, for that matter. She didn't sob or drink, but she didn't let her cigarettes out of her sight. She went about like a robot most of the time, except she developed this annoying habit of hugging us every five minutes and telling us she loved us and couldn't make it if it weren't for us.

She's jangling the keys to the dog kennel. I really, really don't want to pull myself out of my mood. Anger's what keeps me going these days, but I can't make her suffer at my pity party, on top of everything else. I've gotta try and be nice. So, I guess it's time to see if this place is as bad inside as it looks.

It is! It's a super-small, moldy, old ranch house. Dark and dingy inside in spite of the big windows. They're hidden behind hideous net curtains, so it'll be better without them.

"Mom, let's tear these down!" I say.

"Go for it, Carling," she agrees.

And we rip them apart with a kind of atavistic glee. It's fun to use some of that pent-up energy to destroy something. We're almost sad the nets didn't put up more resistance, coming away in shreds. We're showered with dust and spiders and dead bugs, but we don't care—it's as if we're going to do battle with the house and win. The panes are filthy—we'll have to do those later.

Next, we head down twisty stairs to the basement. There are two poky bedrooms and a bathroom—all on the dark side even though there are narrow sneak windows high up in each bedroom. Upstairs, there's a funny little room off the kitchen, not much more than a store closet. It's connected to the kitchen through a minuscule bathroom with a doll's house sink and a tiny shower scarcely big enough for a very small child. Glen will have to have this room, even if his bed doesn't fit. And yes, Mom and I laugh—he is a very small child! It's good to laugh, especially with Mom. Can't remember when we last did that.

The kitchen's tight, but it could be worse. All the appliances are older than ours at home; the cabinets aren't that bad, and we wonder if we can cheer them up with a coat of paint. Then there's the living space, open plan, dated and vomit colored—my God, this battle's gonna take some fighting.

Leading off the main space, there's an alcove Mom calls "the den." It's a shoebox compared to ours at home. All you can fit's a desk or a La-Z-Boy, not both. Outside, there's a carport tacked—and I mean literally tacked—to the side of the house and a deck at the back overlooking a scrappy yard. At least no one's dumped a mattress or a fridge there like the house next door.

Suddenly it occurs to me. "Mom—you're not thinking I'm going to share with both Sherri and Brandi, are you?" I'm forgetting to be nice, and my tone's way too sharp.

"I was going to give you the bigger bedroom and take the smaller one myself."

Aargh! I think. I can't stop the expression on my face. I'm devastated. I've just spread my wings, and to have them clipped back this much, this soon. I don't think I can stand it. I don't want Mom to notice how upset I am. So I turn on my heel and walk up the street.

I don't see the street as I'm walking, my head's exploding ... share with Sherri and Brandi. It was hell sharing with Sherri in the old house—how can I live with the both of them? My God, I'd rather die. And on top of that, we have three weeks to clean this place up, get rid of tons of stuff, and move in. I'll never hold it together for Mom for three minutes, let alone three weeks. Oh my God, my life has come to an end.

When I return to the dog-shit kennel, there's a strange car parked there. It's too nice for this street.

"Sandip! Mary, Jesus, and Joseph! It's been ages!" my mom's yelling at the elegant Indian man in our driveway.

So many ages that I don't even remember Mr. Sandip Gokhale or, as I find out later, his petite wife, Astra, though I have a fleeting impression of a couple that must've been them slipping into the back of the church at Dad's funeral. Mr. Gokhale, Sandip—as he wants me to call him—was friends with Dad back in the dark ages. Seems as if they kept in touch now and again—who'd have guessed?

"Rita! I'm so sorry. You must miss Brad," he says.

Mom's crying now—I guess Sandip takes it that he hit the nail on the head. He's wrong, of course, she must hate our bastard of a dad. She's crying because someone's being nice to her. She can stand the pain, she can't take kindness.

He puts a gentle arm around her shoulders and waits until the tears are gone. "It's OK, Reet. How about you show me around the house? I'm here to help. Astra's coming too at the weekend."

We're almost ashamed to show him the dog kennel, although he's nice about it and keeps telling Mom how well she's doing and, annoyingly, how proud Brad'd be of her. We end up on the not-too-bad deck. I want to find a towel so Sandip can sit on it and not ruin his good pants. Since when do I care?

He's easy to talk with and we chat for ages. First, he and Mom do their catching up, then, all of a rush, I'm telling him all about college and how hard it is to leave, and how I don't want to share with Brandi and Sherri. It all pours out even with Mom in the background. Weird … she seems to get it.

Sandip can't wave a magic wand and solve all our problems like a fairy godmother, but he's tons of help. Without Mom asking—she'd never ask this, and she has the hardest time accepting—he offers to take all our unwanted furniture. He's gonna store it in his garage and sell it over time for us. He and Astra have a big condo with two garages and two parking spaces. He says it'll just about fit—making me wonder if he was ever at our house.

"Your dad and I shared a couple of beers last summer when you were all up in Vermont. Your dad missed you all a whole lot. Lonely without his girls and Glen," he tells me.

Another surprise. I don't know what to think, and I'm angry and confused and glad all at the same time. I thought Dad was a stupid, selfish bastard. Did he really love us and miss us, or is Sandip making that up to make us feel better? And why did Dad keep Sandip to himself? God, some people are weird.

Mom's still babbling about the furniture and how Sandip's being too generous and, at the same time, I see her grow an inch or two. Like Sandip just lifted a weight off her shoulders and she's springing back to life.

"We'll be back at the weekend. Where do you want us to make a start?" Sandip asks.

◆

When the weekend rolls around, I've convinced myself they won't be any use, too fancy to do the dirty work.

Sandip rolls his sleeves up, cleans the kitchen, then he goes off to get sanding stuff and paint, and by dinner time he's buddied up with Glen, and they're hard at work on the cabinets.

Astra may look delicate, yet she's strong and wiry, and I wish I could say she hitches up her sari to get down to work, but she's wearing jeans and a T-shirt. She starts scrubbing the windows. I join her and tell her about Madhur. I know it's a cliche given India's huge, yet she doesn't seem to mind. It's cool to talk about my friend and my college life. Astra promises me we'll cook more Indian dishes from her region together, and I've no doubt she means it.

At the end of the day, we sit on the back deck (now inexpertly scrubbed down by my sisters—no complaints from them about coming to clean if they're going to meet Saints Sandip and Astra. We order pizza. Hard work and new friends have given me a shot in the arm, and I'm feeling optimistic for the first time since Dad died. If only I wasn't sharing a room! Brandi's heading off with Julian when Aunt Pat drives up.

She's not come to clean the toilets, that's for sure, and I guess she's here to sneak a peek at Sandip and Astra. Wrong!

"Surprise!" She shrieks, "Tessa had the baby. It's a girl!"

◆

Thanks to Sandip and Astra and some other folks, we do get the house in shape in time to move. It's a helluva squeeze, but at least Brandi begs Mom to let her have the den to herself. We wedge her bed into the nook and hang a thick curtain across the entry. Of course, it darkens the family room as she keeps it pulled, especially when Julian's here. It's kinda embarrassing, even though they whisper, we can hear every word! Never all that interesting. They talk about manicures—peoples' and animals', music and movies!

How romantic!

17

Sherri – January to late 1987

Oh God! Oh God! What am I going to do? I can't tell Mom!

Talk about your life falling apart. Graduate high school, plan on auditioning for a company, you think you know who you are and what life's all about, then *wham*! Someone (thanks, Dad) pulls the rug from under your feet. Mom needs help with the bills, so I'm a dental receptionist by day and a dance instructor by night. At home—this house in no way feels like home—there's nowhere to practice.

I can't stand sharing with Carling. I thought we were done with all that a long time ago. She needs me to creep around all the time being quiet so she can "study." I hear her crying sometimes in the night, so I guess "studying" isn't going so well. I don't know why we're not close, why we can't talk. Why didn't we all have a group scream at Dad after he died? Get it out? I can't talk with Mom either. She's being so brave, holding it together. And she never has a spare moment, what with working full-time at the salon. Thank God there's Micah.

I'm so scared I'll drive Micah away if I act too sad around him, but sometimes I can't help it, and he holds me and tells me he loves me anyway. He's all I've got. All I've got left. Oh God! Maybe he'll dump me after this. My other friends have all left for college now. Well, I guess not all. It just seems that way. Oh shit! Don't let him dump me. I don't know what to do.

117

God! Oh God! I'm at Micah's now. Hope his mom and dad aren't there. It's so cold today, my feet are freezing even in my furry boots. And I'm shaking. I can't tell if it's the cold or the other thing.

His folks converted their basement into an apartment for him. He's older than me, works as an X-ray technician at the hospital. That doesn't sit too well with his folks; they're kinda weird about medical stuff. He makes a lot more than I do, but he thinks he's better off living at home, since his parents leave him pretty much to himself.

He folds me in his arms as soon as he sees me, and I'm already crying on his shoulder. Huge shuddering sobs. His sweatshirt's drenched in my tears in no time.

"Baby, baby! What's wrong? Your dad again? Carling? Brandi?" he says.

I'm crying so hard I have to gulp a few times to get the words out. I must look awful, red and blotchy with snot running over my upper lip.

I went to Rite Aid today. I was so self-conscious I bought other things too and kinda hid the pregnancy test under the magazine and the shampoo. I might have imagined it, but I thought there was an edge to the assistant's voice (and just my luck, it was a guy) when he muttered, "Have a nice day!" after he rang me up.

"Micah, I'm pregnant!" I blurt out.

He just holds me and lets me sob. I don't even feel his body stiffen with anger or shock. When I'm calmer, gulping and gasping, but not actually weeping, he sits down, pulling me on his lap.

"Oh baby, I thought we'd been really careful," he says.

So did I. All I can think is the couple of days I had an upset stomach after I'd taken my pill. And there was the other day round about that time I forgot, and there it was blinking at me from its silver foil packet the next morning, so I took two and thought it would be alright. It's hard keeping this stuff straight when you share a room, and you don't want your sister interfering. Oh God! It's all my stupid fault.

"I only missed one pill," I tell him.

This isn't strictly true. I missed one pill a couple of months ago but nothing happened that time.

"Did you see a doctor? Did you tell anyone?"

"No! I couldn't. I'm too embarrassed." I feel a deep flush spreading under my blotches, and I start to cry again. "Micah, I'm thinking maybe I should have an abortion? Do you know where to get one? You work at the hospital."

"Whoa! Not so fast, kitten!" and he pulls me deeper into him. I get a whiff of the laundry detergent his mother uses on his shirt and a hint of his sweat slipping through his deodorant.

If I had an abortion (how can I even be thinking this?) and anyone in my family found out, they'd disown me. Micah's parents are Christian Scientists; like I said they're weird about medicine. I bet abortion's not on their radar either. I'm sure they'd disown me too. Maybe throw Micah out as well. A baby, though, at nineteen—this absolutely wasn't in the plan. How can I ever be a dancer now? I'll get fat! Am I going to hell? What are we going to do?

I have to say Micah's amazing. He's really, really amazing. He doesn't say we'll get married, or that he never wants to see me again. He holds me and kisses me, little kisses all over my face, even my tear-soaked hair, but not where the snot has run.

"Do you know how far along you are?" he asks.

"I didn't get my period, and then I waited. I think you have to be two weeks late or the test doesn't work right. Then, I couldn't face buying a pregnancy test—I didn't want the store assistant to know, so I just missed a second one, so I had to go to the drugstore today. God! It was embarrassing," I tell him.

"Okay, so it's still early days then. We need to sleep on it, before we decide what to do. Keep it a secret for a bit longer, sweetie," he says.

He's stroking my hair now, and I catch him glancing at my belly—there's not even a little bump yet. Thank God. Suddenly, Micah starts, "Hey, I know this is a mean thought, but I guess it's too much to hope for that you'll miscarry."

I hadn't thought of that, so I jump up and down in our room at home doing exercises, hoping to shake it out. Carling's furious. I tell her I need to stay fit for dance.

"Let's face it, Sherri—the only dance you do now is showing little girls how to skip across imaginary streams and bend their knees without sticking out their bums," she says.

It's true, though I do teach a little boy as well, Lincoln, whose bum's so skinny he couldn't stick it out if he tried. I burst into tears anyway. And this just exasperates Carling even more.

"Get real!" she snarls, thumping her books on the dresser that doubles as a desk, and bruises her knees.

The next time I see Micah, he's clearly done some thinking. He suggests I move in with him just before the birth. He thinks I'll need my mom and my sisters to help me through the pregnancy. Carling ... is he kidding? It's a strain being so serious, making plans when we're both scared out of our minds, so we hold each other for a while, stroke each other's hair. He traces my jawline with his tongue, then our mouths move together, our tongues intertwine. He slips his hand down my waistband, and I quiver with pleasure at his touch. I pull away.

"Micah, should we be doing this?" I ask him, timid, all at once.

Stroking me gently enough that I feel a pulse throb, he whispers, "Why not, kitten? You're already pregnant."

As he slips inside me in that sweet, tender way that's always felt completely natural, never wrong, he murmurs, "God! I love you, Sherri!"

And my body arcs and slides in time with his, until the climax comes, almost together, and we're laughing and crying all at the same time. As I catch my breath, I let a little thought in. It might work out okay. It just might. We have enough love.

We decide to tell our parents and make the best of it. He thinks his mom and dad will eventually come round. Maybe they can babysit, since I'll need to go back to work after the baby comes. I still can't believe we're planning all this. Sometimes I don't believe it's for real, yet now there's the tiniest bulge and my waistbands strain, my breasts are bigger—I hate that but Micah adores them, licking and sucking until I can't stand it and we have to, just have to, make love again.

I do lots more jumping up and down when I get home. Carling's incandescent.

So I tell her.

I swear her to secrecy, and she's totally shell-shocked.

"You're what? Sherri! You've been sleeping with him for how long? Oh my God! My God. I'm not sharing a room with a screaming baby! Oh, Sherri!" she says. And she bursts into tears and throws her arms round me. It's the closest I've felt to her since Dad died.

It's family dinner when we tell Micah's parents. They're a lot older than my mom. They adopted Micah when they gave up trying to have their own child. It's insane; they actually felt God was punishing them for their sin. All that good old Catholic guilt. They were in a real bad place, when a funky old neighbor told them about Christian Science. Promised them God can heal absolutely anything, I mean anything—even cancer and bad stuff like that.

Infertility'd be a piece of cake to the Christian Science God—as long as they gave up trusting in medicine. Well, it didn't happen quite like that, but almost right after they converted, an adoption agency called, and cute little Micah toddled into their lives.

Mrs. Shepherd serves out the turkey meatloaf, oven fries, and side salad. She's a plain cook, but it's usually good. I'm shaking, hoping they don't notice, taking little, panicky breaths, and keeping a clown smile plastered on my face. Micah's dad bows his head; I try not to fixate on his bald spot and the big mole splotched across his skull like a dead tarantula. His hands are spidery too, long tendons and wrinkled knuckles. His ears sprout bristles that suddenly look like insect leg hair. He's always been nice to me. I feel I've let him down, let both of them down.

"Thank you, Lord, for all your blessings, for the food we eat, and for sharing our table with Sherri and Micah. Amen," he says in a gentle undertone.

"Amen!" we mutter in response, and I squeeze my fists tight to stop the tears that begin to brim. He's being so kind, I can't stand to hurt him.

We start to eat in silence. Well, they start to eat, and I start to pick. For the first time, I feel nauseous and push my food around my plate, my fork making little scratching noises like a hungry mouse. Ooh! The thought of a mouse makes me want to retch, and I press my hand to my mouth. They raise their eyes to me with concerned looks.

"Sherri, dear, is anything the matter?" Mrs. Shepherd asks.

Micah swallows a flaccid piece of meat-loaf, half chokes, and splutters, "Mom, Dad, we have another blessing tonight."

Before he's done sharing the "blessing," his mom makes a noise like a strangled cat and rushes out of the room. Knocking over his chair, his dad leaps up to follow her, coughing out little pieces of meatloaf as he goes. I retch again. Fortunately, nothing much comes up, and I manage to keep the vomit in my mouth and not spew up all over the meatloaf. I've never fancied turkey meatloaf since then.

Micah's parents don't come back to the dining room. Our ears grow stalks as we strain to listen. All we can hear are a few muffled sobs and Micah's dad muttering something indistinguishable. We wonder about clearing the table and washing up, but not for long. We slink down to the basement and brainlessly watch a couple of soaps. I nestle into Micah. Am I imagining there's a hint of tension in his embrace? If there is, I can't blame him—that sucked.

It can't go worse with my mom, so Micah comes over after work, and we tell her the next day. I crack open a couple of cans of Coke, and I'm shaking so hard the foam pours over the glasses and splashes on the countertop.

"Sherri! Be careful!" Mom tells me, mopping up the foaming mess.

"Oh, Mom, it's too late for being careful!" I burble. "I'm going to have a baby!"

It's actually a relief to get the words out. They hang pregnantly in the air for a moment. Mom gives out a little gasp, turns pale, and then she cries too. She hugs me so tight I'm alarmed she'll squeeze the baby out. We're sobbing too. It goes on for a long time. I bet Micah feels left out.

"Oh, Sherri, oh, Sherri, my poor darling, I love you, Sherri, I love you!" she says over and over and over again, until I think we're stuck in a never-ending loop.

It seems as if she's forgotten Micah until he takes a big slug of Coke and chokes, coughing and spluttering, with bubbles bursting out of his nostrils. Not exactly the future son-in-law of her dreams.

"Micah, poor Micah! Jesus, Mary, and Joseph! I love you too, Micah!" she says, thumping him vigorously on the back. And tears spring from his eyes as well, though I'd guess he's secretly hoping she'll hold back on the "I love you too's!"

It takes a while before the thumping becomes hugging, and we all settle down. Tears are streaking down all our faces. Micah tells me later it was the choking that set him off. Sure—if that's what it takes to keep his manly pride.

"Micah, it's a blessing Sherri has you in her life. We'll all manage this together somehow," mom tells him.

Before long we're telling her our plans to live together at Micah's, and she's thinking about a gynecologist for me. She's wondering if our pediatrician's still working. I can tell she's a bit shocked even though she's putting a good face on it, but my amazing mom (how could I ever have put her down?) even manages to say, "Y'know, we've had such a run of bad luck, a new baby's something wonderful to look forward to."

No recriminations, no blame, no "And when are you going to get married?" No, "How on earth or in heaven are we going to afford this?"

After we've talked some more and she sees that I'm ashamed, embarrassed, and exhausted, she says, "Would it be easier if I tell the rest of the family for you?"

"No need!" Carling cries from the stairs where she's been hiding all this time trying to eavesdrop. "I already know!"

I'm blown away by Mom's strength, Mom's kindness. Where does she get it from? Oh my God, I'm going to be a mom, too! I burst into tears again. This time they all make a dash to hug me—Mom gets there first so Carling hugs Micah. That's weird!

It feels as if I spend the whole pregnancy in tears, and no, I don't miscarry. The bump grows and grows, and the baby kicks and kicks. Micah and I spend hours watching my belly take on a life of its own. Is it an elbow shoving up now, a knee—its little bottom? I move in with Micah at about eight months.

I shed a waterfall of tears leaving Mom. I hug Glen, who looks totally embarrassed. He hugs me back, trying not to graze the baby bulge, and there are tears misting his eyes. Carling looks a bit spaced out, and I'm sure she's relieved to get the room to herself. Who knew I'd be the first to leave home. (Well, if you don't count Carling going to college.)

Brandi's not there. I think she deliberately arranged to work extra. I'm not sure, but I think she's a tiny bit jealous. Julian still hasn't proposed. (Neither did Micah—we agreed we'd shock the world some more by just living together.) I'd guess Brandi's confused about Julian, especially since Dad died. She needs to feel his warmth even more, though he doesn't lean into her. And that's just it, Julian's super easy to be around, but he doesn't hold Brandi the way Micah holds me. Doesn't pull her in and keep her safe.

Trouble is none of us have any clue about grieving or being with someone whose dad died. Mon Mon and Wuff, Grandma Phyllis and Grandpa Tone are hanging in there. They're all pretty doddery, but they don't dare die—for our sakes—we need them too much.

Living with Micah the last month's kinda fun. Like make-believe, playing house. I've had a really easy pregnancy, and I'm not that huge. (Well, I thought I was the size of a house, but everyone else told me I'm not.) I give up teaching dance when I can't see my feet anymore. The kids all gave me bibs and booties when I leave, and Lincoln gives me a card with a wobbly, blue baby he'd drawn in crayon with enormous feet wearing ballet slippers that look like soccer cleats. He said he knew I'd have a boy baby. I started to have nightmares about the size of its feet after that.

Micah's good about sharing his space, much better than Carling—even though the place is rapidly filling up with baby things. Mom crocheted all these little outfits, and Tess sent over everything Carolina's grown out of that's white, yellow, or light green. I remember being super judgmental of Tess when we were in Vermont and despising her for having to get married. I've had to change my tune a lot.

Micah's parents—I still feel awkward around them ... They ooze disapproval, even though they don't say a word. But they bought a crib and a car seat, and Sandip and Astra came over with a stroller last weekend. Brandi drove Glen here with a small mountain of disposable diapers, and baby's first swimsuit for both a boy and a girl since we don't know what I'm having. The doctor said that as long as I'm healthy, there's no reason to have an ultrasound. At first, I worried about health insurance. Micah has his own, but since we decided not to get married, it doesn't cover me. Thank God Grandpa Tone stepped in and got me a policy. Times change! Used to be his gifts were tickets for the Boston Ballet!

We're all set, and all I have to do is wait for the contractions to start. They can't be all that bad, can they?

Oh yes, they can!

◆

Melody Jasmine Shepherd was born a week late. I started to think I was going to be pregnant forever. Be in *The Guinness Book of Records*. I was in labor for eighteen hours; the Shepherds wanted me to stay home and have a natural delivery. No way! I wanted to hug and kiss the technician when he gave me the epidural. Mom was with me the whole time. How did she do this four times?

Melody is so sweet, I've fallen in love with her.

So has Micah!

So has Glen!

Glen turns into an awesome babysitter. He's swimming for the high school now, and he's got lots of homework, but he comes over on Sundays. It's not long before Melody develops colic; Glen holds and rocks her, and rubs her tummy while we try to nap. He loves dressing her up in the little outfits everyone gave her when she was born.

She keeps us up most nights, and together with the diapers and the constant laundry—oh, she spit up again!—we're wiped. I can't imagine ever being able to go back to work. We need the money more than ever, now Melody's here.

Micah's parents, Mom and Dad Shepherd (I can barely get my tongue around that) are afraid they'll break her if they pick her up. They adopted Micah when he was three and a half, walking and talking (and vaccinated, hooray!) so they've no experience of tiny babies. I still don't feel at home with them. We have to go to their part of the house to use the washing machine. It's on all the time. I mean all the time. The last time I went up, Micah's mom had just taken out their sheets and towels, and she shook her head, saying, "More laundry? Can't you keep that child clean?"

They're exhausted too. And I might be imagining it, but I feel as if they're judging me all the time, wondering if I seduced Micah, thinking that I'm not a good enough mom.

I'm beginning to feel even more worried about leaving Melody with them when I go back to work. The dentists won't keep my job open forever, and it's not as if I was with them all that long or that I finished my training. We have a terrible time switching Melody from breast milk to formula, so I have a hope of going back to work. She screams and screams like she's in a horror movie. The pediatrician suggests I wear a plastic apron or a raincoat when I feed her to muddle up the smell of my breast milk. She's not taken in and screams until hunger forces her to take the bottle. And then she's worn herself out and nods off before she finishes the feed.

Nobody told me how gross your breasts become when you're trying to stop breastfeeding. Mine are the size of basketballs, taut and leaking, hard, and at the same time, really sensitive. You'd think they're a complete passion killer for Micah. They're not—he still adores them, but we're too tired to be passionate anymore. He sometimes strums his guitar after work, and it would be romantic apart from the bawling, the spit-up, the mess!

Anyway, I do go back to work and, just like Micah says, apart from pangs of missing Melody, it's actually quite relaxing! Since we're close to the holidays, it's not that busy, thank God. Nice of them to have me back right now so I can get into the swing of things. Only hours of being a grown-up, and yes, like everyone says, you do grow up fast when you have a baby.

Mom takes care of Melody on Mondays when she has a day off from the salon, and Mom and Dad Shepherd take her on Tuesdays. They don't believe in medicine even for kids, so I'm always praying Melody doesn't get a fever or an ear infection. Auntie Pat offered to fill in the other three days. She's only working two days a week now and looks after Carolina the rest of the time. She said Melody'd be no trouble, and she's even thinking of helping out Aunt Peggy, who gave birth to a preemie late last year. Aunt Peggy's really old. About as old as Mom. She's been taking Danny to a home daycare, but he keeps getting sick. I hope I'm not having babies at her age. I'll have my tubes tied long before then. You'd think sex loses its luster for old people, so maybe I won't have to bother with my tubes, maybe I'll just lose the desire.

That's so weird. I guess I'd better not grow old.

18

Rita – Spring 1988

Carolina's teetering around looking for plastic eggs. She laughs like a drain when she "finds" one—we pretty much put them right under her pert little nose. When she catches on, she holds them out to be twisted open and grabs at the candy inside. Tessa frets she'll choke—so odd to see Tessa's transformation from wild child to over-anxious mom! The candy's only marshmallow—apart from in the green egg, where Pat hid a tiny Brussels sprout. We all chuckle except Carolina, who howls when she sees it, waking up Danny, who's only just drifted off into a nap. He's been grizzly since he and Peggy arrived.

Pat asked if I minded if she invited Peggy and Danny for Easter dinner. Mary, Mother of God! I didn't know what to think, but I guess I can't go around avoiding her forever. Yes, of course, it still hurts. Yes, I feel betrayed and humiliated but, guess what, in my rare generous moments, I realize if it wasn't her, it would've been someone else. Doesn't matter how nice a picture Sandip tries to paint—Christ! I wasn't totally blind to Brad's goings-on all those years.

For a few months he'd been cutting back on his drinking, but he'd really hit the bottle at Tessa and Carlos' wedding—I don't know why … Perhaps he just let go—he did that enough times over the years. Perhaps since he was paying, he thought he'd get his money's worth. Mother of God! He might not even have known who he was with. Or were they having an affair? I didn't see the signs. Not with Peggy, but I know there were others. Do I care? I dunno. Heavens! it's been such a tough ride since he died, I don't even have the energy to bear a grudge. Or do I?

Even that catnap's done Danny some good, and he's pulling himself up, standing, looking delighted at himself as if it's an amazing circus trick. Sometimes he claps his pudgy little hands, then sits down heavily on his bottom, astonishment spreading across his cheeky face. He's still only got peach fuzz for hair—he looks quite a bit like a peach when you think of it. No sign of the preemie left, just rolls of juicy baby fat, a creamy complexion, and a pink rosebud of a mouth, puts me in mind of Sherri at that age. Melody's got a way to go before she'll walk. She's adorable in her cute white dress with the applique Easter chicks around the hem. We all know it won't stay clean for long.

When the Easter egg hunt's done, we go inside and feed the children before we have our Easter dinner, and with any luck, they'll all go down for a nap. Danny's looking tired again now, smearing mashed potato over his face and into the peach fuzz every time he rubs his eyes, and Carolina's half asleep on Carlos' lap sucking her sticky, sugary thumb. Wouldn't count on Melody—she likes to be where the people are.

Pat moved in with Phyllis after Tone died, and this is the biggest place any of us have now. Phyllis doesn't look too good herself, kinda jaundiced, wrinkles chiseled deeply into her face, none of it disguised by the mask of makeup she's hiding behind. She's not eating much, nor talking up a storm like she used to.

Sweet Jesus! I doubt it's only grief that's gnawing at her, though heaven knows she's had more of her share of that these last few years. Can't seem to keep a man alive. I'm not sure how Pat copes with looking after her and all the childminding.

I never pictured her as a caregiver, more of a social butterfly, a giddy flirt. Well, haven't we found out there's more layers to most of us than meets the eye? On the other hand, Pat's wearing an impractical and rather daring lime green dress, with a split up one leg. Looks as if her flirting days aren't over quite yet, though who she's hoping to run into today's a mystery.

We all miss Tone. Bless his soul. He hovered quietly in the background, and it's only now we realize he had a real presence in the foreground too. Tone was someone you could rely on, a calming influence for Phyllis and Pat. He and Phyllis never set up a joint account so, in his will, he left Phyllis enough to make sure she's comfortable, then he divided up the rest. The grandkids and Pat got their share and, bless him, so did I!

He must've figured out I could do with some help. Now Brandi's moved out, it's one less mouth to feed, but my heavens, the other bills keep rolling in.

Brandi and Julian are in the sun lounge wrestling Dandy (they planned on grooming him as a new pet for Pat). It's a crazy idea—he's too much of a handful today, leaping around madly, loving all the attention. They're both worn out from work and worry over Julian's mom, who's moved in with a "stinking, conniving rat" (Brandi's words). Praise the Blessed Virgin, Brandi and Julian got married just before Christmas on Brandi's birthday—a very small wedding at our church. Can't help smiling thinking about it.

◆

Sandip walked her down the aisle, after Glen and Dad both had second thoughts. (Sandip's a Hindu—didn't seem to freak Father O'Malley.) Julian's mom helped with the cost of the reception—Tone passed only a few weeks before, and we didn't have the will sorted out then. The "rat" was ordered to stay in his hole! And he did, so I've never met him. We self-catered—all done on a shoestring. Aunt Monday and Dad did most of the baking—nearly killed them. Pat and Phyllis helped as well, though their hearts weren't really in it after Tone.

I choked up a bit, well, a lot actually, as I saw Brandi—a vision in a dress she'd picked up from a classified ad. It fit her perfectly, better than anything I'd have made if I'd had the time. She carried a spray of pink roses tied with a pale green velvet bow. "Can't do Christmas red, Mom, it'll clash with my hair." (As usual, she was right.)

Gliding down the aisle on Sandip's arm (Who knew she was wearing duck boots under the stunning dress—the walkways were slick with sleet), she looked radiant and a tad relieved … or was it me who was relieved? Julian took his sweet time working up to a proposal.

Brandi and Julian kept everything very simple, with only Carling as a bridesmaid. Carling mouthed off about getting dressed up; even though Brandi let her choose her own dress. My God! There was the day Carling insisted she'd only wear black and carry a wreath. I shouldn't have let her get to me. She was lovely on the day, in navy velvet, holding a few pink roses like Brandi's, and not a hint of black nail polish, lipstick, or kohl. Didn't even get the henna tattoo she'd threatened.

She fussed around Brandi and Julian, charmed Father O'Malley (in spite of what she calls his "piss-joke" religion), and gave Phyllis a big hug. What more could I ask? There was even a little squeeze for me. All the same, when it was all over, I had an inkling the "performance" had utterly drained Carling; coming at a personal cost. Joseph, Jesus and Mary, can't help worrying about that girl.

We raised a glass or two at the reception. Julian toasted absent family in a rather vague way that set Phyllis off, before thanking his mom and me. Finally, he turned to his beautiful wife, brushing her fingers with a kiss, and telling her how much he loves her. A giant, communal sigh, some stage-whispered "awws," and they were off to spend a couple of nights in the Berkshires, courtesy of the vets.

And then, on Christmas Day, like abominable snowmen, during a stinging blizzard, they gathered their meager belongings and moved into the tiny apartment above the veterinary offices that Dean and Shirl offered them for a pittance.

Brandi and Julian don't stay long after the meal. I wonder if they're thinking of starting a family. (Mother of God, please no! Well, not yet!) It's hard being around all these little ones. They just need to take a look at the parents—that'll stop them feeling broody. Sherri, Micah, and Tessa are all asleep in the living room. They look like raccoons with their big, hollow eyes.

Carlos can't relax, he's a bundle of pent-up energy, and hits Brandi and Julian with a *cascaron* as they're leaving. It's a Mexican tradition. You blow the contents out of an egg, slice the top off it, and fill it with confetti. Then you dump it on your victim's head. It's fun when everyone joins in. Brandi and Julian aren't in the mood.

"Knock it off, Carlos," they snap as their parting shot.

I feel sorry for Carlos, he's not spending the day with his family or kicking back with the guys, and he's still so young, he needs to catch a break once in a while. When will these kids learn to use condoms? God! I hope Julian has some—must have, who am I kidding? They've been together for years.

Carling refused to come at all. Haven't had a glimpse of the "sweet" Carling since the wedding. My dad and Aunt Monday just want to go to mass and then stay quietly at home eating roast chicken, cornbread, and greens all on a plate from the supermarket.

Glen's off to spend the afternoon with friends—managed to tear himself away when Melody went down. He adores her. I'm glad he's out. When we moved, he couldn't hang out with the kids in our old neighborhood anymore. He seemed to withdraw into himself and his models, especially in the winter when he couldn't ride his bike.

I'm their mom, so I worry about them all of the time, even when I'm sleeping. But Carling's the one I'm most anxious about right now. She seems a totally different person than the daughter we dropped off at college back then. She told me, "There's no fucking way I'm gonna come. Easter sucks."

When did I allow her to speak to me like that?" It's as if she hates everything, especially herself. Mother of God, keep her safe. Every day she pulls on her grunge clothes and slinks off to hang with a couple of creeps she met at community college. God! Keep her safe!

Pat's done far more than her share of the prep and cooking for this meal, so Peggy and I tell her to put her feet up, we'll clear up, stack the dishwasher, throw the linens in the washer, and clean the kitchen. Pat barely protests, so she must be beat. Carlos joins us, which is cool, but it means we don't get to talk to each other. Can't make up my mind if this is good or bad, I've only exchanged a few stilted pleasantries with Peggy so far today. Kinda weird.

Carlos is good company and tells us all about the Easters he had growing up—usually at his uncle's house, and generally featured a barbecue and flames. His dad was often "sick."

"Know what I mean?"

We don't (well, I don't), and neither of us dares to ask. When we're done, Peggy says in a half-strangled sort of voice, "Rita, would you sit on the porch with me? I'd like to have a word."

I admire her courage, she always did have that. But I'm nervous as hell. Awkward! Once we're settled, she looks me in the eye and says, "I can't imagine what you must think of me. I'm so sorry for what happened."

I mumble something, I'm not sure what. *"What happened ..."* Sleeping with my husband was not alright. I thought we were friends. Both of them betrayed me and humiliated me, but I'm too exhausted to fight. At the same time, I'm in no mood to confront my feelings about her, let alone pretend I forgive her.

Even though I haven't been too conciliatory, she plows on. "I hope you don't mind, I brought you a little something. It's pathetic really, but I hope you'll take it as a gesture, a little peace offering, and if you can't, that's okay."

There's a lump growing in my throat. I don't want to take anything from her, yet her eyes are full of need. She reaches into her purse and, hands trembling, brings out what must be a framed photograph. With equally trembling hands, I unwrap it. It's me on the top of the mountain in Vermont. And yet, it could be another woman in the picture. I'm carefree, smiling, suddenly alive with possibilities.

The lump swells, my chin wobbles uncontrollably, Oh God! I know I can't keep my composure, the hot tears rain down my cheeks. I'm really crying hard. That day on the mountain, it was so good. I look at my flushed face, my tousled hair, my sweaty clothes, and the look of sheer achievement and joy on my face.

And I remember, because of her I did follow the resolve I made on the summit to do more for myself—exercise, carve out time just for me. Less than a year later (*because of her*, I wonder) everything changed. I've had to be strong, seal off my feelings, and give up my dreams.

Clutching the picture to my heart, I let go, allowing myself to feel my pain, allowing myself to feel sorry for myself, to grieve. I glance at Peggy a little embarrassed, and I realize she's sobbing her heart out, too. A momentary flash of anger crosses my mind. *Holy Mother of God, what's she got to be upset about?* I wonder.

And, all at once, it's as if a floodlight switches on full beam. I realize it can't have been easy for Peggy either. Terror when Brad collapsed, public shame and embarrassment, a baby on the way later in life, putting the brakes on her career, being a single mom, and all the dread of the baby arriving too soon, hardly any family nearby, the loss of her independence, and the awesome, precious responsibility of raising another life.

Suddenly, we are hugging one another, soaked in each other's tears. By some miracle (thank you, Jesus), we are laughing amongst the volcanic sobs and the hiccups. I hear a footfall on the porch ... I think it's Pat's. I can't see clearly through the waterspout of my tears. Whoever it is, they quickly turn back.

I feel so much better. I know other less generous feelings will sneak back, waves of anger and resentment, self-righteousness, self-pity, all those things that have been knotted up inside me, and I realize they'll come and go many times before they fade. Now, I've seen Peggy in a new light. She's someone who made a big mistake. Haven't I made my share of those, too?

I'm thinking of Carling as I drive home. I should try to let her talk, curse, scream, rage, cry—whatever she needs. It's daunting, and a part of me wonders if I'm up to it. She might just hurl abuse at me and leave, but it's worth the risk. And then maybe, just maybe, I can break through and find my darling daughter again. God, I hope so.

I've only just got back, when the police car draws up.

19

Carling – Easter and later in 1988

S hit! Mom's driving up, and oh God! Glen's putting his bike away. Couldn't they have gotten here in another half-hour? Then I'd have faked everything's okay. Oh, God! What's wrong with me—I never get any breaks.

The police officer walks up the path with me. Mom's looking thunderstruck. Glen's peeking out from around the side of the carport.

"Is everything alright?' Mom asks in a tight, high voice. She's scanning my face and the officer.

"Mrs. Lenox? We detained your daughter at the police station this afternoon. She was found in possession of marijuana and alcohol and had been trespassing. The owners have decided not to press charges, so as this is a first offense, we decided to issue a warning."

I want to cry, to hang my head in shame. I don't. I toss it a little defiantly, my hair whips round and stings my eyes, spoiling the effect but at least giving me an excuse if anyone notices my eyes are glistening. We go inside.

"Carling, we gotta talk!" Her voice is sharp, still a bit high, but at least she doesn't yell or burst into tears.

I'm so close to tears now, I rush to my room and slam the door. Why the hell did this have to happen? Why can I never, never have any fun? I'd only just got to the shed. Not having a car, I walked, and it's a hell of a long way. I'd had a hit of the weed and a long pull of beer when the cops came and arrested me, Dingo, and Roz.

I'm almost twenty-one, for Christ's sake! Why couldn't they just let us go? Or let me go? Dingo was about to vomit as we left the shed. He managed not to puke on the officer's pants—just.

I'm trying to muffle my sobs under the comforter. Mom's outside my door pleading with me to come out and talk. That's the last thing I feel like doing right now. I slam a chair against the door; she's not coming in. The phone rings upstairs, and a few moments later, Mom's charging back downstairs.

"Carling, it's Dad—I mean Grandpa. He's fallen down the back stairs. They think he broke a hip. They're taking him to the hospital. I have to go. Promise me you'll stay safe. Don't go anywhere! We'll talk later," she tells me.

I mumble into the comforter, and then I hear her running back upstairs. Her car keys jingle, and she's gone.

"You got lucky," I hear from outside the door. It's Glen, he must've tiptoed downstairs. I don't feel so lucky, I feel like shit. I didn't need this. Mom sure didn't need any of this.

A week later, I'm at the hospital with Mom and Mon Mon. Grandpa's developed pneumonia. He looks older than the dinosaurs, saggy and gray. The others came this morning, maybe wore him out. Mon Mon strokes his wrist. It makes me want to cry. A brother and sister who are tender towards each other. Where did we all go wrong?

Mom kisses him gently on the top of his head, she's crying without making any noise. She doesn't want to upset him. As his only child, in a quiet way, they've always been close. She knew he'd always be there for her. We're all scared he won't survive this. And we all kinda know he won't.

"Carling," he rasps, "you're a good girl, you'll go places, my love," and I can't hold back my tears, choked with guilt and shame. I'm not worth his love. I'll always find trouble. He doesn't seem to mind that I'm crying. He pats the back of my hand with his liver-spotted, shrunken one.

"I don't want to leave you all. I know there's a good chance I might not get over this pneumonia. You've made my life very happy. Rita, Betty, and Carling, my loves. After Faith passed, I never thought there'd be any more happiness, but you've all given me a good life. I want you to know about my will. Rita, I've left the house to you, but you must let Betty stay in it as long as she lives or wants to be there. There's a little money for you too. It's not much," he says.

"Betty, with the house and your savings I think you'll be alright, even though I swear you're going to live to a hundred. The rest, what there is of it, is divided between my grandchildren. Glen's a responsible young man, but I've arranged to put his in a trust towards college or for him to use after he's twenty-one."

It's hard to hear. I don't like thinking that Grandpa Wuff's gonna die. I'm a worm. I'm letting him and Mom and, hell, *myself* down—and he totally believes in me. Totally. My heart's breaking with love for him. We tell him not to worry about all this, to get some rest and make sure he lives for a few more years.

As we leave, I kiss him good night, and I cross my fingers till they throb, willing it not to be goodbye. Mom kisses him too, and after Aunt Mon Mon brushes his chin, always practical, she says, "I'll get the nurses to give you a shave in the morning!"

He lives long enough for a few more shaves. He's asleep mostly when we visit him for the last time. And then, the next morning, with only Aunt Monday at his bedside, he slips away.

The church is almost full for his funeral mass. I manage not to get high that day, though there are lots of moments I think I can't get through it without help. There's this screeching hole inside of me where I didn't think I had room for any more holes. Each hole shrieks with another loss—Dad, my sorry life, camp counselor, college, good daughter, Grandpa Tone, and now, Grandpa Wuff. I'm like an old lace curtain. In shreds.

The Shepherds are here, Julian's mom and ratface, lots of Carlos's and Tess's relatives, the Gohkales, Auntie Peggy and Danny, but not Auntie Pat—she can't leave Grandma Phyllis—and most of the geriatric population of Watervale. They're all spiffed up with their walkers and their wheelchairs. All the disabled parking spaces are filled. I knew he was special for us, but I didn't know he touched a lot of other people's hearts ... I just didn't know. Funny what you can make of an ordinary life.

Brandi, Sherri, Glen, and I—we're all losing it at the reception. Mom's mobbed with people, Auntie Peggy hugging her (hmm, that's a surprise), other folk telling her what a wonderful man he was, how he loved her to bits and was proud of all of us, what a good job she's been doing, or sharing a little story about Grandpa's myriad acts of kindness.

Together with Julian, Micah, and Melody, we cluster around Mon Mon. She doesn't seem upset at all. She grew up with him, lived with him for decades, turned her life upside down for him, comforted him when he needed it, even went on vacation with him, and now she's calm and smiling.

"Don't you miss him?" Brandi asks her tentatively.

"You bet. I miss him every moment of the day. It doesn't make me sad, it makes me happy. Not everyone gets to share their lives with as decent a man as Wilf. I've wonderful memories. He died, loving and knowing he was loved. You can't ask more than that, not in this world," she says.

I am blown away. How can other people have it together? How do they figure out their emotions? I want to be like Mon Mon. Or hell, do I? She never married. She gave her whole life for her brother? I dunno. It's all too difficult, I make this lame promise that I'll try to be nicer to Glen and the others.

Mom's worn out when we get back home. She suggests we curl up and watch M.A.S.H. on TV. For once, Glen doesn't go off to tweak a model, and I don't slink off to be with my friends or smoke a joint. It's nice. Family time. But, I decide, there's no way I'm going to give up my life for Glen! He's a total pain.

I know this is dumb but, as I go to bed, I tell Mom, "Mom, I want you to know, you don't have to worry about me anymore."

But I'm too weak, pathetic. I can't keep my word.

I can't concentrate on my studies. I seethe with resentment at being at this totally crap college, having to waitress in my spare time to help cover the fees. I despise the fake smile I plaster across my face as I slap down someone's all-day, all-greasy breakfast. Some of the professors aren't that bad for Christ's sake. Professor Sachs reaches out, but there's no way I'm gonna let her in.

I'd had a taste of another life. Been to "real" college, turned out to be popular, a good student (well, good enough). Community college sucks. I build an invisible fence around me that screams, "Stay away. Don't come near me." I paint my fingernails black and mostly, I wear black. I plan on dyeing my hair black, too. I can't do it. It's the only trace of my old identity. I desperately want friends, but I push everyone away.

Sharing with Sherri's the worst thing. I'm super relieved when she moves out, and her being pregnant keeps the attention off of me. God, I'm lonely. And I let myself believe Mom's swallowing my lie that everything's fine. My grades are barely enough to keep going, but I'm getting close to an associate's degree—hell, I don't know which direction I'm headed. Going nowhere, fast.

◆

There's this one evening in January, I miss the commuter rail and decide to wait for the next one in the warmth of the student lounge instead of down at the frickin' freezing depot. Dingo and Roz are the only other ones here. They've cut their evening class and are openly smoking something I soon discover is weed.

I'm starved for company, and their edginess appeals. Dingo has a tattoo round his neck with a tiny dagger and the words "Cut here." Roz's hennaed hair escapes a strange black beret, and her nails are blood-red with little pictures of skulls and crossbones on them. They offer me their roll-up. I take my first drag and float home in a haze of happiness. Happier than I've been in forever.

Trouble is, in no time, they share a whole lot more with me. Dingo actually shares himself—thank God he's got a condom! Gross. Dingo's dad has a disused RV on a lot near their house. We hang out there, and they tell me all kinds of weird shit, like when they gave a tramp rotten meat from a dumpster, or when they stripped naked and started making out in the front window with a neighbor staring at them. Maybe true, maybe they're messing with me. (Hell, it works).

One time, Roz tells me they have an open relationship. They can screw other people if they want. I'm stunned, but I try to act cool. I am so far from screwing anyone, the shame of it! Shoulda taken my chances at college, damn that uptight Catholic upbringing—I'm mad Sherri has this over me. Not long after Roz tells me that, we've been smoking and drinking more than ever, and Roz falls on her face. So Dingo and I make out right there, with her snoring on the bench. It hurts and it's disgusting. And they call this love?

I'm repelled and attracted by Roz and Dingo, yet it's how I spend my Saturdays for a while. I'd've gone there most nights too if I didn't have to waitress. Mom's working, and Glen's always at meets. I say I spent the day at the library or college. Nobody cares. Nobody seems to smell the drink and the drugs. Dingo's parents decide to sell the RV after one hell of a row, and when they discover the state it's in, they change the locks.

That's when we find the shed. At the bottom of a long yard in an upscale neighborhood, we can reach it from some wasteland at the back. Spring's on its way so at least we don't leave footprints in the snow, but it's freaking cold in there. After we're busted, I decide to quit—and I'm honestly disappointed in myself that I can't. I hate myself, and that only drives me to do more. We need to find another place. So we start "visiting" Roz's granny—we "hang out" with her for five minutes while she forces homemade wine on us, then we go down to her basement to "watch TV."

It's at Granny's that Roz and Dingo progress to coke. I really, really resist for a while. I'm scared shitless. Then they threaten to abandon me, and they're the only friends I have. So I think once can't hurt.

You're damn right, it isn't "once." And it's expensive stuff. Waitressing isn't cutting it. I have to agree to "deal" to pay for my share.

I can't think about it without fear knotting my insides. I tell myself I'm tough, totally cool, I've got this. The fear insists I'm way out of my depth, but I'm in too deep and I do it.

The police pick me up outside Franklin State. I thought I'd blend in with the crowd there, but I stuck out like a stupid idiot. It's my first time dealing, and I haven't a clue. They put the handcuffs on me. The clang of those cuffs locking never stops echoing in my mind. I'm under arrest. Christ! How low can you go?

I get off with three years in jail since, thank God, I was carrying powder, not crack.

The prison gates slam shut.

20

Rita – August 1988

Jesus wept! Phyllis died the day Carling went to prison, not of a broken heart as I'm sure I will, but of pancreatic cancer. I fell apart.

I don't like thinking of those days. I don't recognize myself, hollowed out, haunted by grief. Thank God for Julian and Micah, they were completely clueless, but somehow they comforted Brandi and Sherri. And little Melody, bless her heart, our ray of sunshine. Glen threw himself into the pool and when he came up for air, cycled over to play with Melody, or eat chocolate chip and sour cream cake with Aunt Monday.

My friends, Astra and Sandip and Peggy saved me somehow. Holding me when I was a watery mess, dragging me out for walks, bringing meals (that usually I couldn't eat), and movies (that usually I couldn't watch), and taking me to aerobics class and right back again when I couldn't face it.

Astra drove me to the prison on visiting days. *What in heavens name did those corrections officers think about her Mercedes?* She waited for me, and there was always an iced coffee and gulab jamun ready for me in the passenger seat to soak up the tears. (I don't want to seem ungrateful, but at first, I craved Aunt Monday's chocolate chip and sour cream cake. Before I knew it, I was looking forward to those sticky gulab jamuns.)

Now and then, Astra and Sandip visited Carling. She liked seeing them, they didn't push her buttons. Mary, Mother of God, they never uttered a word of judgment, never seemed embarrassed or overburdened by our troubles.

One day, I'm over at their neat, modern condo, so neat it could've been featured on an ad for Mr. Clean. Astra's cooking chapatis when Sandip comes home and immediately takes her to one side.

Although he speaks softly, I can't help overhearing, "Honey, did you suggest it already?"

"I'm sorry, I couldn't bring myself to do it," she replies in a whisper. It's then, I realize she's seemed on edge, preoccupied.

"What's up?" I ask, trying to make whatever they have to say easier for them.

"Rita, we don't want to intrude, hope you don't mind, but we think it would be good for you to see a grief counselor."

Jesus! This is something I haven't even considered. I'm taken aback. Do they think I can't cope? I don't know a soul who sees a "counselor." Is that a polite way of saying "shrink"? Do they think I'm out of my mind? And "grief" counselor ... this isn't all about Dad's death, or Phyllis—My God, I miss Carling. I'm scared for her. I let her down.

My thoughts are scrambling as Sandip plows on, "There's no shame in getting help. After all you've been through ... Astra and I saw someone when we found out we couldn't have children. It helped, eased the pain. Lots of couples split up after that, we ended up more in love than ever. Um, I know you'll take offense at this ... We'd like to pay anything your insurance doesn't cover. And if you think it'd help Glen, we'll take care of that, too."

Holy Mother of God! I am so off-guard, I don't know what to think. Inevitably, we burn the chapatis in the confusion, and the smoke alarms start to scream.

━━━━◆━━━━

I have a plan to walk with Peggy and Danny at the weekend. When I get to her immaculate townhouse, Danny's taking a nap. I glance around the kitchen and family room. I'm always stunned at how tidy Peggy keeps it in spite of all the baby stuff. There's not even a whiff of diapers. We'd have drowned in clutter if Aunt Monday hadn't whipped us into shape. Peggy offers iced tea, and we sit at her stripped-pine kitchen table. I'm so distracted I plop onto Danny's booster seat! (It's very clean, smelling slightly of bleach.) Peggy launches into some local gossip, before she notices I'm uptight.

"Hey, Reet! What's up?" she asks.

" Er ... it's just, well, do you think I'm crazy?" I wonder aloud.

"Crazy, Reet? Hell! What brought this on? And no! I don't think you're crazy—except perhaps for hanging out with me." Her eyes widen as she flashes a broad smile.

This is sweet of her, so I explain, "Astra and Sandip ... they want me to see a grief counselor—isn't that a fancy name for a shrink? Aren't they for people who're off their heads?"

"Whoa!" she says. "I never heard of a grief counselor, but it doesn't sound like a bad idea. Astra and Sandip always tell me they think of you and the kids as family. I'd say they're only looking out for your best interests."

"Yeah, I know, but ..." I reply hesitantly.

"But what?" Peggy interrupts

We hear a snuffle on the baby monitor, nothing more. I take a sip of tea and sigh. "Oh, I don't know. Christ, this is awkward. I sometimes think they look after us to honor Brad's memory. I never know how much Sandip got it about Brad. I mean the lying and the cheating. It's like he's "Saint Brad' to Sandip—maybe he'd not care so much if he knew the real Brad. I'm sure they didn't bargain for all this, especially Carling. They do too much. I'm uncomfortable accepting more."

Peggy squirms a bit at this since we both know Brad cheated with her. A flush rises up her throat, and she picks at the neck of her T-shirt before recovering enough to say, "Reet! You old worry-guts! Sandip's smart as a whip. Sure, he read between the lines about Brad. I guess he just chose to ignore the bad parts. Anyways, I swear he and Astra want to help because they love you and your kids. You've been through more than anyone deserves. There's no shame in accepting their help."

All this kindness is making me tear up. I desperately want a cigarette, but I don't smoke in Peggy's house or around Danny, so I take a big gulp of iced tea instead. Peggy busies herself getting together the myriad things we'll need for a simple walk with Danny. I know everyone's trying to be kind, but my brains are mush, and I've some resentment. I've grown really independent over the years, especially since Brad died. Been rough, but it's a part of who I am now. Peggy's not the one needing to accept help. It's me, and I tried so hard to make it on my own.

Peggy's putting an entire change of clothes and shoes in the diaper bag, along with diapers and wipes, juice, a packet of Goldfish, a small truck, plastic book, some stale bread, and extra bags. As she adds sunscreen, bug repellent, a comb, and a couple of cereal bars for us, she says, "Hey, I know your mind's whirring. It's not easy, nothing's been easy for you in forever, and it's far worse with Carling in jail. I know Brandi and Sherri left home, but they still need you, and Glen and Carling. If a counselor can help you be even stronger for them, hell, it's worth a shot."

I don't tell her right away—she heads upstairs as the baby monitor's chattering away—but I'm sold. If this has a chance of helping the kids, I'll give it a go.

You can guess how the walk to the park plays out. Danny teeters to the lakeside to feed the already obese ducks, slips, gets soaked in water and mud and starts to howl. Peggy scoops him up to comfort him, her own T-shirt soaked, too. Once he's calm she pulls out clean clothes from the magic diaper bag, and hey presto! They're clean and coordinated, unlike me!

Danny struggles, pushing the stroller uphill to the playground. It takes an age and when we get there Jesus, Joseph, and Mary, the little kid swings are all taken. Danny's working towards a meltdown until we distract him with the teeter-totter, the baby slide, and the bouncy turtle. Then an eternity of pushing the little kid swing while tyrant Danny shouts "want more, more, more!" I've no arm strength left to push the stroller on the way home, but Peggy's still fresh, fresh enough to squat down to retrieve Danny's "twuck" every time he tosses it out of the stroller.

As he settles and looks drowsy, Peggy suddenly says, "Oh, can't believe I forgot. Did you hear the latest about Pat?"

"Tell me!"

"She's engaged! I only just heard," Peggy says raising her eyebrows.

"Pat's engaged! Who to?" I ask, dumbfounded..

"The oncologist who was treating Phyllis," she tells me.

"What?!" I can't believe it.

"Yes, they kept it very hush-hush—were afraid of an ethics complaint."

I'm blown away. Not just that Pat's found another man, but also that Pat can keep anything "hush-hush."

Back at Peggy's I tell her I'm okay with seeing a grief counselor.

"You go, girl," she says. "And now you're in the mood for new ideas, I've a couple of suggestions." Her eyes sparkle and she flashes the broad smile again.

"Oh no! What the Blessed Virgin Mary are you thinking?" I ask.

"I was wondering if you can't kick back a bit, cut your hours at work? Take some time for yourself. It'll do you good," she says as if she's been thinking about it.

Well, this is rich coming from Peggy, who holds down a demanding, full-time job and raises Danny singlehandedly, and for a moment I'm resentful. Maybe she'll always rub me that way. I don't want her life, yet I'm jealous of how she makes everything look easy. She sounds smug.

Hiding my resentment, I say, "And do you have a plan for what I'll do with all my spare time?"

"Hmm ... as a matter of fact, I do. It's my other idea," Peggy says.

"Spit it out then," I tell Peggy, and Danny obligingly spits out his goldfish crackers—which isn't quite what I had in mind.

Mary, Mother of God! She wants me to go on a cruise with her. A cruise! Is she out of her mind?

21

Sherri, Brandi, and Glen – Labor Day 1988

Sherri

Melody's all dressed up in a cute outfit Grandmom Shepherd found for her. I've the diaper bag packed with everything a kid could ever need, including the kitchen sink! I'm super excited about going to Brandi and Julian's, we never go anywhere young people hang out. Then Micah tells me he's not coming. I want to scream at him.

We've been over this before. Yes, Julian's cooking ribs on his new smoker, but Brandi's gonna make cheese sandwiches and egg salad. Micah rarely eats meat now, but there'll be tons of other stuff. I'm bringing chips, salsa, and homemade guacamole. Mom's sending Glen with mac and cheese, creamed corn casserole, and who knows what else.

"Sherri, it's not that—Dad needs me to help him fix the fence. We can't have Melody running out of the yard when she starts walking," Micah lies.

It's just an excuse, and we both know it. He'd rather spend time with his dad than hang out with my family. Super annoying. Hell! It's not worth arguing over, it'll only end in a fight. Thank God I learned to drive. Micah can't stop me taking the car since he's going to be working on the fence.

I strap Melody into her car seat and load all the clutter. I'm going anyway. It'll be more work and less fun without Micah. He planned on bringing his guitar (some of Julian's friends are in a band, sounds cool.)

I pull up in Dean and Shirl's driveway. Brandi and Julian live in the apartment above their offices. The vets are letting them use the back yard today. It's too much for Dean to manage anymore. (Julian or Brandi mow the grass for them and pull up a few weeds.) Brandi spots me as soon as I park. Her face falls when she sees Micah's not with me. It's not the first time.

"Where the hell—" she starts, but Melody's fussing for a big hug with Brandi, so I get her out. Brandi says, "You didn't need to bring anything, there's enough food to feed a starving nation." (It's a phrase she's picked up from Mon Mon, and suddenly Brandi seems old.)

"Micah's fixing the fence with his dad. I think he just needs a break," I say.

We all do. Though for me, *this* was going to be the break. Hanging out with people my age, laughing, celebrating with Brandi and Julian on his promotion, admiring the smoker he treated himself to, and of course, showing off Miss Melody. I'd guess Brandi prefers a new-to-you car over a smoker. What the hell! We're all too practical. Christ! It's time to live a bit.

Brandi holds Melody while I get the stroller. They're pulling funny faces at each other, having a ball. Melody doesn't want to go in the stroller; she wriggles and wriggles like an eel. She wants to be with Brandi. She's a really, really, outgoing little girl, and Brandi's special. After a lot of coaxing, I hang the diaper bag on the stroller and pass the food to Brandi.

Quite a lot of people are here already. Funny to see a gang of guys and a coupla cute girls around Glen. I guess my little brother's growing up. So weird! They're all hanging by the smoker—until the girls see me, or rather, Melody.

"She's adorable," they shriek. "Can I pick her up?"

"Hey, look at that little pixie face!"

"My God, that's the cutest dress!"

I head over to the old quilt Brandi spread out. Melody's reaching to hug the giggling girls. She's got fluffy curls now, big blue eyes, and a tiny chin that actually does make her look like a little pixie. In Grandmom Shepherd's pretty sundress and matching floppy hat, she's adorable. I've put loads of sunscreen on her so she won't burn, even though Brandi chose a shady spot for the quilt under the old apple trees. Melody took a nap already, and she's doing great, charming the girls and some of the boys.

As they're busy "baby worshiping," I look around. It's gorgeous back here, with all the maples and blue spruce and dogwoods. Julian's talking with a group of people I don't know, older than us for the most part (well, Julian's twenty-nine already.) I think they're from the lab where he works at the hospital. Weird to think he and Micah spend all their time in the same place, and never meet!

I recognize a few guys from high school, mostly Brandi's year. And, oh my God! Wonder of wonders! Someone else's just arrived carrying a baby in a backpack. Thank God, I'm not the only mom here.

Well, technically Dr. Shirl's a mom, you know what I mean. They (Dr. Shirl and Dr. Dean) are sitting on a bench on their patio, watching what's going on. Glen comes over, and Melody reaches for him. He's her true love, even more than Brandi.

"Aww!" the girls sigh. He doesn't even color at this. He looks kinda pleased and carries her around like a princess. She's an instant hit. She wants to hug everyone, even the vets. Dean's awful shaky, but he doesn't drop her even when she grabs at his glasses. Shirl joins us on the blanket, enthralled with Melody.

"Sherri, you're doing such a good job with her. It's not easy. I remember," she tells me.

I almost cry. It's all been so hard. Micah's parents give me the impression I'm a hopeless mom, doing everything wrong. And now there's something else to criticize, the "Carling factor." They try, but they can't hide their disapproval.

Brandi

It's a ton of work throwing a party. I don't know how Mom and Auntie Pat pulled it off all those years. Don't get me wrong, it's awesome too. We've never done this before. Feels like we're finally grown up. Julian was on the young side for the promotion. He's talked of nothing else apart from the smoker since it arrived, and we eventually managed to put it together. He's entertaining his friends now with all the smoker stuff. *Yawn!* What kind of pellets, cooking times, rubs and sauces, what the auger does, what a "mop" is! I'll be glad when it's smoked and we get to eat. The ribs smell phenomenal.

Oh! It's Jill coming up the path. She had a baby! Wow! I didn't know.

"Hi, Jill, who's this little munchkin?"

Jill's a friend from school. We lost touch. I suppose things changed in her life, too. She's followed by a guy I do recognize, Miguel. He was a year or two above us. Pretty much everyone—well, the girls and even a few boys—had a crush on him. Mine wasn't too intense, thank God!

"So when did you guys get together?" I ask, and I glance at their hands to see if they're wearing rings. Jill has an engagement ring. It's about three times the size of mine. No wedding ring.

"We ended up at the same college," she laughs. "Well, actually I went there because of him. I didn't care which course I took as long as I was somewhere near Miguel. It was wicked good. We started dating his senior year. When he graduated, I moved in with him and, snap your fingers, Felipe's on the way!"

We chat some more, and she asks, "Hey, Brandi, what about you, you old married woman? Thinking of following your sister's footsteps and having a baby?"

There's a lot I don't tell her, such as how I have to tempt Julian to "perform" in bed, how he fell asleep on our wedding night! I just say, "We haven't the money."

"No one's got the money." She laughs again. "Knowing you, I bet you'd rather have a pony first!" This stings. If only she knew.

The "chefs" are done. Smoke billows across the yard and with it an incredible aroma. If Dean and Shirl had any neighbors, they'd come flocking.

Once we've eaten and eaten—and eaten, Miguel tells us he's brought a plastic paddling pool and asks if they can set it up. Dean's gone in now, but Shirl says sure and shows them where the hose and outside spigot are. Somehow it's Glen's crew who take over. The guys manage to soak the girls to the skin, and it's easy to tell who's not wearing a bra!

Eventually, it's all set up, and they've poured in some hot water to take the edge off. The girls try to get their revenge and spray the guys, but they just end up getting wetter. Sherri changes Melody into the little swimsuit Glen bought her when she was born! Jill slips a pair of plastic pants over Felipe's diaper, and we lower them in. Melody giggles and giggles, while Felipe screams his lungs out. The girls are so wet they're headed off to get dry, and Julian's group's dwindling too. He takes sopping Felipe and cuddles him close to his chest.

"It's alright, little man," he coos.

And, at last, Felipe's volcanic sobs subside, with only a minor eruption here and there. Looking at Julian with the baby, I think there's hope for us, and we've lots of time. Sweet little Melody looks concerned for Felipe, but she doesn't cry, and when he's calmed down, she leans towards him and gives him a kiss. Then she's splashing everyone and chuckling like a geyser.

People are trailing off now. I go over to Shirl to thank her for letting us do this. "Sit down by me, Brandi, why don't you ... let's visit. The clearing-up can wait." She gestures for me to sit next to her.

"What a lovely afternoon. Thank you for doing this. Dean's tired—he asked me to tell you how much he enjoyed himself. We don't get to be around young folk too much these days." Shirl pauses and then adds in a serious tone, "You'll have noticed how unsteady Dean's getting."

You can't miss it, even when he's not holding a baby. In fact, I've known for a long time, he doesn't do surgery anymore. Shirl does it all. Some old-timers used to prefer Dean; almost no one asks for him anymore.

"Hmm" is all I find to say.

"Dean's got MS, multiple sclerosis—you'll have heard of it, I guess. He can't carry on much longer."

"I'm so sorry," I stammer, and she plows right on.

"I want you to know we're selling the practice. A condition of the sale is that they keep you on as practice manager—don't worry about your job. We're going to live here as long as we can, and the apartment's yours too, for a while, at least. We'll likely have to move into assisted living one day. By then, you and Julian'll be able to afford a bigger place, especially if Julian keeps getting promoted. I bet you'll be glad to get out of our rabbit hutch when the time's right."

I give her a big hug. I'm so sorry for Dean and Shirl. It's good of them to protect my job and think about us. I'll miss them. It's another blow on top of Grandpa Wuff and Grandma Phyllis' deaths, and of course, there's the "Carling factor."

Glen

I was nervous how the guys would react going to Brandi's and Julian's. We're a lot younger than them, they've already shuffled into middle age! Helluva long summer this year, no chance of going anywhere, and everyone else out of town.

God! Carling, you've a boatload to answer for. Ironic thing is that Easter Sunday when the cops came the first time, it coulda been me. I'd been hanging with some high school jocks. The dumb farts offered me pot and glue. I felt a total wimp, but thank God, I said no.

Since the "Carling factor" (hell why'd she do it, I miss my sister!) ... Since then, I don't hang out with them anymore. My buddies here are from my old middle school and a coupla kids who work with me at the hardware store. I got a part-time job there this summer to take my mind off of "things."

Mr. Cousins, who owns the store, remembered me from the time Grandpa Tone and I went to ask about photos for my first-ever model. Well, that turned out to be the bathrooms, but Mr. Cousins doesn't know that. He asked me to bring in the one of his store. Oh, man! He was all over it. He put it on display by the till. Mega embarrassing!

Anyways, I shouldn't've worried about the gang. They said the whole entire afternoon was super cool. Julian's a cool dude, and the smoker's totally awesome. Nearly everyone knows Dr. Dean and Dr. Shirl from when their pets get sick. Dr. Dean looks as if he's gonna croak. Don't drop dead, Dr. Dean. Nobody else's allowed to die right now.

The girls—and the guys, (they won't admit it)—all literally fell in love with Melody. No one like sniggered 'cause Sherri's young for a mom, and she must've done "it" with Micah. No one asked about the "Carling factor." Thank God! Melody's a sweetie. I like dressing her up in all her baby-doll clothes, and she stole the show in the teddy bear swimsuit I bought her.

When we got the girls wet and we could see their nipples through their T-shirts, I couldn't keep my eyes off of them. My "thing" started throbbing, and I had to splash cold water all over me to calm it down. Don't think anybody saw. How the hell am I gonna handle high school swim practice? There'll be all those older girls, with their bouncy breasts and tight buns! (Kinda sad the girls got wet 'cause they left after that, and then everyone else drifted off.)

I'm helping Julian clear up. He told Brandi to sit down with Sherri, Jill, and her guy. Their baby's okay, but not half as cute as Melody. They're draining the paddling pool. Melody loves to see the water swirl down the drain, but she's started to rub her eyes. Even so, she has to give Felipe a kiss bye-bye as they leave. He howls. Pathetic. Melody's wiped. Time for a nap or a meltdown. Better be a nap!

22

Rita – A few weeks later

My God! Can this really be me? I'm wearing an emerald swimsuit and a floppy straw hat, lying on a lounger next to Peggy. We're on the deck of the "Mermaid of the Seas," sipping Calm Breeze cocktails. They're baby blue with tiny yellow umbrellas. Decadent and delicious.

I'm doing it. Doing it all and enjoying myself! My life's already changed a hell of a lot. I have to smile when I think of the first time I went to Dr. Forrest.

◆

I climb three flights of stairs to reach her office, my heart's pounding from the exercise and because I'm scared silly she'll see right into me with laser eyes, judge me, or expect me to change in ways I can't. When I enter her office, it's like penetrating a jungle, with lush plants trailing all over the place, hanging baskets with tendrils swaying as the AC kicks in. Plants dangling from the filing cabinets, the coffee table, the coat rack.

There's so much greenery, it takes me a while to focus and find the doctor sitting in the shade of an enormous Swiss Cheese plant. She's wearing a purple kaftan and some lumpy jewelry I later learn is homemade. There's a tank next to her with a bearded dragon, I guess

I'll hear tree frogs next. To my shock, I stifle a laugh, wondering if she has clients with phobias about being strangled by rampant plants.

She's caught my expression and chuckles. "Yes, Rita, I can't abide a soulless office. The plants are relaxing, don't you think?"

Really and truly, I don't know what to think, but I already suspect we'll get along. In fact, I come to look forward to visiting her rainforest, hearing her wise words, and discovering that although I've been a dry husk, I can blossom like her precious plants.

So, take a look at me! Sweat trickling between my breasts and a pink, freckly flush creeping over my skin.

◆

To say none of the kids expected me to go on a cruise is an understatement. Holy Mother of God, they were dumbfounded. Recovering from the shock, they were happy for me—except Glen. He dreaded tagging along, babysitting Danny, who's not in Melody's league as far as Glen's concerned. No way! Sandip and Astra came to his rescue, offering to have him stay with them. He's ecstatic, gets to live in their super-cool condo, eat super-spicy food, and be the freshman superstar on the swim team. Glen's idea of heaven!

There've been changes at work. Margaret sold the salon a while back. The new owner Julieta is going back to Ecuador to look after elderly relatives. She offered to sell me the business at a decent price. Oh, sweet Jesus! The irony of it! Once upon a time, this was my dream. Now, when I actually have the funds, I've moved on.

It's all Peggy's fault. She ruined my work ethic, dangling cruises and time to myself. Julieta's cool with me talking with my regulars, almost all are good with me coming to their homes to fix their hair. That way, I can organize my time better. It'll mean less money, no walk-ins, but I think I'll like it. I can always go back to the old way if it doesn't work out.

◆

Peggy's dozing—not surprising. We went to a Pilates class this morning. I'll be stiff tomorrow, and Danny woke up at some unearthly hour today, so she read to him and built block towers. He's in the daycare center right now. I thought he'd scream and yell, but he races in there to take command of the black Lego motorbike and the car transporter.

I slip into the deck pool. Icy cold at first, and gooseflesh sprouts. Then I stretch out my stroke and swim a few laps. I haven't watched Glen all these years without learning a thing or two, and I was a pretty good swimmer in my younger days. As I heave myself out, I'm aware of my cleavage, but as I'm dripping past the man sprawled in the deck chair, he mutters, under his breath, "Nice ass!"

Tomorrow, we sail to Antigua, our last island before we head back to Puerto Rico and home. We've booked a trip to Shirley's Heights and English Harbor. Hope there's some shade. Danny burns in a nano-second, and he's cranky when he's hot.

◆

It's absolutely gorgeous at the top of Shirley's Heights, and we can see for miles. Little winding roads to the harbor below, pastel homes draped with bougainvillea, palm trees everywhere, and the turquoise ocean reflecting a bluer-than-blue sky. Danny's dancing to a steel band, and there's just enough breeze to keep him happy. The locals are entranced with him. Not too many redheads in these parts. The drummers notice Danny and seamlessly switch from the "Hallelujah Chorus" to "Twinkle, Twinkle, Little Star." Danny beams bright as a star, "singing" and dancing along.

Everyone tries to sell us rum punches. We only take the fruit version—two women with a child, we're vulnerable. We eat lunch down in English Harbor. I never ate much fish at home, but here it's fantastic, and Danny obligingly falls asleep in his stroller. Even Practical Peggy's pinching herself at how amazing this is. We stroll through the market, the stall holders accosting us on all sides. I'm looking for T's for the girls and little Melody.

It's hard to realize these tie-dye shirts and wrap-around sarongs won't fit in back home in Massachusetts. In the end, I find a little dress for Melody with a pineapple on it, and conch shells and anklets for the girls. I hesitate over Carling—Christ! It'll be so long before she can have gifts. With a nod and a wink, the stall holders tell me they can get special conch shells stuffed with *ganga*—Jesus! What would Dr. Forrest say? Back on board, I wrap my empty shells in all the excess sweatshirts I packed when I couldn't imagine myself in paradise!

Peggy hires a babysitter for our last night, so we can have a civilized meal in the main restaurant. We usually eat buffet style in the cafeteria with Danny, then push him around the decks until he falls asleep.

It's cool ... My God, I'm having so much fun! Putting on a nice dress, make-up, and twisting up my hair. We have a lingering, indulgent meal. The silverware really is silver, and there are crystal chandeliers over each table. Everything's fabulous, and we're soon laughing and joking with the other couples at our table.

After dinner, we stroll round the deck, sipping Calm Breezes, and hang over the railings gazing at the stars reflected in the rippling ocean. Mary, Jesus, and Joseph, they dance in the waves. It's mesmeric. Rod Stewart croaks out, "I Am Sailing," over the loudspeakers. Cheesy, I know, but I'm happily swaying along. Eventually, I notice the man from the pool deck's edged closer to me. Peggy's a few steps away, making space for him. She's wearing a wicked grin.

"Wish I'd met you earlier. Like to come to my cabin for a nightcap?" he whispers in a silky voice.

Jesus! I politely decline, and not long afterwards, find my way back to my own cabin. Peggy, with more stamina than me, heads to the casino. You go, girl! Although I'm not attracted to "pool dude," I'm flattered. I haven't had male attention for so long, I'm not sure I'd know what to do! *Who am I kidding* ... As I remember that afternoon with Jarek. I glance at the mirror. The woman who meets my gaze is relaxed, attractive, and there's a hint of mischief. And it's me!

23

Carling – December 1990 and mid-1991

I am a stray dog cowering in a corner. My hair is matted with blood and mud. I cannot stand up for myself. The only one to mistreat me is myself.

I am snot that needs to be wiped away. I am invisible, an empty carcass in a fleece of shame. There is no reflection in the smeared windowpane or the crazed mirror. Who am I? I can't recognize myself. I have no guts. I deserve to be mocked, humiliated, spat upon. When my family visits, I see them through vacant eyes. Were we once related?

Okay, so it's self-absorbed, self-pitying, melodramatic, and all the rest. It's part of an essay I wrote in a creative writing class. Guess I've had to grow up a lot since then. The teacher prompted us: "What was it like when you came to prison?"

"Which time?" one of the inmates asked.

She's on the "installment plan." Some time in, some time out, some time in again. She's not such a bad person. It's just really hard once you've got a record, to get a job, housing, and ride the stigma ... And so you fall back on dealing again. And it's a sick joke to say prisons are here to give you second chances. They're not so enlightened. They're not "correctional" centers, they're punishment centers.

It's a bit better in a women's prison. There's only one in our state, so we don't get moved around like they say the men do. Even so, it's hard to get into classes; they keep cutting funding, and classes and recreation are the first things to go. I sign up for everything, and I think I'm lucky if I get into anything, or if it actually runs at all or for the whole course.

Oh! The bell's ringing. They're going to count us again. It's an obsession of theirs. I suppose it looks bad if they "lose" anyone. After count, I need to do my shift in the kitchen.

A corrections officer unlocks the kitchen for us. There's another shift leaving, so they get escorted back to their blocks. Everyone on my crew knows each other, but we don't say much; it's easy to be triggered in here, so if you don't want to get a longer sentence for fighting or something, it's best to keep yourself to yourself. We're all coming to the end of our time—that's why they trust us with knives and pans of boiling water. My job today's peeling potatoes. My hands get red raw. I don't mind too much, the TV's on loud in the background, and the time passes pretty quickly, which isn't always the case in prison.

When the meal's ready, we line up to be servers. Another bell rings, and not long after, the chow line forms. The CO's are watching. A lot can happen at mealtimes—someone can knock your tray out of your hands to cause a distraction to cover a drug deal (yes, they're here in prison). The more everything's screened, the more ingenious the women get at smuggling drugs in. Scores can be settled when you're in line waiting for the food. Someone who's bored or mad can take it out on you because she doesn't like your face or the color of your skin.

Kitchen crew eat early. You get used to not choosing your mealtimes, not choosing anything much here. We stay after everyone's done to load the industrial dishwashers, mop the floors, scour the countertops, and get everything back in its place ready for the morning. Then we're walked to our blocks and back to our cells.

"How you doin', darlin'?" Mama Bear asks me when I get back to the cell. She's my cellie. Her real name's not Mama Bear; she's one of the oldest women here.

The older and sicker you are, the less likely you are to commit a crime. If you've worn out your family's patience or you've outlived them when you get out, most likely you'll end up homeless or worse. Mama Bear's been in and out of prison most of her life. She's got a rap sheet as long as your arm, but her real crime's being born black and poor. She's the best cellie I've had. All the others were twisted with anger or bitterness, trying to play the system and dragging me into trouble with them.

The CO's can search the cell for any reason or no reason at all. One time, they took all my classwork and my tampons. They're on edge right now, the annual inspection's due, and they don't want a thing out of place. This means we have much less recreational time, we're not allowed access to the gym or the library, and we have to stay in our cells all the time when we don't have a work shift.

If you think about it though, you have to feel a bit sorry for the Corrections Officers. They get paid next to nothing, no respect in the community, they spend their whole entire lives saying "no" and being suspicious. They end up as institutionalized as the rest of us. No wonder the suicide rate among them is grim.

"I'm fine, Mama Bear. Did you get to call Kaeisha today?" I ask. Kaeisha's her granddaughter and heading to follow in her grandmother's footsteps if she's not careful.

"Nope, I had me a pass for the phone, an' I stood in line a coupla hours. Li'l Nancy's a-screamin' at her lawyer, an' Hornet's tryin' to tell her six-year-old to fix the toilet. Then they ring the bell for 'count,' an' I'll need another pass tomorrow. Kaeisha's suppose' be in after-school then, so's my guess, she ain't gonna pick up no phone," she tells me.

"I'm real sorry, Mama Bear." I want to give her a hug, but I don't. If a CO's walking by, that'll cause no end of trouble.

The inspection happens just before Christmas every year. There's not much holiday spirit here—most of us are trying not to think about how we used to spend the holidays. It's Brandi's birthday and her anniversary, too. Another thing you miss.

Some church group sends in shoeboxes with gifts and a card. Some of the women cry when they get them; others pretend they don't care. But we all use the stuff they pack. Flip-flops for the shower—never quite the right size—a writing tablet and envelopes. Some years, there are stamps—depends if the authorities think drugs are being smuggled into the adhesive or not. There's always a little bottle of shampoo, toothpaste, and a bar of soap (never scented).

The card's often homemade—hand-drawn, maybe by kids. They can't make collages in the non-adhesive years. Nobody signs their name on the cards. They must think we're all serial killers and we'll track them down when we get released. In the case of serial killers, I guess they don't get released, but you get my drift.

I suggest we write a note to Kaeisha. Mama Bear can read and write fine, but she's got arthritis in her hands so it's easier if she dictates and I write.

She pours her heart out to Kaeisha, telling her what a wonderful young woman she is, how proud Mama Bear is of her, and so on. She asks the good Lord to bless her and give her a wonderful Christmas and a whole heap of blessings in the New Year. Then she gets stern. "You make sure you stay out of trouble, finish your schooling, and don't mess with no gangs." She signs it with a big heart, a badly drawn holly leaf, and a swarm of kisses.

When the inspection's over, I'm on the home stretch. Six months and I've done my time, paid my debt to society. I can't tell if I'll ever feel I paid my debt to my family.

There goes the bell, and across the loudspeaker, they announce a list of numbers. The loudspeaker's so fuzzy you can't hear if it's your number. We both think Mama Bear's been called, so she heaves herself up and out. Seems likely they want a urine sample.

Christmas is pretty bad. I don't go to the chapel service where the holy rollers tell us how great everything is and what an awesome God we have. And I take the big step of asking my family not to visit me over Christmas. I think I'll get through the holiday better without seeing them. Visiting hours are cut back anyway to give the CO's a break, so I needn't have bothered. All I've done is get everyone mad at me. Aunt Monday sent me a nice card with a note saying, "You do what you need to do for yourself, Carling. I'll always love you. God bless."

And Sandip and Astra sent me a card with a jolly robin on the front holding a sprig of mistletoe in its beak. The rest of them are not that understanding, and I feel badly for reopening old wounds.

◆

It gets even worse in the New Year. I get back from my shift to find the CO's are tearing the cell apart. The robin card goes flying, Mama Bear's overlarge undies are strewn everywhere, our Christmas shoeboxes are torn apart, our socks are separated, the book I've been reading's flung across the cell.

They heave the mattress off my bed, and then they find it. A VCR player! I recognize it immediately. It's the one from the classroom that only works when it feels like it. I'm horrified. Even worse, there's a tape. Apparently lesbian sex. The CO's start to drag me out of the cell.

"I didn't—" I start to say, but Mama Bear cuts me off.

"She din' do nothin'. I stole it. I got lonesome, I needed watch somethin'."

It's a complete lie. Someone planted it on me. I'm always in the classroom. I have an idea who it is, but I don't snitch.

Instead I say, "Mama Bear, you didn't do this. With your arthritis, you couldn't get up on that chair to unplug it."

But she says sharply, "Hol' your nonsense, chil'."

The CO's aren't listening. They hustle Mama Bear out of the cell. I'm hoping that at her age they don't put her in the hole. Of course they do. She gets three days in solitary, which is less than most, an extension to her sentence, and I get a new cellie.

She's a skinny, little Hispanic woman. I think she forged her boss's signature on checks made out to her boyfriend, but she has so little English I'm not sure. She cries most nights, like I did when I first arrived. I was a complete wreck, especially after Mom and my sisters visited. They assigned me a psychotherapist—an elderly man with tufts of hair growing out of his ears. He crossed his legs like a woman and laid his hands on his knees. Long, bony, white fingers, liver spots, and yellow nails. He looked weak and wispy, but he didn't suffer fools. He got my number.

Somehow, I listened when he told me there were reasons for what I'd done, but I couldn't make them excuses. I had to take responsibility, and the only way to make it up to my family was to pull myself together, quit the self-pity bullshit, and make sure I got out of here in one piece. Easier for him to say than for me to do. All the same, gradually I came out of my funk.

I met Sister Claudia first in the "Alternatives to Violence" program. I didn't commit a violent crime, yet I just apply for everything, like I said. I probably got in to make the numbers up and keep it viable. Anyways, tiny Sister Claudia was there wearing her gray habit. She was the kindest and the toughest instructor. Months later, I'm in her creative writing class. She sure is the most diminutive nun I've ever seen. For such a small person, she has a whopping great spirit.

She made us write about all the tough stuff in our lives, and if you bullshit Sister Claudia, she gives you a withering look that's worse than any criticism I ever got at school. Mostly, she liked my work, and I liked pleasing her. The only time I lied through my teeth was when she gave a prompt, "Write about your Higher Power, or whatever gives you hope." I wrote this sweet little piece about how I loved the Catholic church. When she handed it back, I got the look, and she'd written, "Don't mess with me, and don't write any more c---!"

One day, I'm at the education block a little before the others, and we start to chat.

"Carling, you ever thought about college?" she asks in a way that isn't as naïve as it sounds.

"College was my dream, but I messed up. There's no undergraduate program here—no one will look at me once I'm done with prison, I'll be lucky if I land a job," I explain.

The others are beginning to file in so she tilts her head, cocks her eyebrows, and smiles all at the same time.

A while later when the loudspeaker blares, I think I hear my number. Alarmingly, I'm escorted to the assistant governor's office. *What the hell did I do?* I've never been here before. Turns out, I did something right! Sister Claudia's put in a good word for me. The assistant governor, peering at me over the kind of bifocals that perch on the end of a haughty nose, explains that there might be a way for me to go back to college after my release.

"Er, thank you. I can't go to community college. That's how I ended up here," I reply sheepishly.

"You mustn't blame community college for your offense. Plenty of people do very well there. However, as it happens, Sister Claudia was thinking of something else."

"Isn't it too late?" I say, excitement mounting in spite of myself, because truth be told, I'd daydreamed about becoming a psychiatrist or a psychologist. Figuring myself out, and helping others at the same time. I'd dashed those dreams away. Seemed a sick fantasy.

We talk for a while. It's unnerving. She peers over her glasses and down her nose at me. I feel intimidated and childish. Eventually, I screw my courage and tell her my dreams. And she doesn't laugh in my face. There's a series of quick nods that almost dislodge the glasses. I can't help but smile.

"So glad you're still ambitious, Carling. I needed to determine that before I share Sister Claudia's proposal." She continues, "The sisters have a college scholarship fund. It's usually offered to promising high school students. She's considering recommending you for the fall."

I gasp. She smiles and continues, "It won't cover anywhere near a full ride, and you'd have to persuade an admissions officer to give you a chance, but please consider it very seriously. It's not often—in fact, I can't remember ever having an opportunity like this before."

I am stunned.

You can bet your life I spend whatever time I can in the library researching college courses. I still can't believe this is going to happen, and, at the same time, I quiver with excitement that it might.

I'm sitting here chewing my pen, chewing my nails, chewing my lip, the insides of my cheeks—anything I can chew on—screwing up the courage to write my application letter and essay. I found an alternative college on the outskirts of the city that has rolling admissions and takes non-traditional students. They offer a course leading to a career as a licensed chartered social worker; I can be a counselor with that when I qualify. It's a long shot, and I want it so much that I'm chewing my hair now.

Sister Claudia checks my work, looks at me seriously, and then murmurs, "May the Lord you don't believe in, be with you. You'll knock it out of the park!"

I'm worried something will go wrong before my release, especially after the incident with the VCR. I barely see Mama Bear again, and I try to thank her with my eyes when our paths cross. My cellie learns a few words of English. I help her all I can, and I keep out of everyone else's way.

Nothing else bad happens.

And with conditions, I'm accepted! They need me to take a foundation course starting late August. If I do well in that, I can sign up for my "real" program early next year.

OMG! My new life starts here. I'm shit scared. I can't blow this.

◆

The last count. The last blurred loudspeaker calling my number—this time for dismissal. I am handed my paperwork and a few personal possessions. The prison van could transport me to the train station, but Mom said she'd meet me. I begged her not to set up a "prodigal daughter" party, yet when I walk through the gates, they're all there. Mom, my sisters, Glen, Aunt Monday, Melody, who charges at me for a humongous hug, Aunt Pat, Tessa, Carolina, and her baby brother. Sister Claudia's off to one side talking with Sandip and Astra.

It's overwhelming and, suddenly, I feel shy. We've all changed in different ways. I realize it will take time to readjust. For now, I let the tears flow and remember what it's like to be squeezed so hard you think your ribs will crack.

24

I'm numb with fear. Micah's gripping the steering wheel with bone-white knuckles—like he's going to tear it out. I have to remind myself to breathe. My stomach's turning pirouettes, and I'm clenching my teeth.

"Babies on the bus go wah, wah, wah," Melody sings innocently from the back seat. Oh my God! It's surreal.

Micah's parking technique's off today, so we scarcely have room to get out.

"Damn!" he swears.

"Damn!" Melody chirrups back.

I want to yell at Micah to watch his language, instead I bite my lip.

We strap Melody into the stroller. Although she's big enough to walk, this isn't our hospital. We might have miles of corridors before we find the doctor's office. Micah glances at the instructions again. Neither of us hold them in our heads. There's a map. But Micah can't orient himself. Shows how jittery he is. Reading a map's like reading an X-ray; usually it's a breeze.

We're cold by the time we get to the main lobby. The weather's got a bite to it, and nerves are sapping our energy. The entrance is framed by trees, beginning to dress themselves in their autumn colors against a crystal-blue sky. There are stark shadows like the Hopper paintings I studied back in high school art when life was sweet. How can I be thinking of art at a time like this? Is this what they mean by an out-of-body experience? Watching myself while I'm on auto-pilot?

We follow a maze of elevators and corridors to a bleak waiting room. Smells of disinfectant and fly spray. Melody immediately gets down from the stroller and walks across to the big window. Canada geese fly by almost at her eye level, forming their weird V's and honking like it's time to leave. She thinks it's cool and starts clapping her hands and honking like the geese.

Whoa! Reflected in the window, we look odd. Micah's shrunken, and I'm like Melody's big sister. She's cute and wide-eyed; we look like hollow-eyed migrants. We love her to bits, but she transformed us overnight from carefree to careworn.

She's found the box of toys. There's a yellow plastic keyboard with red buttons. She can't resist. It plays a tinny version of "Teddy Bear's Picnic." She squeals in delight and does a little twirl. She presses another button. "Ring Around the Rosie" rattles out, and this time Melody joins in with her pretty, clear voice. The last button releases "Three Blind Mice," and we hear these in rotation for half an hour as we wait for the doctor. These silly songs mess with me. They're kinda ominous. I don't know about Micah, but I want to throw the keyboard at the plate glass window a long time before we're called in.

We expect to be handed reams of paperwork listing Melody's medical history in excruciating and baffling detail, as we have done at all the other appointments, where the professionals seem incapable of explaining the findings. This time we're mistaken.

Dr. Scanlon sits in the open space in his office, not behind his desk like the others. He's an older man, white hair ringing the dome of his bald head. His eyes twinkle. Embarrassingly, Melody runs to him and gives him a hug. I cannot get her to understand that this isn't appropriate behavior, but so many people are charmed by it, I don't get any reinforcement. I'm so wound up, I already want to cry. The doctor smiles.

"What a beautiful daughter you have," he remarks with a little chuckle in his voice that helps me relax a bit. Then, there's some small talk about how we got here, what the traffic was like, the weather, our plans for Halloween.

When's he going to get round to examining her? I wonder. She's now pulling off her shoes and socks to fiddle with her toes.

I get up to put them on again. Dr. Scanlon gets down on the floor and plays "This Little Piggy" with her. Melody's giggling and giggling and, to my horror, reaches out and pats the doctor's bald head. After a bit more play, he distracts her with an owl that hoots when you press its tummy, and he takes his seat again,

"I have a good idea what's going on with Miss Melody, just by watching her," he finally gets around to saying.

Normally mild-mannered Micah snaps, "We didn't bring her here for you to look at her." (*To whit, to woo!* hoots in the background.) "Aren't you going to run some tests? Examine her? All the other doctors agree there's something wrong, but they don't know what."

Melody's been missing her milestones all her short life. Late to sit, to walk, to talk … Now she does talk, there's no stopping her.

Dr. Scanlon smiles at Micah, but his voice is serious as he says, "I'm so sorry, I didn't mean to give you the impression that I'm going to do all the necessary tests and examinations, beyond those that are already in her file. There are some characteristics I can observe that are indicators." (The owl hoots, apparently in solidarity with Dr. Scanlon.)

"Let me explain. Melody's a little peanut. I see you," he gestures at me, "you're petite, so that might account for Melody's size, and yet again it might not. She has a beautiful little face. Some folks have probably called her a little elf or a little pixie with those sparkling wide-set eyes. Notice she looks as if she has stars in her irises, and that upturned nose and tiny chin."

We both glance at Melody and at each other. I can feel Micah's resentment. I bet he's thinking, *So what's wrong with having a pretty little elf face?* After all, Dr. Scanlon himself looks as if he's Doc from "Snow White and the Seven Dwarfs."

"She has a very outgoing personality—no clinging to her parents when she's in a new environment," he continues, unaccompanied by the owl now, thank goodness. Meanwhile, Melody's investigating the rubber plant. "And then I was sorry to keep you waiting while I reviewed her notes, I had to see to an emergency earlier—I couldn't help overhearing that she has quite the affinity for music."

We look at each other dumbfounded. The doctor seems to be saying that there's something wrong with having a pretty, petite little girl who loves music. (So, Micah plays the guitar, and I'm a dancer—she could've inherited that.) She loves everyone, even strangers. My God! These are her strong points, aren't they? When the hell's he gonna stop playing around and get to her medical issues?

It turns out (pray God, no!) these characteristics may be indicators of a genetic condition named Williams Syndrome. Dr. Scanlon explains that a test has been developed in the last few years, called a FISH test, that will be conclusive.

I start to cry, and Melody puts her arms around me. Micah's fighting back emotion too—he's likely scared, frustrated, angry, and sad all at once. We're not taking it in. It's unbelievable—and what was that he's going to do with a fish? Maybe we should've accepted Grandmom and Grandpa Shepherd's offer to come with us. We wanted to be the parents and, at the same time, we were still hoping against hope that nothing was really wrong after all and Melody'd grow out of all her problems.

Dr. Scanlon gives us a leaflet about Williams Syndrome. He says he doesn't want to go into detail now, in case he's mistaken. He'd like to discuss it again with us once the FISH result comes back, and he makes an appointment for the following week. He offers early morning or evening, so we don't have to take more time off work, but we know we won't be able to concentrate for worry that day, so we choose mid-morning.

As we're leaving, the doctor says, "This is a very difficult time for you. Please try and keep in mind you have a delightful and remarkable little girl. Enjoy her and love her as much as you can."

As we're gathering up Melody, I'm crying all the more. In my heart, I know the doctor's suspicions are going to be right. At least he recognizes she's a sweetheart. All the same ... My God! How are we going to cope? It's way, way too scary.

As soon as we get to the car, Micah breaks down and sobs. We're upsetting Melody, so we turn on the radio and find some bouncy music. Then we pore over the leaflet. It's full of pictures of other kids, pretty much all like her, with these cheeky, cute, fairy faces. The leaflet tells us very little more. Williams is a rare genetic disorder that causes physical and developmental issues. Oh my God!

I don't know how we live through the next week. Micah and I alternate between holding each other so close it's as if we're welded together, and needing our own space. There's never much of that in our tiny apartment, but Micah spends a lot of time in the medical library at work. Most nights, I don't dare ask him what he's found out. Grandmom and Grandpa Shepherd are gonna need knee replacements after all the praying they do.

By the appointment, even though we scarcely admit it to ourselves, we all know, deep down, that Dr. Scanlon's right. The tests confirm Williams Syndrome. I can't really explain it, and maybe I'm a bad mom, but after all the anxiety, it almost comes as a relief. Melody doesn't care. She's her wonderful little self, stretching her arms out to give me a hug. Who could ever live without her?

Aunt Monday can't, as it turns out. She invites us to Sunday lunch together with Mom and Carling. Glen's "hanging out," and Micah doesn't come either, he says he's got a lot of thinking to do—he can't roll with it like the rest of us. He can't enjoy the present for fear of the future. I worry that he's so withdrawn these days.

Melody's very happy putting apple slices in the pie crust and telling herself a whole entire story about the mommy apples and the baby apples until she pops a coupla slices in her mouth and almost chokes with laughter. Mon helps her spoon the cinnamon sugar over the apples, and we quietly notice that her fine motor skills aren't too great. Then Mon closes the pie, and we make a little heart shape out of the leftover dough. Melody puts it on the crust,

"That's my piece!" she squeals in delight.

Mon Mon has the chicken and vegetables ready, so we can pop the pie in the oven. "Little Miss Melody," she tells her, "did you ever hear what Auntie Carling put in the oven when she was a little girl?"

"Mon, no!" Carling cries out. She's heard this story once too often.

Over lunch, Carling tells us she's moving out of Mom's house.

"Where you going?" I ask, my mouth full of chicken and beans.

"There's an apartment above the gas station where I work," she explains.

I glance at Mom's face, she looks relaxed. I was wondering if Carling's safe to live alone. Will she get into trouble again? Mom must see my questions written across my brow as clearly as if I'd spoken them out loud.

"I think you're doing the right thing, Carling my love. You needed a home base for a couple of months until you got settled, but Jesus, Joseph and Mary, you need your independence, your own place now."

Although she's only moving closer to college, it's a blow. Now the awkwardness of her having been in prison's less, and she's adjusted to fit in with our lives, I'd looked forward to having Auntie Carling around. God! How things change! Remember the days I couldn't stand sharing a room with her?

"Hey, Sherri, don't look so glum. I'm not going to abandon you and my favorite niece," Carling says.

"Knees," Melody parrots. "I got dirty knees!"

We help Mon Mon with the washing up, she still hasn't got a machine. She's nearly as old as the century, and there's barely anything wrong with her ever since she got her cataracts done. Still, I can't help worrying about her. Maybe she'll live to be the world's oldest woman. Sure hope so.

It's Halloween, and we dress Melody up in an M and M costume. She chose the purple one. She breaks everyone's hearts, and we could carry off a ton of candy if we wanted to. It's super fun, even though Micah's still not with the program. Then we stop at the Shepherds' neighbors. Mr. Watson opens the door, leaps out, and yells, "Boo!" Melody screams her lungs out. And once we've got her home, it takes ages to calm her down.

Finally, when she's settled, Micah's all serious. Then he says the most dreaded words in the whole world, "Sherri, we've got to talk."

I'm not sure he's going to be able to—he's shaking and crying already. I reach out for him but he pushes me off.

"Sherri, you're gonna hate me. I'm sorry, really sorry. We have to make some changes," he says.

Oh my God! My heart stops. I think he's going to leave me and Melody. Oh, fuck!

Kinda. It's been really tough living below his parents these last four years in a minute apartment. It's driven me crazy, and I know it's made it super tough for us as a couple. I hoped one day we'd move out into a place of our own like Brandi and Julian. But the living situation's only a part of it. There's Melody.

Since Melody's diagnosis, Micah ... My God! Micah! He's been doing a whole lot of thinking. He can barely keep his voice steady when he reminds me we don't have the money to raise a special-needs child. Who knows what extra help she'll need, tutors, a special school, medical bills? Who knows? Micah's been pissed off at work. He can't see a career path there. No way to make more money.

Incredibly, he wants to join the armed forces, and he's been in touch with a recruiter. Christ, he'd wanted to sign up when he was younger, but his parents talked him out of it. He'll make better money, health care for Melody, education, a pension.

My brain's racing. No way! I didn't see this coming. It's too much to take in. All the same, I see a chink of light. We'll live in military housing. There'll be other young parents around. Melody'll have friends ... Can I take her away from family? I can't think of it.

Micah's two steps ahead of me. He thinks it'll be too much for me to cope with Melody without family support. Too much moving around won't be good for Melody. She'll need to see the same doctors who understand her needs. She'll need consistent schooling, she'll need ...

I cannot believe what I'm hearing. My God! My heart's an open wound. Micah's leaving us. He promises to send money for Melody, and he'll see her whenever he's on leave. That's it. He loves me—and he doesn't love me. He doesn't need to tell me I'm not the bubbly, spontaneous girl I used to be.

I scream at him, "You bastard, Micah! You think you haven't changed. God! You were a sweet, tender guy, now you're friggin' cold as ice!"

We're both sobbing and screaming now. I'm surprised his parents don't tell us to quiet down. Later, I realize they must've known what's going on. In the end, it's Melody who interrupts. Rubbing sleep from her eyes, she pads in wearing her pink footie PJ's.

"Mama, Dada, don't cry! Did a naughty man say boo?"

"Yes, sweetheart, he did," I tell her.

25

Romance – Spring 1992

Rita

Jesus, Mary and Joseph! Thank God! Nico calls a break. I'm hot and sweaty, and I lurch between elation and frustration. We're learning some new figures, and they just don't come easily. Truth is, nothing comes easy since I started taking tango classes, it must be six months now.

Annie, one of my clients (well, they're not clients anymore, they're all friends), suggested we sign up for the session, and Peggy was keen to come too. She drops Danny off with Sherri at my place. Sherri gets him to bed in Glen's old room, and Peggy stops by in the morning to take him to daycare before work. Peggy does the same for Sherri on Saturday nights, so she can go out and feel young again.

I'd babysit in a heartbeat. They try to give me a break, bless their hearts, and they tell me it's good for Melody. Well, what d'ya know! Melody adores it. She gets super excited for her "pajama party." It gives her a chance to be around someone her own age, though that young lady isn't lacking in social skills. Just the opposite!

Tango's pretty daunting at first (still is). Thank heavens, we're all three of us beginners. I love it now. Always did like to dance. Most of us go for a drink afterwards. Night life! Makes me feel young again too.

We're in Centennial Hall at the Arts Center. It's a big, dusty room with wainscoting and chipped crown molding. Stepping in there the first time, it's overwhelming. I have all these stupid fears, like everyone'll be better than me. What was I thinking? I'm a beginner! Jesus!

That first night we thought Nico'd hate us—three single women. Usually there's tons more women than men in dance classes. As it turns out, he couldn't have been more welcoming. He's got a couple of guy friends who hang out for free. There's a widower who looks about seventy, but he glides like Fred Astaire. And now and again, another dude named Jorge, who has a slicked-black ponytail, joins us when he's in town. Most weeks, we all get partners, no problem.

"Going to the bar later?" one of the regulars asks.

Peggy and I agree, Annie can't. She's a lawyer and needs to review a case she's defending in court tomorrow. I cut her hair in all kinds of weird places, not only her home, but also her office and once, in the courthouse car park. She's type A—an overachiever, and a perfectionist. She struggles more with tango than even I do. The woman's role is to follow the man's lead. We women all want to take over, do it our way, Annie and Peggy more than most.

It's truly a dance about communication. The guy makes you sense where he wants you to go with a hint of pressure. You can dance in open hold or close hold. Close hold's embarrassing at first. You can feel your partner's muscles flex, his chest rising and falling, the warmth of his thigh, the angle of his hip. My God! It's a sensuous dance, just right for all those passionate Latin Americans.

Why on God's green earth am I so drawn to it? I'm from the cold Northeast, practical, ordinary. Maybe I'm starved of passion since the early days with Brad when he rode me into the sunset, my heart tucked in his motorcycle jacket. I guess tango's drama and intimacy transport me to the Lions' Club dance hall and that starry night.

Nico calls us back to the floor. My partner's Frank, the widower, and Peggy's with Martin, one of Nico's friends. They're having an animated conversation. Martin's kinda cute when he grins, and Peggy's lapping it up. Holy Mother of God, wonder what that's all about. Annie decides to head off so she can concentrate on her brief before turning in. We wave her off, making plans to see her next week.

I do like dancing with Frank. He knows what he's doing, his leads aren't forced, but they're definite, and it feels as if we are dancing with one mind (his). Finally, I get the figure Nico's been teaching. It's a complicated step that ends with me hooking my foot under Frank's knee!

"Bravo!" Frank tells me. If I wasn't already glowing with all the effort and excitement, I'd flush.

"Switch partners!" Nico calls, "We'll end with free dance."

He switches the music and comes over to dance with me. Peggy claims Frank—like me, she enjoys dancing with him, although he's a little quiet for her taste and she still can't entirely resist trying to lead him around the dance floor.

It's even more fun dancing with Nico. I used to feel awkward about it, as I'm a beginner and he's amazing. I'm over that now, and of course, I've improved some. There's a great atmosphere in the room as the music ends with a crescendo. Nico spins me off in a final flourish, and we all laugh and catch our breath.

I hate pulling on layers of winter clothes just to walk across the street to the bar, but it's pretty chilly, in spite of officially being spring. The bar staff like our group. We come in as everyone else is going home, so we extend their hours, but they don't mind. We're in such a good mood from the dancing high, we tip well.

Peggy brings me a glass of water and a margarita. Someone makes the old joke, "margarita Rita!" Peggy gets the same for herself. I'll buy next time. We'll most likely refill the water, but we rarely have more than one cocktail—we're both driving, and there's work to do in the morning. Nico's friends, Martin and Lance, join us. This isn't unusual. It's just a bit surprising no one else does.

After the usual banter, Peggy gets up to refill her water, though she hasn't finished. Lance goes to the Gents, and Martin leans closer to me. I suddenly become aware they're playing "Lady in Red" in the background. Glad I didn't choose my red shirt tonight because I feel awkward and self-conscious.

"I was watching you dance tonight. You looked great. You've improved a whole lot." Then he adds in a rush, "I was wondering, any chance you'd have dinner with me?"

Although he's speaking quickly before the others return, he's fairly relaxed about asking. Jesus! I am not the least bit relaxed about answering, I haven't dated in years. There've been too many responsibilities—I don't think I know what to do. I hadn't thought of Martin or any other of the guys in that way. I probably look like a frightened rabbit. All the same, I manage to blurt out, "Yes, thanks, that'll be nice."

He searches his pocket for a card. "Great! Write your phone number on that, and I'll book something."

I find a pen in the bottom of my purse and scrawl my number. I can't believe I'm shaking. I've taken a glance at the front of the card. He runs a construction company.

No sooner have I pocketed the pen than Peggy comes back with her water. I must be as red as the lady in the song. She gives me a funny, knowing look. Lance returns from the Gents. *Am I imagining it? Is he scrutinizing me?* It's not possible to turn any redder! Lance makes an excuse, then leaves soon afterwards. I'm sure he looks at Martin as he goes ... And yes, he smiles and winks.

Glen

I walk out of class and she's there waiting for me. She's wearing an oversized Peruvian sweater, jeans, and sneakers. She's got that hat on with earflaps matching the sweater even though it's not that cold. I try and flick off the hat, and we chase around teasing one another. I like to see her chestnut hair spread loose on her shoulders.

She lets me brush it now and then and doesn't think I have a hair fetish. Hey, she's wrong about that. I do have a hair fetish, I keep my body smooth shaven, sometimes even my head. Weird, I know—it's what you've gotta do when you're a competitive swimmer. Reduces drag.

I'm here on a swim scholarship. I'm a good enough student, especially math, but Audley might not have looked at me if it wasn't for the swimming. I'm the shortest guy on the team—again! I'm lucky to have gotten the scholarship; they usually look for big guys. I switched to distance when coach realized I wasn't going to get a last-minute growth spurt. It's less popular, so the competition's not as strong.

It's cool being at college on an elite team. We practice early morning and often again in the evenings. Gotta avoid the frat parties. Means I've an immediate group of friends across the disciplines. Thank God! I was wicked shy and overwhelmed when I first got here. Literally, I wouldn't have spoken to anyone if it hadn't been for swimming.

No one has a larger retinue on moving-in day than me. I wish they hadn't all come. It's mega-embarrassing, and I don't want them to notice if I tear up when they leave. There's Mom, Sandip and Astra, Brandi, Melody, and Aunt Monday. She makes it up all the steps to my room, not even huffing and puffing. Apparently (Melody tells me this over the phone), she slept all the way home in the car, snoring gently.

Luckily, my roommate doesn't arrive 'til late in the evening. He's on crew, a humongous guy. We're sharing since he needs to get up early too. They break the ice in the winter. Makes swimming seem like no sweat—okay, we're wet, but we're indoors.

I'm an architecture major. I literally didn't even have to think about it. And they laughed at my Lego models! The models forced me to look hard at buildings—scale, proportion, style, decoration, and all the rest. I developed the math skills to get the scale and the engineering right and, after that, math was a breeze..

"Coffee shop?" Lisa prompts, and I'm cool with it. She wants to tell me about a lecture she's been to by Rasheed Choudary. I'm clueless about him until Lisa explains he's a former president of the UN. I literally pinch myself. This is my life now!

I study architecture in a place super rich in architecture, it's like I time-traveled to an old cathedral city or something. World-class leaders come to speak, there's a stunning girl holding my hand, and it's me, Glen Lenox from nowhere school, nowhere town. My sister went to jail, and my mom was so poor that my sisters gave her all their wages. Fucking insane!

We grab our coffees and blow at them until they cool. Steam spirals, and Lisa blows hers into my face. She's mega excited about the lecture. She's "undeclared" at the moment, maybe political science or finance later. We each have a break before our next class. She knows my schedule better than I do myself.

"Wanna see the Bollywood movie Sunday afternoon? You don't have practice or a meet," she reminds me when she's done obsessing over the lecture.

Works for me. I don't know why Lisa puts up with me. She says she likes that I know who I am! (And hell, I thought she was bright.) She likes being part of a couple and at the same time, having enough freedom to explore her own interests—find out who she is. Friggin' amazing. That's who she is!

A couple of her friends join us at the cracked Formica table. Maybe this is my attraction. She's with me, but I don't crowd her. College relationships get super intense. When they split, guys soon figure out they've no other friends.

"Hey, Lise, tell us how you guys met," Tory asks. She knows the scoop—she's asking for Eric's sake because she wants his attention.

"Well," Lisa says, and you can hear the smile in her voice—she likes telling this one. She looks out of the corner of her eye at me. "It was freshman week. Everyone else seemed to know where they were going, what they were doing, and I felt like a dork because I didn't."

The others smile. They didn't have a clue freshman week either. We were all winging it, faking everything was cool.

"Anyways, I noticed the Indian Society was having a buffet lunch. I was too scared to go to the cafeteria on my own, it seemed ginormous, and I thought everyone'd stare at me sitting all on my own, so the Indian Society was like the easy option."

"You scared, Lise? No way," Tory says. Lisa just nods. Admitting her fears. One of the things I like about her.

"An Indian buffet?" Eric says with fake laughter.

"An Indian buffet lunch!" we parrot back.

"What did you wear—a sari and all?" Eric plays back, unaware Lisa's stepmom's from India..

"No, you loser. So I went to the lunch, and there's, well, Indians there," Lisa says.

"My God! Why am I not surprised!" Eric retorts.

"And there's this one white guy with seriously short hair, looking like a nerd, except he's holding a plate groaning with food, and I ... like, l have to go check him out," she says.

We're all laughing.

Yup. That's the deal. We were the only non-Indians at the Indian Welcome Buffet. I'd gone for the same reasons as Lisa—didn't want to go to the cafeteria on my own. I'd avoided it, and now I was beyond hungry. I'm not as honest as Lisa, couldn't admit I'm a wimp even to myself, told myself I was being smart trying new shit. Bullshit! Whatev, we ate lunch together. I finished way before her.

"Want my naan?" she offered, seeing I was having trouble not stealing it from her plate.

They were clearing away the buffet by the time we left. By then, she knows about Sandip and Astrid and my lame life story. I know her dad's second wife is Bengali, and think Lisa won't want to waste time hanging around me anymore.

"So, Glen, can I like see you again?" she stuttered as we left the center.

Fuck yes! I think, and I say, "Hey, that'll be cool!" Been cool ever since.

After the movie on Sunday, we go back to her room. Jake, the rower's gonna be asleep in mine—he's a party dude. I don't know how he pulls it off. Thank God Lisa's roommates are out. It's a suite for three students, quite spacious compared with mine and Jake's. Lisa's applying for a single next year. She wants her privacy. (Well, shit, our privacy.) We throw off our jackets, and I'm kissing her in the middle of the room. I run my fingers through her hair, and she presses her breasts to my chest. Christ, can she know how that makes me feel?

We break apart and decide to have a little liquid refreshment. While Lisa's in the kitchenette down the corridor, making hot chocolate, I sneak a peek at the girls' clothes. Mostly jeans, sweatshirts, and regular stuff. They all have "best" dresses, and Lisa actually does have a sari. She swears her stepmom made her bring it. I dunno. It's a gorgeous concoction of turquoise chiffon and gold thread. She'll look amazing in it. I stroke the delicate fabric and then hear her coming back with the hot chocolates.

We're not as naïve as you'd think, we spike them with vodka. So, we're under age, and yes, I'll forfeit my scholarship if coach finds out—but hell, you gotta take a risk now and again. Spiked cocoa's nothing compared with what the others do.

As we warm up from the cocoa, we peel off more layers, until she's in her panties and I'm in my boxers. Her fingers caress all the rippling muscles across my chest and back. I'm going crazy as the little hairs around her tight nipples brush my smooth chest. Her breasts are unreal. God! She slips her hand to feel my thigh, and lets it stray to my throbbing penis. Its heat excites her.

She gives it an exquisite squeeze and murmurs, "Hmm, Glen, you ready to go all the way?"

God, yes! I think, moving toward her bed.

The door bursts open, and Esther, one of Lisa's roommates, rushes in. "Oh my God! Sorry. Couldn't you guys get a room?"

We all laugh, and I'm painfully aware I'm bright red—to the tips of my ears.

Sherri

I drop Melody off with Brandi at the stables. We find a wizened old apple for her to give to Andy, the one-eyed pony she rides. Brandi runs a class for disabled kids on Saturday afternoons with another instructor and loads of volunteers. Melody adores everything about it, the horses, the people, the ripe hay, and the smelly poop! She's stronger now, got muscle tone.

I can't help feeling sorry for Brandi. She and Julian still can't afford to board a horse. She rides some of the other boarders when their owners can't exercise them, but it's not the same. Melody showers Brandi with hugs and kisses, "My bestest, super-special Auntie. I love you."

(Don't worry, she says some version of this to Carling when she sees her too.)

Melody marches off to give Andy his apple. She knows just how to do it, approaching from his good eye, and putting the apple flat on her hand. Andy pulls back his velvety, whiskery lips and delicately gobbles up the apple with his big yellow teeth. Melody giggles and giggles, but she's learned not to hug and kiss Andy—too much slobber. We go through our usual parting routine.

"Bye-bye, best Mommy in the wide, wide world!" Melody says.

I won't see her until tomorrow because Aunt Peggy's picking her up and keeping her overnight. I leave the car seat for Peggy and a bag packed with more than everything Melody could possibly want, including the Audley teddy bear Glen sent and a strange toilet roll cover Aunt Mon picked up at a craft sale. Melody plays with it like a glove puppet, forcing her fingers through the holes. She chatters away, inventing a whole adventure about Glen Bear and Prinderella.

I've already changed into my dance gear, and I can't wait! Jeez! Having great childcare is totally awesome. I was this fussy mom at first, feeling guilty and hating to leave my little girl. But she's so safe and super happy.

When I went back to Mom's, it was tough. You know, moving back as an adult when you left as a kid. Remembering all the little ways Mom got on my nerves. Feeling a big fat failure since Micah left. Needing Mom to look after us ... I was one hot mess. Was kinda nice having Glen in the house before he went to college, and it was good for Melody to have her special guy around so she didn't miss her dad so much. I have to say it's bittersweet, watching Glen eat up his freedom. He never fucked up.

Now we've hit a routine, I gotta admit it's a helluva lot easier. No Shepherds spying on me. Mom's always ready to babysit. She takes Melody with her on her hairdressing rounds. Melody's a little star, and they all spoil her rotten. They'll miss her when she goes to school.

She's going to St. Irene's. It's private, and she'll be a year older than the other kindergartners. If it doesn't work out, we'll think again. It's pricey but they're very supportive. Micah agrees it'll be a good fit for Melody—and he's good about sending me money. We have this whole agreement drawn up by a proper lawyer. Broke my heart. I couldn't bear Micah actually going. How the hell could he leave me and Melody? Still stings ... but not so much.

I love that Peggy set up the baby-sitting swap-off. Gives Mom a break, though Auntie Peggy sometimes looks as old as the hills. Swear I'll never be an older mom. When I first got time to myself, can you believe it, I didn't know what to do with it! I wanted to take a Pilates class like Mom. (Pathetic, isn't it?)

There wasn't much on offer on Saturday afternoons, until I found an adult ballet class. Duh! Why didn't I think of that? Wow! I was totally sore. Sure, I'd gained some muscle from picking up Melody and heaving her car seat around, but I'd lost my dance muscles and my flexibility. No way I'd lost my love of dance. It's been about three months since my teacher noticed I have talent. She pulled me aside after class and told me about this avant-garde dance company they're setting up. She invited me to try out.

So it's a more experimental and contemporary style of dance than I've done before—super intense and a whole lot of fun. After the session, we go to each other's homes and watch old movies and drink beer, or just hang. Last week in practice, I was writhing across this guy Ben's knees—we were sea creatures, seaweed and anemones, all tentacles—when he leaned forward and kissed my forehead.

"Great move!" Francesca, our choreographer, yelled, "Keep that in!"

I'm pulling into the studio now. Adult ballet, a break, and then (I can't wait) company practice, when I can guarantee being kissed! Afterwards, Ben and I decided not to hang with the others. We're going to "Lemongrass," the new Thai restaurant that's just opened.

Over dinner, I'll tell him all about Melody—and then I'll know if he's boyfriend material or not.

Aunt Monday

It takes me longer to get the chores done these days. The washing-up's laughing at me from the sink. It'll just have to wait. I need to sit down and catch my breath. What was it that Polish man used to say? "Can't complain," something like that. Who would have thought I'd live this long? If the good Lord spares me, I'd like to last a bit longer.

I want to see Carling successful and happy. She's giving it her all. Comes to see me most weeks and tells me about her coursework.

Nice to have someone who doesn't treat me as if I'm gaga or a little child. We have sandwiches for dinner so there's not too much work or washing up. I hope she can get it into her head she needs to pamper herself. I'm not the world's best role model for that. Well, I suppose I always did buy the lovely lemon soap and the good Irish butter.

It's grand seeing the rest of the family doing so well. Glen at Audley and with a young lady friend too. Sherri's dancing again—always a good sign—and Rita whispered to me that she's going on a date! I didn't quite catch if it's Rita or Sherri going on a date. Good news either way. Brandi's practice manager, and she and Julian have a new place. Little Melody's going to start school in the fall. She may not end up doing rocket science, but she'll do far better. She'll always draw people to her and bring happiness.

And I'm happy with a quiet life. There's women's club lunches on Mondays and then the Council on Aging. They drive me to the grocery store so I can do my shopping. If it gets too much for me, they'll sign me up for the delivery service, at least I won't starve. Sandip and Astra made sure I have handrails at my steps, and tactfully suggested a chairlift for inside the house. I had to swallow my pride—it's going to be installed next week. Hope I figure out how to work it, or it'll be in my way and I'd better not fall trying to push past it!

I'd best keep going to chair yoga to make sure I bounce and don't break my neck if I fall. The yoga teacher's a riot! "Don't let the old lady out!" she chides. Can't she see the wrinkles? I guess I shouldn't think of myself as old—I'm maturing! And there's bridge at the Council on Aging two afternoons a week.

Last Tuesday, something funny and a bit surprising happened. I'd dabbed a bit of rose water behind my ears when I got dressed that day. We were all sitting around looking at our cards when old Father Clemence dropped his. Took him a while to ease himself off his chair, then he went scrabbling around on the floor. We left him to it for a while since your hand's a secret, but he really couldn't manage, so I bent down to help. The chair yoga does have its uses! When we finally picked up the cards and straightened up, he was out of breath and a bit red in the face. The other two had wandered off to the bathroom, no point in hanging around, we couldn't finish the hand.

When he caught his breath, Father Clemence said, "Betty, you do smell nice."

I was taken aback, and then he continued, "I've watched you, Betty, over the years, and I often thought that if I ever was to leave the priesthood, it would be over you!"

Well, I never!

We had a good chuckle over that!

26

Glen and Lisa – 2003

G*len*

Gotta keep my eyes on the road. The clouds are bursting open like floodgates, rain's slooshing down the windshield. These pathetic windshield wipers on this damn U-Haul can't cope. I'll have to pull over until it passes. Hope Lisa's alright, she's driving our car.

We didn't have a car for the longest time. Not much point in New York. When we started making serious money, we bought a secondhand VW bug and rented an ultra-expensive, super inconvenient parking space. We found out even though New York offers us the world, we loved getting out of town! Getting out for good now.

Still can't believe it. We're literally moving to Raven's Creek, Central Mass., maybe forty, fifty miles from Watervale where I grew up. Everyone's stunned at how much the new house cost, but when you've lived in a condo the size of a golf-cart garage for the last six years, at nearly the same price, it doesn't seem too bad. And the new place's well-built. That matters to the architect in me.

Sure, we could've sprung for a removal company, but we had so little stuff. We called up Jake and a coupla other friends, and we'll get it done ourselves. Sherri's Ben and Lisa's brother Ramsay are showing up tomorrow. Won't take long. Tonight, we'll get a good night's sleep at the B and B down the street.

You can guess it's a long drive in a U-Haul. It's got the aerodynamics of a brick, and I've seen slugs with better acceleration! The bug's a race car in comparison.

Hey! No surprise, Lisa's here. Wonder if she went round the house already. I make sure the truck's in park with the safety on, before I jump down. Ouch! Hurts my ankles—must've stiffened up with all the driving. Well, at least it's stopped pissing it down.

"Hey! Mrs. Lenox! How's your new home?"

"Waited for you, Mr. Lenox," she replies, knowing I love her for waiting. (I love her for a whole lot of other things too, never stop pinching myself this beautiful, clever woman's my wife.) She pulls out her keys and fiddles with the lock. You'd never guess a smart woman like Lisa's challenged by locks.

We giggle until the door creaks open. (WD-40'll fix that.) I scoop her up and carry her across the threshold. More giggles. I tried that at our condo after we got back from honeymoon, nearly dropped her—no where near so much fun as this.

We flick on the lights and look around. Yes! It's ours! We live here! We already spent a couple of weekends here—had a sectional delivered, but it feels different now. Inevitably, we both need the bathroom after the trip, and I grin as I remember Lisa brought toilet paper last time we were here. I've always known she's smart!

"Glen, aren't we lucky!" she says, clapping her hands and kissing me! I love how she flips from serious businesswoman, suit, heels, hair up, to my amazing wife, her eyes on fire, her chestnut hair flying.

We've been together since freshman year, graduated together, moved in together in a student apartment even tinier than the condo while I did my post-grad work. I felt bad letting Lisa support me. Luckily, she landed a great job with an ad agency. (And actually, she didn't need luck, she's super smart.) Eventually, I got a junior position with a prestigious architectural firm where I'd done my work experience. I sweated it at first, designing stairwells, elevator shafts, utility access and the like. I did a hell of a lot more complicated and satisfying work as an undergraduate.

When I passed my exams, I got a sweet promotion and, thank God, moved on to interesting projects. Guess you could say, I made it! Me! An architect! Finally, starting to pay off my loans and share the bills. I love sparking ideas off my team. We joke around, but we know how to work our balls off when we have to. I'll sure miss those guys.

The first coupla years Lisa was based in New York. Then she started traveling to clients. I didn't mind it much, working late most nights, and occasionally, I indulged my secret. Lisa spent four years at Audley, waiting for me to towel off after a meet or a practice. Now, it's my turn, waiting for her. When I look back, those early years were mega-stressful. And we made it through. Gonna be way sweeter in our new home.

Lisa

Finally, I see him rumbling up the driveway, a smile flits across his face when he notices me, then he concentrates again, careful to make sure the van's safe. That's my Glen, kind, focused, and extra careful. I turn off the radio, cutting "Do You Know Where You're Going To?" mid-track. Hope that's not bad luck.

I always had a thing for Glen. Wasn't just physical attraction, though. Hell! I adore his sleek, sculpted body, his short, soft, feathery hair, the dancing blue eyes, and his gentle hands even though they reek of chlorine! For an athlete, there's no way Glen's a jock. He's modest about his successes, seems almost surprised by them—well, apart from the out-of-this-world victories, when he leaps up and down like a demented kangaroo. Defeats drive him to train harder or smarter.

Over the years, he's shown his smarts, adapting his swimming, to stay competitive against the bigger guys. What I really love best about Glen's his wonder. It's innocent, childlike. Sweet.

"How can all this be happening to me?" he says, totally awestruck.

No swagger, no "I did it my way." He forgets he's where he is through a boatload of effort, persistence, self-motivation, damned hard slog. He's kinda cute around women. Must be all those sisters and his little niece. Sad, thinking about Melody.

Glen's just Glen—even at Audley, he didn't try to impress me or act different around me. He's his own person, not someone acting like who he thinks he oughta be. I envy him that. I'm still finding myself, business tycoon, outdoors girl, control freak? It's partly why we're making this move. New York was a trip at first. I'd be pitching to rich clients—my ideas taken seriously, leading a team, controlling a budget. Promotion, challenge, respect. A rush for sure, and yet, is that all there is? I wonder what kind of a life we'll build together here?

They all said our relationship wouldn't last, not through college, not living on top of one another in New York, not with me making all the money, and not when I traveled so much. Ha! They were wrong. Sure we had our moments, nasty little spats when my controlling instincts clashed with his competitive ones, but they were triggered by exhaustion. Glen studying too hard to dive into a pool, go for a run, and me, cooped up in the executive suite, missing the pine-laced air of Maine.

We figured out a lotta things together, not only the finances, how to give each other space, when to back off, and the tough stuff, like working through loss. We took up jogging. (Okay, Glen runs when he's not with me, and I power-walk when I'm not with him.) It's something I can do wherever I travel if the weather's good and I don't get lost! Keys and maps aren't my thing. And there's a treadmill jeerimg at me in pretty much every hotel.

We did the New York marathon a few months before getting married. Glen slipping into a training routine easily, super careful not to patronize me slogging along. We didn't have numbers, so we ran for the Williams Society in Melody's memory.

You know, I sometimes think Glen loved Melody even more than me. Bullshit! What am I saying? He loved her differently, but it sure as hell ran deep. She had all kinds of developmental delays and, so what? She was the most engaging child you ever met. Bubbly, happy, bursting into song, hugging you, telling you how much she loved you. Adorable.

Turned out there were physical problems. A constriction of the blood vessels to her heart, I think. The medics should've picked it up when she was diagnosed, but they missed it, or it got a lot worse as she grew. Poor little thing needed surgery—and she didn't make it.

I'm sure Glen cried more than Sherri and Micah (Sherri's ex), though everyone was torn apart. I was scared Glen'd never come to terms with her death and it might be the one thing we couldn't handle together. I didn't know what to do, what to say. I felt guilty for being healthy. Glen was in a trance, and I couldn't reach him, couldn't comfort him. Then, almost in desperation, the whole family connected with the Williams Society and Glen channeled all his grief into doing something to help other Williams kids.

He ran like a crazy man. I hadn't a hope in hell of keeping up. I swear I'm never ever going to run a marathon again. I'm shivering in the holding tent, it's early morning, I'm wearing a rag-bag of clothes over my running shorts, and a garbage bag over all that. Not quite the look I usually aim for. We're all crammed in, and I'm super-nervous. All the others look like runners. I'm hopelessly out of my depth. This is an insane idea.

I raised a lot of money. You have to commit to that for a charity number. Luckily, in advertising you meet some wealthy people. Even so, I strained our pockets and my parents', my brother, old school friends, my childhood dentist—anyone I could think of. Now all these people are counting on me, and am I even ready? I'm the world's biggest idiot deluding myself I can run this, but there's no escape now, I gotta go for it.

It was even harder for Glen to raise the pledge, none of his family makes much—even Carling with her new doctorate. His "Auntie" Peggy (I've never understood that relationship) did her best, and Auntie Pat helped out. Her husband's in the medical profession, and they'd both fallen in love with Melody (who didn't?). Anyways, if it hadn't been for Sandip and Astra, I don't know what Glen would've done.

❖

Eventually, they call my group, and I throw all the rags into the trash bag and give it to volunteers who relay it to dumpsters. Then,

192

you stand about in cohorts, shivering, teeth chattering, thinking it's about time to go home. Finally, the cohorts inch up to the start, and you're off. No one can actually run at the moment, through the huge pack, but after an age, it thins out, and you eat up the miles. "Eat up" is definitely an exaggeration in my case. My feet hurt right from the start, my breathing gasps until I hit a rhythm.

Once I get to the halfway point, I develop a stitch and leg cramps. This is hell. I slow to a walk for about three miles. I'm getting cold, I'm going so slowly. Then, I crawl into the first aid tent, they rub my muscles and give me Gatorade. I drink gallons of it and feel better. I'm jogging again, maybe I can finish this, I let myself believe until I worry about finding a Jiffy John—all that liquid! I've never gone beyond twenty miles before, that nearly killed me, and at twenty-two, I'm about to give up.

I'm so tired, my feet are pulp, I don't think I can go on. Suddenly, Glen's by my side. He finished ages ago and worked his way back to find me. That's how we cross the finish line together, my legs wobbling like spaghetti. There's a photo of us, swathed in a silver cape, hugging and crying. I'm near collapse. Glen had a very respectable finishing time, but being Glen, he asks the officials to register him at my time. God! He's awesome.

◆

As I said, I vowed never to run another marathon. You won't believe it, but I came close to changing my mind almost immediately. My step-mom had breast cancer years ago when I was little. I'm sure she didn't forget about it, but we all had until it came roaring back.

She didn't tell us how sick she was until after the marathon. When we went up to visit for Thanksgiving, she couldn't hide it. Rounds of chemo and radiation had tortured her body and robbed her lustrous hair. Right after Thanksgiving prayer, Glen went down on one knee and proposed! I was speechless! Tears were running down his nose! We were all sobbing our hearts out.

It seems when we arrived the day before, he'd seen how weak Mom was and drove into the village to get to the jewelers before they closed. And I thought he was buying a toothbrush! I didn't tell him I'd almost given up hope of getting married—hey, what girl doesn't dream of her wedding?

"I love you Glen, you, you pea-brain! Yes!" I sobbed when I got my voice back.

He looked a bit sheepish, whatever that looks like. "Lisa, Lisa ... God, Lisa! I'm a lucky bastard!"

I'd dreamed of a fairytale wedding—at the beach, under a bluer-than-blue sky, the waves rolling in the background. Seagulls wheeling above us, not making deposits, photos by the lighthouse, violins ...

It was a bitter cold January day. We got married in the living room of my family home. Now and again, we watch the shaky video Sherri filmed. We always cry seeing my step-mom propped in a recliner, her tiny body in a sari nearly hidden beneath the exquisite mohair shawl Rita crocheted.

I smile when I see my dress. It came from the Macy's sale. No time for a fitting. It's a skimpy, strappy number left over from the summer. Not at all the dress of my dreams. The camera jerks and gives a clear shot of the ceiling. No water stains! We watch the pastor walking towards the front windows, stroking Mom's hand as he passes. He joins Glen, my brother Ramsay (Glen's best man), and Zephyr, my bridesmaid (from high school days). They're shoulder to shoulder, looking self-conscious.

I remember wondering how Dad and I were going to fit in, too. Sherri jerkily pans the room to catch Glen's family squeezed in between the dining chairs and the hutch. The camera sweeps to the kitchen where Dad and I are waiting together with Ben and Ramsay's girlfriend, who can't fit anywhere else. I take Dad's arm, shivering in the flimsy dress, and nerves kicking in. We're ready to walk down the aisle we've made through the open-plan living and dining room. With a great jolt, Sherri turns to Glen. Everything's out of focus except the tear dripping off his nose!

The camera bounces around and the world turns upside down as Sherri moves to the front to film our procession. You can't see Dad squeezing my hand or hear him say, "Love you, Lisa."

There's a burst of background noise, then Ben starts singing Noel Paul Stookey's "Wedding Song." Soon, they all join in. The sound quality in the video's awful, but as they sing, "There is Love," tears glisten and Dad and I walk down the aisle.

Later, when we're alone, between kisses, Glen whispers, "That was an awesome wedding. Thank you for being my awesome wife! I thought I'd never dare ask!"

He can always melt my heart, and right then, I realize it was the most awesome wedding. Way better than in my dreams.

Our honeymoon's nothing like the romantic ideas I'd dreamed up either. No gondola in Venice, no frescos in Florence, ruins in Rome. We stayed in Maine, to be close to Dad and Mom, spending a few days skiing! Glen's never skied before, so there were lots of laughs … Causing a pile-up at the ski lift, some spectacular falls, too scared to turn, zooming into the glade.

All the same, he's a natural athlete—I guess his dad played football, maybe that's where he gets it. It didn't take him long to chase me down the easy slopes, but he was no match for "Maine-iac Lisa" on the black diamonds.

We splurged on the best hotel on the slopes. A modern take on a log cabin, open fires everywhere, even in the bedrooms. After skiing, we jumped into the hot tub. Glen pretended to be a giant squid making the little kids squeal.

Steam spiraled into the air, and we gazed at the myriad stars sparkling in the sky. Everything smelled of pine and Glen's favorite scent—chlorine! The moon hung like a mirror, and snow crystals vibrated in its light. When we headed to our room—I'll draw the curtains here, except to say we were warm, cozy, tenderly active, and toasted our marriage with hot chocolate spiked with vodka!

Honeymoon over, we stopped at home. Mom's bed had been moved to the living room, the furniture rearranged after the wedding. Dad had the bed face the windows so Mom could watch the firs sway in the wind. We sat on her bed, she had shrunk to almost nothing. Dad, his eyes moist, told me how much she loved our wedding, and when I held her hand, her fingers felt for my ring. She relaxed as she touched it, she'd no energy to speak. Darling Glen offered for us to stay until she passed, but Dad wanted to be alone with her.

"Goodbye, I love you." My last words to her.

The phone call came a week later. Glen held me and stroked my hair as the tears fell.

Glen

Can you believe it, we're all moved in! I guess I'll get used to it, but we have so much space. You can take a long walk around our house. And the yard—unbelievable! Our own maples, a blue spruce, rhododendrons, azaleas, space to kick a ball around. Wow! I blink at it all and when I open my eyes, I see a swing set and a coupla kids running around!

27

Brandi – To 2005

I t's a raw morning, the type that cramps your fingers even with riding gloves. Steam's rising in funnel clouds from Malachite's flanks and nostrils. I guess if I pause to think, I'm sending out wispy smoke signals of my own. We already had a dusting of snow this season, but today, it's just frost. I try not to tense or transfer my nervousness to Malachite, who's clearly enjoying the ride, and as it's Thanksgiving, it's all he's going to get today. I can't help being hyper-vigilant for ice ever since the accident.

The trail's wide, passing through a mix of pines and deciduous trees. A flurry of birds rises from a copse as we approach, a late chipmunk darts out across our path. The sky's a pale, yet sharp, winter blue, with a lemon-drop sun breaking through. This is the best part of the day as far as I'm concerned.

Later, we'll be cooped up inside, stomachs groaning with food and drink, then we'll snooze in front of the game, or try to entice the kids to separate from their game console and play something more sociable, poker perhaps. And I'll feel a bit odd. It's the second Thanksgiving without Julian.

We're approaching where it happened. Where the trail divides and the left fork borders the road. I nudge Malachite down the ill-fated track. Straightaway, we hear the hum of traffic. Subdued, likely due to the holiday—only a low rumble. No screeching brakes, sickening skids, no sudden smash, splattered glass, that metallic burning smell, the hanging silence, and then the wail of sirens—like that time. Today, we carry on scrunching dried-up pinecones and pounding leaf litter as we go.

That other time, I was riding Orion, who's very steady. As the sirens screamed, he reared, spooked. Normally, I might have held him, calmed him down, but I'd been feeling queasy, not quite myself. My reactions were a tad slow, my muscles weak. I felt his hoof catch a pocket of ice, the metal shoe clinking as it made contact. We lurched violently, and then we were down.

I fell punishingly hard, landing on my hip and elbow. My head ricocheted against the frozen ground. I was likely out for a second or two. When I came around, Orion had scrambled up and was ambling off in the direction of the pond. I took my time, sitting for a while, my head spinning, before I attempted to stand. I felt really shaky, but as far as I could tell, nothing was broken and, at least, Orion was up and walking, a good sign. (Today, I have my cell phone with me so if anything happens and I have signal, I can get help, but they weren't so common then.)

Fearing more black ice, I picked my way toward the pond. Orion had already calmed down. I looked him over. He let me run my hands over his legs and withers, but bending low made my head swim, so it wasn't a very thorough check. He seemed to be in better shape than me. I didn't dare mount him, because my hip hurt so bad, and I worried I might be concussed. It took a long time—we'd gone some distance before the fall. I was feeling pretty sorry for myself, until it crossed my mind that someone might've been killed in the traffic accident. All the same when I made it back to the barn, I was weak, Jell-O-legged, and totally nauseated. Thank God, Gretchen was there, almost ready to take a last-minute ride.

"Brandi! What happened?" A note of hysteria rose in her voice as she secured Orion.

I remember swaying and hitting the straw, the sweet, sickly smell of ordure, then the rancid smell of vomit. My vomit. From the fog of my faint, I might have registered Gretchen and the barn girl talking about calling an ambulance, deciding it'd be quicker to take me in the Jeep.

I came round as they were loading me into the Jeep. A searing pain seized my belly, and I felt the blood. Then nothing.

———————◆———————

Later, I feel the crisp sheets pulled taut, sniff the disinfectant. Julian's here bending over my hospital bed. His lovely face is stretched taut. He kisses my brow and squeezes my hand.

"Sweetheart," he chokes, "Brandi, I love you."

And then, in a tight little whisper, "Brandi, the nurses said you might not realize you had a miscarriage."

Tears roll down his cheeks as he squeezes my hand again, harder this time. I feel the pressure but not the pain—there's too much pain scouring my mind.

Had I known? Just before I passed out, did the realization pierce the fog? Most of the fog's evaporated, leaving a light, medicated haze—and I sure know now. I wish I were unconscious again. I want to be in Julian's arms. I want to wake up from this nightmare. My body howls at the vacuum inside me. Julian strokes my hair, my face damp with his tears. I want to sit up and let him hold me.

"You have to lie down. You're concussed and you have some awful bruises. They want you to lie still," he tells me.

I close my eyes. Tears shower my face like rain, and I begin to convulse with sobs.

A nurse appears. I'm given a mild sedative, and thankfully I sink into dreamless sleep. The next time I wake, Mom's here. She smells of nicotine, and it makes me slightly nauseous as she brushes her lips against my cheek. I'm propped up against a hill of pillows now, so our eyes meet. There's no stopping the tears.

Nothing's fuzzy anymore—I am too aware that I lost the baby. It helps to cry with Mom, to talk about it, spill it all (well, not all). She hadn't known I was pregnant. We hadn't told anybody just yet. I was two and a half months along, and there wasn't even a telltale bulge.

I'd felt queasy, out of it. I had no other symptoms, not even the terrible tiredness some of my friends talk about. And believe me, I'd heard way too many pregnancy stories. We decided to wait to share the good news until the early, critical months were past. And they almost were. I don't know if we really feared I'd miscarry. I don't know if we actually planned not to tell anyone if I did. How could we imagine it would ease our pain? I guess we didn't think we'd handle the pity.

Even Mom couldn't truly know how much I wanted this baby. Julian and I'd been married forever. At first, there was no question of a baby. We saw what it did to Sherri and Micah. We'd no money. And we needed time to get used to being together.

A nurse in the hospital comes over. She sits on my bed and wipes away my tears and makes me blow my nose.

"I know you can't hear this yet. This happened to me—well, without the concussion. I had a miscarriage, and within a year I was pregnant again. I've got a little boy—he runs me ragged. There's no reason why that can't happen for you."

Well, with as disengaged a lover as Julian, I know there are plenty of reasons. After the miscarriage, he has all the more excuses to keep away from me, claiming he doesn't want me to "get hurt." It was months and months before he touched me again.

◆

Time passed.

Julian's promoted again. He loves his job, whatever it is he does all day, peering through ever more powerful microscopes.

Dr. Dean and Dr. Shirl have retired. They were as good as their word, and the new vets kept me on as practice manager. Odd at first, getting used to other people's ways. Dr. Jack and Dr. Zach (yes, confusing—especially over the phone) went to veterinary school together and bought the practice. After a year, they hired another vet, Dr. Leroy, two veterinary nurses, and an assistant for me.

We're where it's at. The whole town brings their animals to us. We have all the latest technology, and the vets are hot on research. I nearly went bald when we computerized the records. Now, it all runs itself—most of the time! And finally, I'm not the only one cleaning up the pee and poop all the time.

Jack and Zach figured out I can do lots of stuff, as well as running the office. Although I've taken a bunch of courses, I'm not a registered veterinary technician. Even so, they joke around calling me "Dr. Brandi" and telling Dr. Leroy he's got to listen to me. Now and then I go with them on their rounds—especially if it's a sick horse.

There's the downside of being part of a team. We all had to clean up after Dr. Zach poured charcoal into a baby goat who'd gobbled up poisonous leaves. Just like a baby goat! It's supposed to induce vomiting, but this little goat exploded, spraying black bile over the walls, the ceiling, the cabinets, and the floor! The baby goat was fine—just shook his head in surprise. We all pitched in to clean up the mess, except Dr. Zach, who had a sudden emergency to attend!

Somehow I resisted bringing any of the strays home, until the day a litter of the sweetest kittens was abandoned on our stoop. Their little squeaks and hopeful eyes were adorable, and they must have some Burmese in the mix, judging from their velvet coats. I always wanted a Burmese.

No, I didn't take the whole litter, just a tiny female with an odd-looking ear. Julian fell deeply in love, naming her Rhapsody for her blue, blue eyes. After two days with Julian sneezing and sneezing, I had to bring her back to the office. Seems Julian didn't know he's allergic. My chin quivered when the new owners took Rhapsody away.

Life with Julian's always laid back. What he lacks in passion, he makes up for in kindness. He loves surprises! One birthday, I arrived home smelling of dogs and guinea pigs (better than Chanel if you ask me.)

"Get changed, sweetheart!" and he whisks me into Boston for dinner with Ben, Sherri, and Melody. They're in on it, and Melody thinks it's a blast Julian kept me in the dark.

"Surprise! Surprise!" she shrieks, rushing for a hug as we enter the restaurant, "Aunt Brandi, Aunt Brandi, we're going to the ballet." She does a practice twirl, and the other diners melt.

Everything about *The Nutcracker*'s spell-binding. The theater gleams with gilt and glass chandeliers, and the ballet's exquisite. My favorite's the Coffee Dance, but Melody loves watching the Christmas tree grow. "Let's get one like that for our house!" she tells Sherri and Ben. Any time spent with Melody's special, but that night is super-special. (We'd no idea it would be one of the last before she passed, poor angel.)

She sparkles—and I mean sparkles—like a whole galaxy of stars. She's wearing a darling dress Mom made her from navy satin. At the interval she pirouettes and twirls in the main lobby, gathering a little crowd of admirers.

"Young lady, you'd best audition for Clara next year!" a fan tells her. She rewards him, to his surprise and delight, with a Melody-sized bear hug!

Another time, Julian comes home on Friday night, tells me we've got weekend plans and to pack a bag. We go to an inn on the North Shore, where the entertainment's gliding! I had no clue how much I'd love this. It's so peaceful up there, like floating. Toy town below or out over the ocean—you ride the wind differently offshore.

We spend a nice evening at the inn, sipping merlot and holding hands. When we go to bed, I'm sure Julian'll want to make love celebrating the weekend—and it's a good time of the month for me. Why haven't I got used to this? He just rolls over and says good night.

◆

We move across the tracks, to a dated duplex. There are two bedrooms, so I kind of assume one's for a nursery when we get round to starting a family. Amazingly, we have enough money to enjoy ourselves, two second-hand cars, and a new guitar for Julian, who's playing in a band.

There are five of them altogether, a gay couple, another man, and a female vocalist. You can hardly see her body for the tats. Romany told me she has them all over (I mean all over) a kinda stylized Japanese scene complete with cherry blossoms, a pagoda, and Mount Fujiyama—the crater's her asshole. Cringe at the thought. Hell, whatever turns you on. She sings with an ethereal, breathy voice that's out of this world.

Then, finally, I'm pregnant again. Julian came home in a super-good mood after band practice—been jamming with Taz—and I plied him with fine wine (judging by the price). He was so mellow he didn't roll over that night.

By the morning I know I'm pregnant! I just know. As soon as it's possible to get tested, it's confirmed. I'm ecstatic. My gynecologist assures me everything's fine, and the baby will come early in the summer. Julian's blown away, and pleased in a stunned, cautious kind of way. I bombard him with baby names, baby clothes, baby books, baby gear.

"What are we going to do if the baby doesn't sleep? Cloth diapers or disposables? What if it doesn't take to the breast? Hey, I found this super-cool car seat, shall I buy it? God, Julian, I'm scared of giving birth! It's gonna be awesome going to the playground, isn't it? You okay with a pacifier? How about preschool?"

After he storms out to go jam with his buddies, it dawns on me I gotta back off. He needs time to warm to the idea of being a dad. I hold everything back and follow his stupid advice not to let anyone know right away. I carry on as normal, except I don't go riding in the woods.

I'm heartbroken when this pregnancy ends the way of the first—without an accident to blame. Just like Julian wanted, I didn't tell anyone again, feeling somehow ashamed, until we visited Glen and Lisa.

Lisa and I are walking in the park without the guys. Julian and Glen always get on well together, and they're off to check out the latest grills and smokers. Lisa's looking a bit down, not her usual self.

"You alright, Lise? You seem a bit quiet."

"Oh, everything's fine," she starts to say, but her voice quakes and suddenly she's sobbing her heart out.

Turns out, she just had her last round of IVF, and it failed. She's a lot younger than me, and boy, do I feel her tragedy. We're hugging each other, there's a reservoir of tears, and we're shaking with sobs.

"Oh, Lisa, I didn't know," I stammer. "Oh God! Lisa, I just lost a baby!"

We're almost propping one another up as we cry. It's so sad and so comforting to hold each other, even if the passers-by give us funny looks.

Time's ticking on for Julian and me—we're not kids anymore, we've settled down. Time's ticking on for the rest of the family too.

Sherri and Ben adopted twin boys from Korea. Although the odds of Sherri having another child with Williams Syndrome are infinitesimal, especially with a different partner, she couldn't face it. She trained as a special ed teacher for children with disabilities and, inevitably, she's good at it. She does it partly in honor of Melody, and partly because she loves the kids. She couldn't do it without Ben. Thank God they found each other.

I hint to Julian that we should think about adoption too. He's caught off guard, color rising up his throat when he says, "I'm sorry, Brandi. Unless it's our baby, yours and mine, I can't love it the way a parent should."

I'm shocked. I've seen Julian with plenty of little kids. He's sweet, silly, and natural with them. I have to wonder if I've been missing something that's been glaring me in the face.

And then I can't miss it ...

We're run off our feet at work, short-staffed, short-tempered. Leroy is out sick, and the vets are lurching from one emergency to another. Everything gets rescheduled over and over. It's not going down well with the owners, who transfer their frustrations to their pets. The office's full of growls, snarls, and hissing. The same's true of the human animals!

Anyways, a call comes in. A deer's thrashing about in the scrubland at the outskirts of town. She's got tied up in some wire, and she's panicking. Dr. Jack offers to hold down the fort and keep working through the list of cases we can't turn away.

"Brandi, I'm going to need you and Les," Dr. Zach calls.

We leave Zoe, my assistant, in charge of the office, grab our things, and head out. This is the kind of thing vets don't get paid for, but it certainly makes for an exciting time, and I'm glad to be included. We pile into the Land Cruiser. We're amped up and a bit tense—this is a wild animal out of control, could spell danger.

A guy from Fish and Wildlife flags us down. He looks freaked. The deer's a doe, thank goodness, with fencing wire wrapped around her rear leg. Her eyes stare wildly, and every time she thrashes, she tightens thewire, driving it deeper into her leg. The Fish and Wildlife guy suggests we shoot a tranquilizer dart, but Dr. Zach's worried that might stimulate cardiac arrest. She's getting crazier and crazier, and Zach's concerned one kick of her hoof will slice into our flesh.

Time's short, Zach tells us the plan. As soon as she's even a little calm, the two men tackle her, and I'm ready with the wire cutters. Les squirts antibiotic spray over the wound. It's over in an instant and we all spring back letting her go. Bucking and lurching, she's back on her feet and bolts away toward the bushes. As long as the wound doesn't get infected, she's got a good chance.

My whole body's alive with adrenaline and, for a moment, we're pacing about, laughing, high-fiving, and taking great gulps of air. Super-charged. I feel better than at any time since the miscarriage.

As we park back at the office, Zach takes a good look at me and Les. We're both covered in mud and leaves. There's a feral animal scent coming from us that we hadn't noticed until now, and I'm drenched in antibiotic spray.

"You guys go home—it's been quite a day," Zach tells us, (though in truth, he's in worse shape than us.)

It's a couple of hours before my usual time. He's right, we can't work in this state. I need a long, soapy shower and to throw my clothes in the wash.

I should've noticed Julian's car on the street—not in its regular spot, not far off—but I'm heady with the adrenaline rush, and I don't register it. I unlock the door and undress to my underwear, tossing my clothes in the washer before going upstairs.

Our bedroom door's closed ... hmm, that's odd—we usually leave it open ... and what's that noise? I burst in, and there's my husband and Taz from the band. They're both naked, and it's obvious they've just sprung apart. They have that deer-frozen-in-the-headlights look. Should be the stuff of comedy, two naked men and one woman in her underwear. Of course, it isn't. It's the stuff of tragedy.

My tragedy.

28

Rita, Carling, Glen – Thanksgiving 2005

"Hey, Mom! Happy Thanksgiving!" Brandi greets me, juggling a homemade pumpkin pie, a tub of vanilla ice cream, and her signature cranberry relish. She sets it all down safely in Pat and Phil's enormous gourmet kitchen. We hug each other. She's looking good, rosy cheeks, a sparkle in her eyes, some stray wisps of hair flying from her ponytail.

"Been out for a ride?" I ask, and she nods with a smile. *Thank you, God!* I think.

Last Thanksgiving, she was sending out "don't touch me" vibes, and even though she looked at you, she barely saw you through haunted eyes. Poor baby, she was hurting so bad. Oh, Brandi! It's not as if I guessed about Julian. Now when I think about him, I see all the treats, the outings, the trips, were his way of making up for not loving her the way she deserves.

"God, Mom! There's no space in the fridge," she says, putting the pie and the relish by the sink and taking the ice cream to the freezer in the butler's pantry—funny name, even Phil and Pat don't run to a butler. On her way back, Brandi can't resist scratching behind Puzzle's ears. He's Pat and Phil's arthritic dog.

"How're you doing, old boy?" she asks, "Gonna be a bit wild here today." He wags his tail, already begging for scraps.

Pat spots Brandi. "My, my—you look good enough to eat. Met someone special yet? Or you want me to fix you up?"

Typical Pat! It's a mark of how far Brandi's come that she laughs it off. "Happy Thanksgiving, Aunt Pat, did you forget I've sworn off men?"

"Sworn off men?! Good God! There's no way I'm swearing off men—hey, darling." Pat laughs as Phil sidles up, draping his arm across her hips.

Ooh! He's giving her butt a squeeze. A cheeky look sweeps across his face, and Pat's smothering a squeal. She's wearing kitten heels and a pink silk dress. (Pink in November, for heaven sakes!) Phil, a good bit older, is conventionally dressed in gray pants, a blue checked shirt, and an exquisite gray sweater—merino wool, I'd guess.

Time to baste the turkey. It's my specialty—that and fixing the gravy. The bird's huge this year, almost too heavy for me to lift out. Jesus! It smells divine! We've a big crowd today, tables set up everywhere. Tessa's kids watch me struggle, and Carolina comes over to help me drain the fat.

They're already devouring chili con queso, trailing queso all over the counter. We wrestle the turkey back into the oven, and I join them. How can they eat so much and stay slim? The cooking smells make me ravenous. I dip a chip into the queso, a cheesy thread drips down my chin—it's so good! Brandi moves over to sample it, too.

"When d'you say Sherri's coming, Mom?" Brandi asks.

I register the question. Not sure if it's tough for her to be around the twins, when she doesn't have kids of her own.

"They're hoping to make it in time for dinner. Depends on the boys' naps," I tell her.

Wham! The kitchen explodes! Jesus, Joseph, and Mary! Oh, hell! The queso bowl slips off the counter, smashing on the tile floor and splattering warm, sticky queso all over the place, including Brandi's pie, and there's a million glass daggers. I grab Puzzle's collar before he walks through it, spreads it everywhere and cuts his paws.

"Carolina, Juanita, Sam! Don't just sit there! You gotta clean this up! Quick!" I yell at the kids.

They stare at me as if I just dropped in from Mars, as if cleaning's a totally alien concept. Carlos appears, says something in Spanish, and they get right to it. This is a new side of Carlos. You'd think he's a big kid himself most of the time. Evidently, they know who's boss.

Puzzle is a bit puzzled to be dragged outside, but nothing fazes him these days. The house is in an upscale development, so upscale I mistook these homes for mini-hotels when they were first built. It's on a rise, with a view over the golf course. Phil's home before he met Pat. I'd have bet she wouldn't like living in another woman's house. Wrong! All she needs is a lavish redecorating budget.

Makes my little ranch seem like a joke. Suits me, and I have it to myself now unless Martin's over. He's a good guy, we dance together (in more ways than one), travel together, stay over when we want to. Both of us like it this way—Mary, Mother of God! Listen to me ... What became of the good Catholic girl I used to be in some other life? I light a cigarette—another sin. I'm doomed.

"What you doing out here, Reet? It's cold!" Peggy says, climbing out of her car. She's balancing a couple of casseroles and a stick of French bread.

Quickly, I stub out the cigarette, take the casseroles from her, put them down, and give her an extra-long hug. The French bread's pretty limp afterwards. The bread-crushing hug's because of Danny.

He's joined the Navy, doing basic training. It's Peggy's first Thanksgiving without him, she's gotta miss him. If the Navy doesn't kill him, it'll save him. He crashed Peggy's car last spring, totaled it—and he's going through his smoking and drinking stage. (Why didn't I "go through" my smoking stage? Everyone else quit.)

I fill her in on the queso crisis. We're all cold out here on the stoop—even Puzzle's shivering, and he begins to paw at the door. We pick up the casseroles and turn to go in, when a taxi draws up.

Carling

OMG! Pat's new place is amazing! I thought the taxi driver was taking me to the wrong house, but there's Mom ... who's she with ...oh yes, it's Aunt Peggy. They haven't seen me yet. Why're they outside? It's freezing.

"Hey, Mom, Peggy, Happy Thanksgiving!" It's cute, watching their reactions.

Mom's jaw drops until it just about hits her knees, and then she screams, "Carling!"

Peggy has some presence of mind and brandishing a bent stick of bread, says, "Wow! Happy Thanksgiving, Carling!"

Then the others are all at the door (my sisters were in on this, and word must've gotten around), they yell, "Surprise!"

Mom's hugging me fit to crack a rib! She thought I couldn't get away from Denver. I've a few private clients, I teach one class, but mostly, I work at the prison. Told Mom I couldn't get away over the holidays—tough times for inmates.

Mom's probably got a thousand questions, but all she can manage is, "Carling! Carling!" And occasionally, "Carling, you're here."

We haven't seen each other in a couple of years. It really is difficult to get away.

Pat's house is a palace. They should feature the kitchen in a magazine. I'm hanging there with Brandi, Glen, and Lisa, and a whole bunch of other guys. My mouth's watering at the roast turkey aroma when Peggy nudges Mom. "Time to check the bird, you don't want Carling to get a burnt offering."

I'm too much in the thick of things to break free and help out. The fat spits and hisses, and as Mom eases the enormous turkey pan out of the oven, there's a rush of steam and heat. Then the front door bursts open. Two adorable little boys charge in. They launch themselves at Mom's back, shouting

"Mimi, Mimi!"

Mom wobbles, and before Ben can pry the boys off—you've guessed it, she drops the turkey.

Maybe not best to feature the kitchen in a magazine right now, dripping with grease! By some miracle, after its short, abortive flight, the turkey lands right side up on the newly cleaned floor. Mom, only a touch splattered, gets up and reunites turkey with pan, saying, "Thirty-second rule!"

Scared, the boys are wailing and are now in Sherri's arms. In the pandemonium, we rush to help, slipping on the floor. Pat's screaming directions, but it's Peggy and Pat's husband Phil who take over, banning the rest of us from the kitchen while they clean up the mess. Phil strips off his sweater, and Peggy grabs an apron. Tessa's kids've made themselves scarce. I guess cleaning a kitchen once in a day's more than enough for them.

Later, the meat's really delicious, what little I get of it wedged at the kids' table with Theo, Teddy, Ben, Sherri, and Mom. They clearly adore their Mimi, but they can't get it into their heads that I'm her daughter just like their Mom and Auntie Brandi. Once I've coaxed them into eating a few bites of food, pretending the spoon's an airplane, or a rocket, or a train about to land in their mouths, I'm a fave too.

"Come play, Auntie Carwing," they beg. So we bundle them up, take Puzzle and a ball, and head outside. They're awfully cute boys, happily immersed into our family. The professional psychologist in me hopes it will stay that way, at the same time, I know one day they'll inevitably have questions about their birth family, who they are, where they come from. Fingers crossed that'll all work out when the time's right.

Glen

"Lise, you full yet?"

"Not so's I can't squeeze in a piece of pie with those intriguing cheese tendrils," she replies.

I don't think I can swallow another mouthful, but I get her a slice. Been a surprisingly good Thanksgiving. I'd doubts when I heard how many Pat invited, typical Aunt Pat, loves a party. Didn't feel at all bad about bringing Lisa's dad. He's having a ball chatting with new friends. And the Carling factor's priceless! Mom's face! And her tears. Used to get on well with Carling, wish she was nearby. It's good to see her again.

When Lisa's done with her pie, we decide we'll help clear up. Everything was delicious, and all we did was bring wine and beer. We're delivering the first stacks of plates to the kitchen, where Peggy's already rinsing and loading the dishwasher. Mom stops us.

"Those can wait! Come sit down with me—you too Peggy, you've done too much clearing up already. I've hardly had a minute to visit with you guys all day," says Mom.

We gather round the mahogany dining table where Brandi's chatting with Sandip and Astra. Before long, Mom starts asking Peggy about Danny. Yup, I thought it's odd he's not here. I lost track—maybe Mom told me he joined the Navy. It'd gone clear out of my mind. Distracted by in vitro worries and other stuff.

"D'you have that picture of Danny in his whites?" Mom's only got to ask, and Peggy's fumbling in her pocketbook for what turns out to be a large photo.

"So handsome!" Mom sighs, passing it round. After a lot of oohs and ahs, it makes its way to me. I'm so shocked, I'm speechless.

"Anything the matter?" Lisa asks in an undertone.

Everything's the matter. I stutter, "God! He's grown up, looks great in uniform." And I pass the picture along as fast as I can.

I cannot believe the idiot I've been all these years. The lighting in the picture, combined with the white uniform and Danny's cropped hair, shows planes and angles of his face I never noticed before. I'm the biggest dickhead! Danny's no random lovechild. He's my half-brother. And I'm sure everybody else figured it out years ago.

I can't look Aunt Peggy in the eye. I feel Brandi and Mom's eyes boring into me. To hide my confusion, I tell Lisa, "Let's get on with clearing-up, your dad'll want to go home soon."

She's about to protest since her dad's clearly having a blast, but with the tiniest glance she reads my face, and nods, "Sure, time to do the dishes, we'll need to hit the road before long."

I'm surprised I don't drop the dishes. My mind's racing the whole time we're clearing up—and it takes forever, we used all the plates and bowls in the entire universe. Danny. Danny. Dad's son! And Mom joined at the hip with "Aunt" Peggy. How the hell had that happened? How come I didn't figure it out before? What planet am I on? Mom's giving me furtive looks. I'm sure she figured out I only *just* figured it out. What a dufus!

Leaving's not easy, we have to divide up the leftovers, and although most of the neighbors have already left, there's all the lingering goodbyes with family, especially Carling. I'm totally wiped when we make it to the car.

"Hey, what's going on?!" Lisa asks as soon as we edge away.

I tell her.

There's silence, then both Lisa and her dad yell, "Oh my God! Oh my God!"

29

Lisa and Carling – 2009

Lisa

It's surreal.

"Mr. and Mrs. Lenox, did you decide on the two embryos?" the technician queries, her voice flat. She's said this so many times, it's routine for her. Not for us, even though we've been down this path before. How do you choose between one cluster of cells and another? We're picking our children, for God's sake, isn't it a serious decision? Will this one be a genius or a serial killer? And more to the point, will they choose us? Will we pick the lucky winners who'll burrow into my womb, develop normally, grow to term?

Christ! We've been here before, clinging to the hope that these living cells will become our child. And then, nothing, no baby. Failure, the ultimate rejection. Glen and I choose one each, trying to stifle the flicker of excitement, knowing we'll likely be torn apart again.

This is definitely our last round of IVF. We thought we were done with three. The preparation, the procedures—they're relentless. I can cope with the physical toll, it's the emotional cyclone that gets me—and Glen. And it's the ultimate passion-killer. Don't imagine "making a baby" this way is romantic! Forget the candles and the soft music, cue the sterile (sick joke, ha-ha) clinics, the monitors, the white coats, and gloved fingers. And, no matter what, there's the bill.

We can't come to terms with not being parents. We've a good life, yet there's a hole in it deep enough to reach China. Work, sports, community—they're all substitutes for what we want most, a little Lisa, a little Glen.

"Y'know, Lisa, we can be around kids without being parents. Don't know where I'd be if it weren't for Sandip and Astra," Glen says.

He's grasping at straws. It's no help. It doesn't take away the hollowed-out feeling we have. Perhaps we oughta talk with someone. Hard to know who.

Sherri can tell us about adoption—not ready for that. And my brother Ramsay, he's got five kids. He wouldn't understand. He's nearly bald, has dark circles under his eyes like a sad old spaniel. He walks around with bits of cloth diaper on his shoulder to soak the spit-up, he forgets to lose them when he goes to work. Doubt he can speak in full sentences anymore. Lucky bastard.

Glen's aching for a baby as much as me. He'll be one helluva dad. Remember how he was with Melody? If we do ever have a child, I'll be lucky if she even notices she's got a mom.

A mom?

Now, it's definitely surreal! The doctor's looking at the ultrasound with us. A lot of milky waves. The tests confirmed I'm pregnant, and Glen and I are holding our breath. Glen thinks he spots a frog in there—is that a fetus? It's early, and the ultrasound's so fuzzy. The doctor agrees froggy's a baby, a real baby! He can't find another in the swirling depths of me, so it looks as if only one embryo implanted. Even one's a miracle.

I've never been pregnant before. We're amazed and terrified, stunned, overwhelmed, deliriously happy, panicked. Are there any emotions we don't feel? The doctor shakes Glen's hand—that's too little a gesture for this moment, and Glen gives him a bear-hug, smashing his stethoscope into his sternum and squeezing the air out of him. I'm sure he heaves a sigh of relief when we leave.

"Let's tell everyone!" Glen bursts out. "I'm so tired of burying our pain. I think it's worth the risk."

I'm not so sure. We wait until the next ultrasound when it's absolutely certain there's just one baby, and then we share the news.

I'm terrified it'll jinx the pregnancy, put extra pressure on us, make us feel we've failed others as well as ourselves if I lose this baby.

When we tell them all, it makes a whole load of people super-happy. We realize we've a community of people there for us. Who want to share our joy and who, in most cases, will stick with us if we have to go through more pain.

On the downside, everyone nags Glen to look after me. I already feel as if he's wrapping me in cotton wool, padding me with bubble wrap, and treating me like a feeble-minded invalid who can't be allowed to lift a finger. He doesn't want me to go upstairs, climb into an SUV, or stand on a stepstool in case "the baby drops out!" I want to scream as, in fact, I feel good—no morning sickness, no fatigue, completely able to carry on my daily life and be in charge of my own body.

The weeks and months creep by. Glen adores stroking my belly, and it's not all about the baby, he strokes my hair too, showers me with kisses, makes love tenderly since the doctors assured him it won't hurt "Algernon." We'd nicknamed the bump "Algie" or "Algae" for short (well, he did look like a frog at first). I have second thoughts about this. I've heard of couples who named the bump and weren't able to think of any other names after the baby's born.

We photograph Algernon from every angle. I expected to feel horrible about being fat, but all I can do is celebrate this new life growing inside me. I let strangers pat Algernon—a complete invasion of my personal space, but I don't care. After the first few months, Rita's crocheting up a storm, and Ramsay and Sherri are showering us with advice and hand-me-downs.

I'm thirty-seven weeks when I get the flu. The real flu, not the heavy-cold kind of flu people complain about. Fevers, chills, muscle and bone aches, razors in your throat, ribs that threaten to splinter from coughing. The doctors reassure us the baby will be alright as long as I drink enough fluids and my blood pressure's normal. Flu can be a problem earlier in pregnancy, but I'm so far along now, everything will be alright.

I sleep a lot. The first couple of days, Glen takes off work. I dream, wild, disconnected dreams. Torrential rain, Glen flitting in and out in my robe, me falling hundreds of feet, turning, twisting, landing in a huge lotus, finding a tiny infant in its petals. The dreams come and go, and gradually my temperature levels, and I begin to rally.

I was thinking the sickness'd bring on an early delivery, as they warned it might, and I worried I might not have my strength back in time but now, five days after my due date, I feel like a beached whale. Winter has us in its clenched grasp. It's early this year. A nor'easter's forecast, and Glen and I are scared we won't make it to the hospital if the baby finally decides to put in an appearance.

My OB's concerned too and decides it's time to induce. Glen's way more afraid than me. He doesn't admit he's got sympathetic labor pains, but he sure looks like he has. He's more wrung out than after his most nail-biting swim victory, far more than after the marathon, than after he found out about Danny. And there are hours to go!

Glen swears he'll stay with me, although he's squeamish enough he might faint. When he admits being light-headed, one of the nurses is about to march him out when he says, "I'll be okay, I'll just watch the monitors instead of my wife," and he does, right until he hears, "Congratulations! It's a boy!"

Husband, baby, they're both in my arms, and we're all three weeping—Alistair, with a lusty, angry yell that drowns our sweet tears flowing with joy and relief. And yes, we manage to call him Alistair in honor of his Scottish Lenox roots and not "Algae." even though he's like an amphibious creature at first. (A future swimmer like his dad?)

His cries echo round the delivery suite. My God! It's true, we really do have a baby!

Jesus! There are some incredibly long days in the early months—and long nights. I grope around in some kind of fog. Alistair's a fussy baby. He won't sleep, he won't feed. He spits up when we want to go out, and I have to change him *and me* all over again. He screams in the supermarket, his bowels explode into his diaper at all the inconvenient moments.

Someone tells us to put him in his car seat on the dryer so the vibrations will lull him to sleep. He doesn't sleep, he throws up.

Someone else suggests we drive him around in the car. I do this, and when he eventually drifts to sleep, I park in the state park and sleep blissfully (for a few minutes) until a ranger knocks on the window to check if we're alright. I could scream! That's the first sleep I've had in days, and predictably, Alistair wakes up and howls.

If Rita or Brandi visit, he behaves like an angel, and I'm scared they'll tell everyone I'm an unfit mom, can't cope. When Glen's home from work, he rocks and rocks Alistair, who rewards him with a colicky burp, spit up and throw up before eventually nodding off.

We're exhausted—and besotted! Ridiculously proud to take him out in the stroller once he's settled. Ridiculously proud when a passer-by peers at him and whispers, "Aww!" Ridiculously awestruck at his baptism, with all the family gathered round, feeling a rare sense of religious wonder at this furious froggy boy who's miraculously come to change our lives.

In spite of me freaking out, he gains weight, gives us a gummy, gassy smile, rolls over, reaches for keys, earrings, glasses, grips our little fingers as if he wants to snap them off, giggles like a drainpipe and, on cue, sits up. We're doing it! We're parents! The pregnancy was normal. He's normal. Everything's going to be alright. Until it isn't.

It's Friday night—thank God, Glen's home. Alistair's been fussy all day. Nothing unusual. I'm worn out—nothing unusual either. Finally, we get him down, and Glen opens a bottle of wine, to celebrate the peace and the weekend. The wine's good, a few sips and it goes to my head. I've drunk so little with all the IVF, the pregnancy, and the need to function on almost zero sleep. I'm just winding down when there's this god awful shriek from the baby monitor.

We dash to his room, finding him soaked in sweat and very flushed. Do we give him baby Tylenol? He's our too-precious child, so we call the emergency pediatrician. In a flash, we're off to the emergency room. As they take him from us, we're terrified, clinging to one another. It's after one a.m. when we get home. They pumped fluids into Alistair, antibiotics and fever reducer. He looks a whole lot better. We, of course, look a whole lot worse.

We collapse into bed, and Glen is snoring gently within seconds. It takes me much longer. I'm roused from sleep a few hours later. Alistair's crying again, not the piercing, fever scream like before, more of a fretful cry. I roll to the edge of the bed to go to him before I realize Glen's on his way.

In a while, the crying stops. I put on the light so Glen can see his way back. When he enters the room, I notice he's wearing my robe. This is odd. There's no way he could mistake it for his terrycloth one. Mine's a Japanese kimono, painted with exotic flowers and teahouses. Not practical around a baby, but sometimes I need something to make me feel good about myself.

I stare at Glen, who seems utterly unconcerned. He hangs the robe on my hook and climbs back into bed, falling back to sleep in an instant. What have I just seen? I remember my dreams when I had the flu—Glen in my robe. What the heck does this mean? Am I seeing things? Hallucinating?

Eventually, I sleep again. It's fitful sleep, not the blissful, deep kind and, all too soon, Alistair wakes again. I go to him, Glen's out cold, and I'm still confused, questioning if I really saw what I saw.

We'd planned on bundling up and taking Alistair to the playground with the baby swings he loves, but since he was sick last night and I barely slept, we stay home. Glen makes waffles for breakfast. Butter and maple syrup seep through them, and the smell's sublime. We put Alistair in his baby-bouncer chuckling like a clown. We must look like the ideal family.

By some miracle, perhaps thanks to the meds, Alistair takes a long nap around lunchtime. It's my moment. All the same, I dread to ask … but now I've had other disturbing thoughts, my closet not always seeming the way I left it, my dresser disturbed.

"Glen, you were wearing my robe last night. Did you do that when I was sick too?" I ask.

His hand trembles as he takes a long swallow of water. Then, he looks me in the eye, a flush rising up his throat and spreading across his face. Even so, he holds my gaze and, shaking, stutters, "Lisa, I'm sorry. I should've told you years ago. I'm a coward. I like wearing women's clothes. You were asleep, I didn't think it'd hurt …"

I'm dumbfounded. Devastated. I thought I knew this man. The one man I was sure has it together, comfortable in his skin. My God! Oh, God! I married a pervert. I had a child with a pervert.

"Lisa, say something, darling."

I can't. I begin to cry, and I run upstairs to our bedroom. Ugh! Our bedroom, where I sleep with this freak, this betrayer. I glance at my robe, my closet, my dresser, I feel vomit rising, and I rush to the bathroom, where I only manage dry heaves.

He comes to me and puts an arm around me. I throw it off.

"Lisa, Lisa, I'm so sorry. I love you, Lisa," he says.

But I can't hear him.

I can't speak.

I can't think.

I'm sitting on the toilet, and I can't move. I scan the bathroom, my eyes land on my makeup bag, my perfume. Does he use these too? If he does, he's really discreet about it. The doubt eats at me. The deception. The invasion of my privacy. The shattering of our trust. It's all swirling around in my head. I can't help it, my mind swerves to an image of Glen's penis peeking through my lace underwear, Glen's chest straining my bra.

Like a lightning bolt, another thought explodes, is he a pedophile? Suddenly, I'm on my feet. I go to the bedroom and throw open my closet. I can't tell if anything is out of place. I pull my dresser drawers open. My underwear's untidy; it's no proof, it's always a mess. It maddens me not knowing. I want to lash out at him, confront him with everything. Be cleverer than he is. I want to hurt him as much as he's hurt me.

He's at the doorway watching me. I don't want him there. I'm on my knees rifling through the drawer and sobbing.

"Lisa, I didn't tell you because I thought you'd hate me. I like to wear your clothes. I like it because it feels like I'm closer to you," he tells me.

Now, I can speak. I yell at him, "Don't give me that crap! You're sick. You destroyed my life. You've destroyed all our lives! I hate you!"

Alistair's crying now. Glen goes to him, scoops him from the bouncer, and I yell, "Don't touch him!"

I grab Alistair from Glen, making the baby cry even harder. Manically, I start to pack, throwing Alistair's things into a bag. Diapers, wipes, diaper rash cream, bottles, formula, his favorite bear, any clothes I can grab. I shove a few things in for myself.

"Lisa, where are you going? You can't take Alistair. He's my son too," Glen's half-shouting, half-sobbing.

To be honest, I don't know where I'm going. Not to my dad's—I can't possibly tell him, nor Glen's family. Not to my girlfriends'. The shame is totally humiliating. I need to get away. Get Alistair away. Where? What can I do?

"Lisa, don't do this. Can't we talk?" he begs.

"No, we can't!" I hiss between my sobs.

"Don't go. Hell! We've gotta work this out," he says.

"Not fucking likely," I say.

"Where are you going? Tell me—I need to know." Now he sounds desperate. Good.

And then, I decide.

"I'm taking Alistair to Daisy's Inn," I tell him. The B and B where we used to stay back when we were house-hunting.

"Promise me you'll come back on Monday. I'm not a monster. I'll rearrange my work. We'll talk. Lisa, I love you. I love Alistair. I can't bear to be without you," he says.

I drive away. Alistair's howling in his car seat. For once, I'm so distracted that his cries can't upset me anymore.

Carling

The light's softening now, and long streaks of shadow stretch across the shiny, white slopes. I'm cruising down the last run of the day, taking my time; I'm tired after so many spectacular trails, I don't want to get hurt through carelessness. I reach the base of the gondola when my phone buzzes. I check it, fearing it's work. No, it's Glen. Funny, he never calls, just the odd email every now and then.

"Glen, what's up?" I ask, and I can tell straight away something's really wrong. "Hey! Wait a sec. Let me take my skis off and get to the car. Reception's better there. I'll call you right back." It takes a while to clump out of the resort and get to the parking lot. I load the skis, loosen my boots, and take a few deep breaths before I call him.

To say I'm stunned is an understatement. He's my baby brother. "Mr. Perfect," we used to tease him. Great athlete, great student, and later, great marriage. We all thought Glen's the least affected by Dad's death. The one who gets it together way before the rest of us. And Glen, my kid brother, a transvestite! What the …?

"Say something, Carling," I hear him say and realize there's been a pause, too long of a pause.

"I love you, Glen," I say instinctively, and I know it's the best response I can give.

"And you don't think I'm a monster, a freak, a perv?" he asks frantically.

"I don't know what to think. I'd no idea," I reply, and my mind spins. Were there clues? He'd loved Melody's little dresses, and there'd been some kind of incident with our underwear the first time Julian came over. I only remember because Bradi wasfurious. Hell, not a lot to go on. Were there things I missed?

"Glen, you're sharing this with me because I'm a psychologist as well as your sister?" I question carefully.

"I didn't know anyone else to call. Can you help? Can I even be helped? I've tried to stop—I can't do it on my own." He's pleading, desperation in his voice.

"Hey, this is not my field," I tell him. I'm calmer now, the professionalism kicking in. My more detached tone calms him enough that we can talk more rationally.

It all pours out. He's done this since he was a kid, he always feels totally ashamed, but he can't stop. He's sure he's not gay, he's always been attracted to women, but he doesn't want to be one. He adores Lisa. He says something confusing—that he thinks dressing like Lisa is a compliment.

I don't get this. Lisa and Alistair are his whole world. He's petrified he's hurt them and maybe lost them forever. He hates himself for who he is, what he does, and he's terrified someone else will find out.

It's a hell of a lot to take in. Seeing Glen in a whole new light. Jeez! Awkward! Like more than awkward! Before I hang up, I let him know that although he needs help and support *yesterday*, I'll have to do some research, talk with a colleague, and figure out next steps. And I reassure him he's not a monster and that I love him. Always will.

I cancel my date. Sawyer"s frustrated—he doesn't get many weekends off being in the theater, but he figures it's serious, even though I don't disclose what's up. Weird to worry about client confidentiality when it's my own brother.

I head back to my apartment. The drive, with its spectacular scenery, gives me time to decompress. The apartment's small, but I love it. I love the exposed brick, high ceilings, the original windows and, most of all, the view over Denver. It's likely gonna be a long night, so I make myself a BLT, pour a glass of Diet Coke, and take a bag of gummy bears to my desk.

There's not much in the literature. Every now and again, I lose my concentration, barely able to believe I'm reading this because of Glen, my Glen. How did he hide it so well and for so long? And now his life's falling to pieces, and I've no idea if he can pick them up.

It's midnight before I've read all I can find. Munched a lot of gummy bears in the process. I'll call Ethan in the morning (he's the one guy I think might have insights.) So far, it's clear that Glen's behavior is unusual, but not a sign of a perversion or any mental illness. Nor is it a PTSD response to Dad's death or any other trauma. Nonetheless, it's taken a toll.

All those years of hiding who he is, fearing discovery, smothering his shame. And now it's affecting his family. It's all the more difficult to address because it's not socially acceptable. He'll lose his partnership, the respect of friends and family, most likely, if they find out. And, at the same time, repression—hiding something's not healthy.

After a long and generally reassuring chat with Ethan, I call Glen and explain all this. He sounds relieved.

"So I'm weird but not a freak?" he says. "Carling, thank you for finding all this out. You're a lifesaver. Any idea what I'm gonna do about Lisa and Alistair?"

I don't like the "weird" comment, but I let it go, sensing he's trying to make a joke and knowing on some level, that's a good sign. Of course, I've already struggled in my mind about how to help Lisa. I think he's hoping I'll fix it for him. Make it go away or make it alright so he can carry on. From what I've heard, Lisa's livid, exhausted and revolted. It's gonna take a huge commitment, a lot of hard work from both of them. And is Lisa up for it?

Heart in mouth, I call Lisa three times before she picks up. She's very hostile. "Er, hello, Carling. I'm not sure we have much to say to each other. It's obvious you're on Glen's side."

Alistair's crying loudly in the background. I don't know how I manage to keep her on the line. I'm completely drained when we finally hang up. She did need to talk, yell, hurl accusations, curse, sob. She's been down some really dark alleys. Apart from Alistair, she's alone and afraid. She juggles making a bottle for Alastair as we talk. When he takes it, and I've crammed more gummies (yuck), we can move on.

Ultimately, she accepts Glen's not a pedophile, no threat to Alistair or herself. She'll talk with Dr. Ethan. Given the distance, the time difference, and other considerations, he can't work with them long term, but together they'll make a short-term plan to help her feel safe around Glen and get a conversation started.

I toss the remains of the bag of gummies at the trash. I miss. Too weak after all this stress to throw straight. I should eat something healthy, but I really don't want to cook, and there's not much in the fridge. Another BLT?

The intercom buzzes. It's Sawyer, how sweet. I let him in, and here he is, takeout bags, a bottle of wine threatening to fall from under his arm, a bunch of supermarket flowers in his hand. I want to hug and kiss him, but I'm scared he'll drop the wine and I'll crush the flowers, and then I hear him singing softly. What is it? Something I know. Oh, God! It's "Little Brother."

30

Lisa – 2012

"Lise, can you grab Billy for me? I just know he's going to fall off that slide. I gotta chase Molly, she's heading for the baseball game," Erica says to me.

I check that Alistair and Lainey are alright. There's a cool digger in the sandbox where they're engrossed, and some familiar grown-ups are watching the kids. Then I scamper up the slide like a monkey. Billy does look as if he's about to jump.

"Come here, Billy!" I'm trying to keep the panic out of my voice.

Billy screws up his eyes and shakes his head. I grab him and yank him toward me—a bit violently—against my normal parenting style, but a whole lot better than Billy launching into space, splattering his guts on the ground. His lack of protest suggests he's registered he's in danger. We wobble together, so I decide it's safer if we both slide down the slide instead of maneuvering around up here trying to reverse down the steps.

I aim to arrange Billy between my legs—this is a steep slide for a little boy. Before I'm done, he pushes off, hurtles down, shooting off the end and landing on his rear with a thump. I fly down after him. If I wasn't scared of Billy's hurt, this'd be super-exhilarating. Why do I worry? Billy's already charging back to the stairs. Thank God I'm in shape and I catch him.

"No, Billy. You're not going up there again. No way! This is a big-kid slide," I tell him, and predictably he turns on the waterworks, shrieking, "No fair! I am a big kid. You melon head! Hate you."

Not all that long ago this would've rattled me. Making someone else's child cry, being called names. No sweat now. I'm cool with it and with Erica and her crazy family.

She appears dragging a protesting Molly. "Billy, enough already. That slide's off limits. Non-negotiable," she tells him.

She's more abrupt than I am with Alistair. I guess you've got to be with four kids. Lainey's Alistair's age—nearly three. We met at toddler gym, the kids sitting down in the canvas tunnel, causing a roadblock. I'll never know how Erica manages it. Billy and Molly are twins, the "twin terrors," she calls them. They're only a year older than Lainey. Lainey's "a high price to pay for a moment of passion," Erica laughs. And there's her older child, Lena, a first-grader.

"Hey, y'know," Erica says, "let's bag this and go back to my place. The kids can play and we can visit."

The chances of any adult conversation are nearly zero, given that we'll be watching the kids. And those twins are likely to electrocute the dog, set the house on fire, or flood the bathroom if we don't keep a close eye on them. It'll be fun. Erica's home always looks like a nuclear test site, yet everyone's happy and healthy.

With the usual protests, I extract Alistair and Lainey from the digger. Other kids swoop in to take their places. I guess we haven't done such a good job with the "sharing" concept. I load Lainey into her car seat in Erica's people-mover and get Alistair installed in our Audir.

I like Erica a whole lot. I never would've met anyone like her if I'd stayed in corporate life. I do work three days a week—not the same. I thought the situation was getting dire when I could recite all the words to Alistair's Sponge Bob movies and shows, and when I talked to my dad over the phone in words of one syllable with repetitions like I use with Alistair. (Hey dad dad, we're going bye bye). Way past time for re-entry into the adult world.

Erica's like my antidote. She's where hippy and gypsy intersect, wearing long, floaty, mismatched clothes completely unlike the no-nonsense jeans and sweats I wear around the kids. Her wrists jangle with a dozen silver bracelets, jagged hair extensions snake down her back, she has a pierced nostril and a row of piercings in her left ear. Must be heavier on that side.

She told me once she thought about getting her tongue pierced too, but she worried about what it might do for her sex life. A second's hesitation, and I realized she meant oral. Well, naturally, I colored at the thought, lurid imaginings flooding my brain. Erica noticed, and we both fell about laughing.

I never dreamt parenting could be this much fun. Erica went to college and has a degree, summa cum laude. Surprising, since she claims she never went to class. Not really so surprising. She may be unconventional, but oh man, she's smart—just doesn't like to show it. After college she got a job with an exotic travel company that sent her across the world checking out scuba-diving schools, bungee-jumping outfits, jeep safaris, and all kinds of other wild adventures.

She and Matthew met in Phuket. He was there for a sales incentive "freebie." Apparently, it was "sex on the beach, sex in the tiki hut, sex on the plane on the way home!" You'd never think it to look at Matthew, he's even geekier than Glen.

We bribe the children with Cheerios and juice. Okay, it's not that big of a bribe. Erica's good about not filling them up with candy and cookies.

The twins wander off to devise an animal-eats-human game, splashes from their juice-boxes flecking their trail. They're gathering a lot of large plastic animals including dinosaurs and dragons, who attack Lainey's dolls, a nutcracker, and a stringless puppet. Quite a lot of dismemberment going on.

Lainey and Alistair play with model cars and a garage. The cars come in and out of the garage, generally through the windows, and "fly" onto the roof in an order that's crystal-clear to the kids, and totally baffling to adults. The game's punctuated regularly, though not predictably, by all the cars being gassed up.

Amazing! I never expected to enjoy semi-organized chaos this much. I spent most of my life avoiding chaos of any kind. There's only one thing that bothers me. I don't know whether to broach it with Erica. She always lets her children pick out their own clothes, so I'm used to clashing colors, unmatched socks, and garments back to front. Billy's especially inventive and often wears Halloween costumes with a mix of superhero clothes, the Incredible Hulk, complete with fake muscles on top, Spiderman in inside-out tights below. Today, he's in lilac leggings and a pink top with a ballerina on it that presumably was intended for one of his sisters.

"Doesn't it bother you that Billy wears girls' clothes?" I ask, trying too hard to be casual.

Erica tosses her head back, laughing. "Never think about it. Nothing Billy wears is gonna stop him from growing into a great guy."

"And he does look good in pink," I add to cover my confusion. She's given me more to think about than I bargained.

We've struggled through the past two and a half years since I discovered Glen's "secret." I called it "Glen's secret perversion"—at least in my head, out loud too when I lashed out at him. The therapist recommended I try not to think about it in those terms, even when I was pretending to make light of it.

I've got to admit she was helpful even if damnably challenging and non-judgmental. I had some lightbulb moments—Glen's hesitancy to get married, for example. He worried if I could love him if I knew. Guess he was right to worry about that ... Eventually, I discovered I couldn't stop loving him. Even though I haven't come to terms with his cross-dressing, I compartmentalize it. Not the ideal response, but the best I can do for now.

Little by little, we made some accommodations. Glen ordered a few dresses online—he doesn't "borrow" mine anymore, and we store them at the back of my closet so if Alistair finds them one day, he won't think anything of it. I can't stomach seeing Glen "dressed up," so I take Alistair on "adventures" at certain times. Glen promises he won't leave the house, or invite anyone over, and so far he's kept his word.

In return, I get a regular spa day when Glen looks after Alistair. Now I'm back at work, it's harder to squeeze in time at the spa. Maybe I'll never understand Glen's compulsion, it makes me squirm. And I hate having a "guilty secret" to keep. All the same, this way our family's intact. Glen and I've loved each other so long, I couldn't throw it all away—even if it did take a while for me to trust him again.

And now, I've come across Erica, who's completely unfazed—at least about a boy in girls' clothes. Do I have my priorities and my prejudices in line or not, after all? Will Erica be cool if Billy cross-dresses when he's grown, if he becomes a drag queen? Is it such a big deal?

I don't know.

31

Glen – 2014

Back here at Mom's again. Just me. The other time we tried clearing the house, Lisa and Alistair came along. Bad idea. We figured Alistair'd like going through Mom's stuff. Thought he'd poke fun at all our pathetic old art projects Mom kept, have a ball leafing through photo albums, seeing his dad and his aunties as kids, like poking around in all the places usually "out-of-bounds." What do parents know? We were totally wrong! He wandered around looking bewildered and bored. Too young, I guess.

He was mildly interested in finding one of my old Lego models under the bed. He's seen the best one of the Odeon I keep in my office at home. He didn't know there were others.

"Dad, can I break this up and play with the bricks?" he asks.

"No way!" I snap and, almost immediately, regret it. "That's history!"

"Daddy!" Alistair scolds.

"Glen! Don't be ridiculous!" Lisa sighs, "Why on earth do you want to keep model restrooms?"

She's right in a way. What am I going to do with my old models? Store the lot somewhere out of sight? Pass them down to Alistair? Not likely—and even so, I'm not ready to part with them just yet, especially the restrooms. They were my first ever. They mean too much.

After Dad died and we had to move away from my street and my friends, the models gave me something to focus on. I lost myself in them. Helped me hide my troubles from Mom and my sisters.

Brandi thinks I was the least impacted by Dad's death—there's a lot she doesn't know.

Doubt I'd have become an architect without the restrooms and all the other models. I know, they're a bunch of grubby old Legos, but I can't just throw them out. Well, not yet.

Alistair moved on to the kitchen, absorbed for a while checking out moldy old crackers, jelly coated with fuzzy green fur, a block of cream cheese, still smelling good, and a couple of wizened carrots. He and Lisa found some trash bags and tossed it all out. When Lisa suggested he throw out the rusty baking sheets and battered pots and pans, he lost all interest and begged to watch TV. Even that didn't distract him for long, Mom doesn't get many channels, and he couldn't find Disney. So Lisa took him off to Brandi's to visit Grandma.

Gave me a moment to take it all in. This little house was home during some tough times. I'd retreat to my "room." Not much more than a large storage closet off the kitchen, linked to a tiny Jack and Jill bathroom. No self-respecting architect planned that. We had to take both the headboard and footboard off my three-quarter-sized bed to squeeze it in. Can't see the bed now for the boxes—Mom's futile attempt to start clearing things out before she got too sick.

I shiver remembering my room wasn't properly insulated … I roasted in the summers and froze in the winters. All the same, it was my space, and I grew to like it. Better than the girls—crammed into the den and a downstairs bedroom. Only Mom and I had any privacy.

Back then, we were all grieving in our own ways. Now, I understand why Sherri got pregnant and ran off to Micah's, why Carling got into trouble, and why Brandi drifted into life with Julian. They think I had it easy—I didn't get it about Dad until much later, and I had other distractions. Fortunately, Mom and my sisters didn't know one of my distractions was dressing up in their clothes when they weren't around. Didn't know the guilt that little comfort cost me either. Crying myself to sleep and praying, *God forgive me and make me normal.*

After therapy, I feel less guilt and shame. It's what I do, a part of me. Heaven only knows why. How did I get so lucky Lisa hung in with me? She can't figure it out, but she quit eyeing me with disgust like she did at first. Christ! I hated those looks, hated myself for *being myself*, causing them. It took a while, and she kinda relaxed about it a couple of years ago. Hell, it's totally awesome she's my wife.

"Hey! We're back," Lisa calls as I hear the door click. Since she's been in my mind, I give her a big hug that surprises her. I'm about to ask how the visit went, when I notice Alistair's licking an ice cream, splotches dribbling down his shirt. Odd, Lisa doesn't often let him have ice cream, not at this time of day and in this weather. I catch a glimpse of his face. It's blotchy as if he's been crying.

Lisa takes me to one side and whispers, "He's upset. Your mom's a lot worse than last time. He didn't want to touch her or kiss her, hug her, anything. He was in tears as soon as we left the room. We should head home."

So I'm on my own this time. Sorry for Lisa ... First-grade soccer practice in the cold, then she'll be watching Alistair and his tearaway friends, Lainey and the "tornado twins." (Isn't that what Erica calls them?) I guess Erica has another emergency and needs a place to drop them off. Hope there's a home to come back to after they're done with it. Don't know how Matt stands it. Must be their amazing sex life or something.

Mom's house smells musty, reeking of nicotine and tar. I force a couple of windows open and let the air circulate even though it's chilly outside. The trash cans are mostly full from last time. They're rank, so I take them out to the garage Mom built where the carport used to be.

I start in Mom's room. It's too weird to go through her clothes. It's not as if she's going to wear them again, and I have absolutely no urge to try them on. I just can't deal with them. Instead, I strip the bed and toss the sheets and towels in the washer. It's ancient, but it still works and doesn't flood the kitchen or break down full of cold gray water.

Next, I arrange the trinkets I think my sisters might like on the bed. There are a couple of pictures of Martin and Mom on the nightstand, a few frail airmail letters from him postmarked Auckland. I guess they kept in touch after he moved to be with his son. He was a decent guy. Made Mom happy. I fill a trash bag with things that are begging to be thrown out, find a pile of books I want to keep and vacuum the carpet.

The living room and the den are choked with stuff, piles of magazines, crocheted throws, videos, souvenir ashtrays, bits and pieces from dance trips with Martin, novelty slippers (when did Mom wear Harry Potter slippers?), and old photos—Mon and Grandpa Wuff, Melody, Carling's graduation, my graduation and wedding, Theo and Teddy and, of course, Alistair. I can't face all this right now. I decide to clear my room.

As I was leaving last time, I triggered an avalanche of boxes, some crashed off the bed and they're sprawling over the floor and out the door. I decide today's task is to tidy all this up, sort through the boxes, be ruthless, and actually make some progress rather than drifting down memory lane again. The first few aren't emotionally taxing, old files from school days. There's the odd picture from swim team days where I'm weighed down with medals, or being back slapped by other swimmers who look like grown men compared with me. I still feel a rush of pride. Is that wrong? I don't know.

The next box's full of the girls' stuff—old makeup, jewelry, secret journals, cassettes, a cowboy hat, and their stuffed animals—"Tedoo," "Pinky," and "Mingo." Must have come with us when we moved. Guess Mom had a hard time throwing things away, too. Most of this is straightforward, thank God. I find more of Mom's stuff, hairdressing supplies (rusted aerosols, congealed gel, curling papers, hair dye), and crochet patterns.

Then, I notice them, three grayish turquoise circlets, misshapen now, looking like bedraggled haloes. She kept them. The girls' headdresses! From *that* wedding! Women are an enigma wrapped in mystery—who said that? God, I hope she didn't keep the vile dresses as well. How the eff did she stay friends with Peggy after she knew Peggy'd cheated with Dad?

Oh! And here's the photo that revealed that piece of deception to me. Why does Mom have it? Why does she keep it? It's cracked and crazed now, but it's Danny in his whites, when he signed up for the Navy. The one Peggy passed around that Thanksgiving. Danny's so clean-shaven, and the reflection of the light from his uniform on his face highlights angles and planes I'd never noticed in the flesh. The dark auburn hair, the angle of his eyebrows, a glint in his eye, the bow of his lips.

It hit me like a hurricane. Danny is his father's son. *My* father's. I remember my confusion when it struck me full force. How dumb I felt for not seeing it earlier. How everyone must've known except me. Give me a break! I was thirteen, and in shock. I didn't even think of putting two and two together and drawing the obvious conclusion after Danny was born.

I look again at his picture. I've never been able to unsee what I saw that Thanksgiving. The likeness is uncanny, his build, the set of his shoulders, the flashing eyes, and now I think of it, his tone of voice. Suddenly, another wave crashes over me. There's no doubt Danny's his father's son ... *But am I?*

Who am I?

Now the floor's clear of boxes, I cross to the bathroom. The mirror always was misty. It's worse now, I can't see myself clearly enough. I run downstairs to the other bathroom eager to have a good look in that mirror.

Grabbing a dubious towel and some liquid soap, I wipe it as clean as I can. Then, I take a long look at myself. There's nothing to say I'm not Dad's son, but precious little to say that I am. My sisters are redheads with green eyes, pale complexions, and freckles, like Dad. Sherri's petite like Mom, barely tall enough to have had a shot as a ballerina. Carling and Brandi are medium to tall, broad-shouldered with slim hips, again like Dad.

And then there's me, with my light brown hair and blue eyes, fair complexion, a slim, slightly long face—I could have the same father as Danny and the girls. It's entirely possible. I'm short for a man (that could've come from Mom), I have Dad's broad chest, but is it really well-developed from all the swimming, running, and skiing I've done? And where are the telltale signs Danny has? The arch of the eyebrow, the slight toss of the head, that cheeky curl at the corner of the mouth. Who in the family has a chin like mine, long fingers, a dimple? I keep looking at myself. I can't be sure.

Sandip and a bunch of other guys were always telling me how proud Dad was to have a son, but I felt I didn't measure up in his eyes. The God-awful year he signed me up for football and the coach shook his head after tryouts and told Dad I'd never make the team. The way he feigned interest in my models—he never said as much, but he gave the impression they were a sissy thing to do.

We were both quick at math, but he was only interested when it served his business. Before he died, I outpaced him in tons of math topics. He wasn't too proud then, seemed confused, pissed. *Yes! Pissed.* I craved his love, and all I did was piss him off.

I look again in the mirror. It doesn't give me an answer. Where do I come from? Could Mom have cheated? My Mom? What have I passed on to Alistair? It's eating at me. I have to know. *I have to know.* I march into Mom's bedroom and thumb through the photos piled on her bed. Yes! There's one of Dad, not too far in age from where I am now. His features heavier, coarser than I remember. I stare into his eyes. They look creepy with the red-eye from the photography, but there's still a cocky flash in them, a flash of defiance, or is that disdain? I can't tell, and his eyes keep their secret if there is one. I just can't tell, and now I need to know.

I drive over to Brandi's house to get the truth.

❖

My tough, pretty Mom looks barely alive. Not much left of her now except her tar-choked breath, her fluttering heart, and a mostly functioning brain. Do her eyes betray amusement, perhaps relief that I've figured it out? Is that what the Mona Lisa smile's intended to convey?

When I'm about to give up on her, turns out she needs me to know. She squeezes my hand with her chicken-foot claw. Very deliberately. Three times.

I understand. Brad Lenox is not my father. And when I squeeze back, I'm sure she knows that I know—and that I'll keep her secret even from my sisters.

I'm totally wiped after my talk with Brandi on the porch. Given Mom's news, the cat allergies, and the cold, I couldn't focus on what she was telling me about the funeral arrangements. My head was spinning, almost literally!

Back at Mom's house now, fueled by adrenaline, I'm methodically sorting through Mom's things, making piles, taking bags to the trash. I'm hyper-motivated, and I start forming a plan. I'll need a dumpster for the clutter, and I'll send anything valuable my sisters don't want to the local auction in a couple of weeks. Mom probably won't last that long. She sinks in and out of sleep and scarcely eats.

All the time I'm sorting through everything, I'm searching for a sign, a clue. Who was he? Did I know him? Did he know? Did he watch me grow up and never reach out? Do I look like him? Act like him? Did he have a mean streak, letting another man raise his child? Was my mom having an affair? My mom, unbelievable ... Or not? Did anyone find out? The questions streak around my mind. But there are no answers.

As far as I can tell, there isn't a trace. No photo tucked in the back of her wallet, no hidden note, nothing stuffed in her pockets, no dedication in a book, no engraved keepsake. Nothing. Who was he? I'll have to let Mom take that secret to her grave.

32

Krystyna Sarva – 2014

"Hello, Dad, how are you?" I ask.

"Can't complain, especially at my age," he replies, sounding upbeat. For once, the international line's clear, and since he didn't miss a beat, I'm sure he has new batteries in his hearing aids.

"You never did complain—at any age!" I tell him.

"Well, one of the fish died, I suppose I could complain about that," he says half joking.

"Oh! Which one?" I ask.

"Darter—the black and white stripe," he tells me.

"I'm sorry."

"You know I can't complain ... He lived a good life, for a fish," he responds, and I know he's teasing. I can hear the humor in his voice.

"There you go again, Dad. You know I'm in Boston, right? Well, I happened to pick up the *Globe*. There's an obituary in it for a Rita Lenox. Rang a bell. Could she be that neighbor of ours when we lived in Massachusetts way back when?" I ask.

"Rita? You remember Rita? How old does it say she was?" he asks, surprised.

"Let me see. Seventy-six. From Watervale. That's where we lived, isn't it? Sounds right," I tell him

"Yes. Poor old Rita. What else does it say?"

"Survived by three daughters ... oh! There was a son as well. I can't picture him ... three grandsons, and ... oh, how sad—predeceased by her husband and a granddaughter," I continue.

"Oh! Poor Rita. I don't recall a son either. Just the three girls. Little spitfires, all of them. He must've been born after we left. Brad ... was that his name? He always wanted a boy. When I think of it, I might've heard Brad passed away. What did Rita die of?" he asks me.

"It doesn't say—wait, they're asking for donations to the Williams Society and Dana-Farber, the big cancer center. Must be one of those," I answer.

"Poor Rita," he says again. "Krystyna, I told you I've nothing to complain about when folk a lot younger than me are dropping dead right and left these days."

"Dad, you know what, the funeral's tomorrow afternoon back in Watervale. I'll be all done with my client by lunchtime. You want me to go? I think I might like to poke around our old neighborhood. Seemed so strange when we first moved there," I say.

"I'm surprised you're interested, you were off at college most of the time we were there," Dad says.

"You're right, but I think I'll go anyway. It's where Mom died, after all. The funeral's in the same church. I can tidy up her grave, leave some flowers. Then I'll slip in at the back of the sanctuary. Afterwards, I might take a drive round our old street—if I can find it," I tell him.

"You've a GPS in the rental car?" he wants to know.

"Yes, I'll be okay, even if it's changed a lot. D'ya happen to remember the street?"

"Hmm, let me think. Hill Street?" He thinks for a second. "No, Hall Street. Seventy-two, if I'm not mistaken—second house from the corner. Say a little prayer for Rita for me if you go. She was a good, hard-working woman."

"OK, I'll light a candle too. Look after yourself, Dad."

"I'll be fine. You take care. Don't rush to visit when you get back. Give yourself time to get over the jet lag. You're not so young as you once were either," he says.

"Don't worry, Dad. And y'know, this is my last business trip," I reassure him. "I'm taking early retirement, only got a couple of months left. Feels strange."

"My daughter ... Retired! It felt weird when you weren't in grade school, when you graduated college, but retired?! Makes me feel like an old crock. All the same, I'm lucky. I can't complain."

I feel like a voyeur of my own life, driving out from Boston on roads that are both familiar and unfamiliar, to a town that always did feel foreign to me and, at the same time, exciting. Memory's played strange tricks. Some of the landmarks are still there, like City Hall, Warner Park—yet not quite where I expected them to be or the same scale—everything's smaller.

Oh, I'd forgotten the hardware store—used to love that place, it was like a rabbit warren, I'd pretend I was wandering around a maze. You could buy anything there. I mean anything—condoms to Christmas trees. It's closed now, and so's Dino's café next door, but the buildings are still there. Here's the church—looking the worse for wear, dwarfed by a screen of fir and leathery rhododendrons. They've grown thick over the years.

I park the car and walk to Mom's grave. I've no problem finding it, though it's overgrown and the headstone's blooming with lichen. Someone must've done some tidying once in a while. I read the inscription, speaking the stark words out loud. "Zofia Sarva, Good and Faithful Servant" and her dates. I never liked it. Dad wanted something in Polish, but the stonemason talked him out of it. Wonder why he didn't ship her body back to Poland. I'll ask him when I get the chance.

I clear the worst of the debris, thankful for the clippers I thought to pick up at the gas station, where they had surprisingly decent flowers. I brush my lips across the spray of white chrysanthemums before laying them down, feeling a rush of sadness even after all these years. I hadn't expected this, and I'm reluctant to turn my back on her grave, but Rita's mass is about to begin.

Now my emotions are churned up, I regret planning to attend, but I go in for Dad's sake. Some of the family must have arrived before me, or perhaps I don't recognize them. After all, they were three little redheads with toothy grins back then. The church's filling up. Rita must've been well liked. Dad'll be pleased. He had a soft spot for her.

Hastily, I light the candle and make an offering. The back pew is full already, so I walk down a few rows and tuck myself in by the center aisle. Despite the hushed press of people, it feels bleak here. Guess it always did. I breathe in the forgotten and familiar scent of damp stone-dust, smoky candlewick, and something vaguely metallic I can't identify ... polish, rust, I'm not sure.

All I know, it's calling me back to Mom's funeral. Such a desolate place, its stone ribs encasing the skeleton that'd been Mom. The priest's mumblings about the soul and the spiritual afterlife offered no comfort. I couldn't imagine how Dad and I could carry on, let alone ever be happy. I didn't realize that although we were strangers in a strange land, there were friends here who would help us, amongst them Rita's family. I wonder how they're doing.

I expect organ music. In its place, there's a harpist strumming a haunting melody. Irish or Scottish, I'd say. It's so beautiful I can't tell if it makes me happy or sad. They bring the coffin down the aisle. It's not borne aloft by pallbearers, like the old days. It's on a sleek trolley. Four men accompany it. One's an older Indian gentleman. Another slips into the front pew next to an elegant woman and a little boy. Should the child be here? I don't know, I never was a parent, never gave Dad grandchildren. And, of course, he never complained.

The priest looks startlingly young, not much more than a boy wearing solemn robes he hasn't grown into. He has an accent. South American, maybe. He speaks touchingly about Rita—clearly, even though he's young, he knew her well. Her courage, her vivacity, her devotion as a mother and grandmother. The next eulogist's a family friend. She tells of Rita as a woman with a great capacity to forgive, to be a loyal friend, and a knockout dancer. (Dad will love this detail.)

The man who accompanied the coffin moves to the lectern. It turns out he's the son—the one we never knew. He chokes up from time to time, but he gets through his tribute and I feel drawn to him, Rita, and her family. He talks about the mother who was his rock, who built a home for her kids after her husband's sudden death, who loved them all no matter what.

It's when he speaks of the granddaughter, Melody—I think that's her name—that he really struggles for words. How great Rita was with her, taking Melody to work, sewing little outfits, patiently teaching her to read, soothing her fears. He also talks about Rita and her grandsons, how she could never tell the twins apart, how his son awarded her "Grandma of the Universe."

He's entertaining, sharing when Rita tipped out of a kayak, Rita and a roast turkey that flew across the kitchen. Like the other speakers, he doesn't fail to mention her zest for life, the outdoors, and of course, dancing. He ends with a neat image of his mom and St. Peter tangoing through the pearly gates. I glance around, people are smiling, feeling better.

There's more music—the organ now. "How Can I Keep from Singing" peals around the echoing chamber. Inevitably, everyone joins in, and it doesn't ring hollow. The young priest blesses the host, the communion ritual unfolds, and they all shuffle up for their taste of God. I don't join the procession, lingering in the pew, glad now that I came. It's softened the raw edges of Mom's death, released pain I hadn't realized I've been carrying.

As the coffin glides by, I check my program for the title of this ethereal harp music. "The Water Is Wide" ripples through the air, suggesting calm waters for Rita and new horizons for those she left behind. We file out behind the casket. To my surprise, the son and (I'd guess) a daughter greet us as we leave.

Glen Lenox takes my hand. "Thank you for coming. My mom would've been touched. Forgive me, I don't recognize you. How did you know her?"

I explain, and he squeezes my hand, thanks me again.

I drive to the old house. The street's changed, but the house's still there. It's been so long, and I was hardly ever there so I have trouble recognizing it. Someone's transformed the landscaping, and there's a huge new addition. I park down and across the street from our house and the Lenoxes'. I click a few photos for Dad.

Perhaps I'm overemotional, I'm putting my career in the rear-view mirror, and as I look into that mirror, I see these two homes sheltering regular folk who intersected for a while. I find I'm tearing up, understanding the sweetness of ordinary lives. Take Rita, a hairdresser in a small town, not someone who'll go down in history. Nonetheless, what a life—courage, compassion, and a determined will.

I'm on the plane, headed back to Poland when something odd strikes me. My mind's overtired, and refusing to drift into sleep, so it may be the product of a disorganized brain. All the same, I can't stop thinking about it.

It's the next day when I call Dad. He's full of questions about Rita's funeral, the old house, the Lenox girls. When he asks about Glen, the son, I seize my chance,

"He's nice, has a son of his own. Obviously loved his mom, gave a beautiful eulogy. Funny thing is, must be a coincidence, or I'm tired enough to be imagining things ... He looks a bit like us. Long, thin face, slight build, his handshake. Something. I don't know. It's bizarre," I say.

Dad doesn't reply for the longest time, I wonder if he's alright.

At last, he clears his throat, and in a voice that's barely composed, says, "Krystyna, that's wonderful, Rita had a son who looks like a Sarva. Who'd have guessed? And a grandson as well! My, oh my. Oh my! I can't complain."

About the Author

Originally from the UK, Jean Goulden divides her time between northern Florida and central Colorado. A lover of the outdoors, she is an avid hiker and, despite a retinal condition that limits her sight (but not her vision), has rafted down the Grand Canyon, hiked the Inca Trail to Machu Picchu, and climbed Mount Kilimanjaro. When forced indoors, she has a lifelong yoga and meditation practice, enjoys cooking and spending time with friends, family, and her two cats.

A Glass Darkly is Jean's first novel.

Also by Jean Goulden

Books

*Tracking the Camino de Santiago de Compostela: Memories of blisters
and blessings in pursuit of the headless saint*

*Hiking England's Coast to Coast Way:
Landscape, Laughter and Love*

Jean Goulden's Blog
Salt Spray and Aspens
at www.JeanGoulden.com

◆

I hope you enjoyed reading *A Glass Darkly*.
I invite you to post a review on Amazon
so others may also enjoy it.